ᘓ ᘏ

Belos crouches down, studying me. He sigh

from my face. I wrench my head away.

"You do look like your mother, you know. I see the resemblance, with you bound here before me, as she was before she died."

Somewhere behind me, Horik gives a muffled shout.

I choke on my own horror. Belos's lip twitch with amusement.

"It was almost in this very spot. Do you know, the last thing she ever saw was me lifting you into my arms?" He slips the Shackle's cuff over my pinned hand and says with satisfaction, "You must have always known it would come to this."

Chains of Water and Stone

KATHERINE BUEL

THE GRIEVER'S MARK SERIES

The Griever's Mark
Chains of Water and Stone
Unbound

Chains of Water and Stone

ISBN-10: 8554568565
ISBN-13: 979-8554568565

BOOKS BY KATHERINE BUEL

The Griever's Mark series
The Griever's Mark
Chains of Water and Stone
Unbound

Standalone novels
Heart of Snow

Chapter 1

The battle axe arcs above me, a gleaming Drift-weapon marked with faint blue symbols similar to those on my opponent's face and hands, similar to the one on the back of my own neck. He swings again, too wide, afraid to hurt me, and I punish him for his caution. As the axe sweeps harmlessly past my left shoulder, I spin and slash at Horik's chest with my notched spear. His eyes widen as the blade rips through the fine Runish embroidery of his tunic.

Horik's surprise dissolves into a fierce grin. A faint light surrounds him, and he vanishes into the Drift. I whip around, expecting him behind me, but he reappears all the way across the empty training yard, leaning casually against one of the abandoned, straw-stuffed archery targets. He yawns, feigning boredom, and idly brushes loose straw from the target's canvas covering.

I yell something inarticulate, just noise, venting my frustrations with everything—my powerlessness, my father. My father. What a strange feeling to call anyone that. Better, perhaps, to keep thinking of him as King Heborian.

I have to calm my mind to enter the Drift and only long years of practice make it possible now. I ease along my mooring, enduring the familiar sensation of compression, and slide into the Drift. Around me, the world resolves itself into its bare, essential energies. The dead stone of Heborian's castle and the curving wall enclosing the training yard loom dimly, as though the physical world is a ghost of itself. Under my feet, the earth lies dull and quiet, though not so unresponsive as I once thought it. I begin to sense it more, that deep, buried power. Beyond the castle, the restless ocean tugs at the edges of my awareness. I shut it out.

Within the Drift, glowing silvery-white forms dot the castle grounds, and far more move about in the city beyond. Heborian I recognize in his study because he burns so brightly, with more hints of color. I'm tempted to drift to his side and surprise him. I did it once before, not long ago, on the day he told me who I am. I dismiss the idea when I notice Wulfstan, Heborian's ever faithful dog—I mean advisor—hovering near the king. I can endure Heborian's anger, but I'm not keen on Wulfstan's scorn.

Horik's silvery form, lit with hints of blue and gold, shifts uncertainly beside the dull hump of the archery target as I keep him waiting. The tattoos spiking up his neck and threading along his jaw glow blue. They're less obvious in the physical world, partially obscured by his dark beard, but here in the Drift they burn clearly. I wonder suddenly if my own tattoo, the Griever's Mark on the back of my neck, is as visible. It must be. I don't know the meaning of Horik's tattoos, but he bears them proudly on his face. My own tattoo is nothing to be proud of. It means only that my father rejected me as soon as I was born, resigned me to death when he traded me to Belos. Heborian claims the Mark was meant to protect me, but I don't see it that way.

I'm about to drift to Horik when I notice a still, subdued figure at the edge of the yard. Earthmakers glow more dimly than humans within the Drift because they distance themselves from it. Valuing only the elements, they regard the Drift as dirty, something to serve only selfish desire.

I know the shape of this particular Earthmaker, the calm face, the quiet movements. Bran. What does he want? The sight of him irritates me. A distant part of me knows I'm angry because I only prove him right when I use the Drift and my sparring with Horik to vent my frustration, rather than controlling it as an Earthmaker would do. Yes, I'm weak. Yes, I'm selfish. Does it satisfy him to be right?

I burn more brightly as my anger swells. If Bran wants to see my temper, let him see it. My energy coils as I drift close to Horik, my whole being tight with anticipation as I ease along my mooring, already shaping my Drift-spear.

If Horik is startled by my sudden appearance, he doesn't show it. When I jab the butt of my spear toward his belly, he spins, taking the blow lightly across the ribs. From the corner of my eye, I catch the faint blue glow of Drift-energy around his huge fist just before he drives it into my back. The blow sends me flying, arched with pain. I land on a knee, then my hip, yelling as the impact jars still-healing wounds. Training makes me tuck my shoulder and roll so I don't shatter my arm. I bump and skid across the cool, dewy grass before lurching to a stop in a broad patch of dirt worn bare through years of booted feet circling one another.

I grunt and push myself up, ignoring the pain of pulled stitches in my shoulder and thigh. Three yards away, Horik grins and spins the axe in his hand. Joy flares in my chest. Right now,

I love this man. He knows what I want, what I need, and he can both give it and take it.

We charge each other, his axe high, my spear low. It's dangerous to spar with real weapons, and I wouldn't do it with anyone less skilled than Horik, but there's a reason he's the king's champion. And me? Seventeen years serving Belos taught me well enough how to defend myself.

I jerk my spear up as we collide, levering it against my body. I knock his heavy axe aside just enough to slide under his guard. I can't get my spear around in time to drive the butt into his belly, so I let the spear vanish even as I draw from the Drift. I drive a faintly glowing elbow into Horik's muscled stomach. He flies back just as I did, but I'm not as chivalrous, and I don't give him time to recover. I scramble to my feet and lunge.

Horik lets his axe vanish. He's halfway to his feet and off balance enough that my lighter weight bowls him over. Before I can land my first punch, his foot wedges into my belly and launches me. I have only a second to register surprise at the big man's flexibility before I realize his hand is also clamped on my wrist, preventing me from correcting my fall. He slams me to the ground like a sack of grain.

He doesn't hit me but he does grab my waist while I'm still stunned. He throws me again. I tumble, landing in a sprawl of limbs. I scramble to my feet with a snarl and charge. I try to slide under Horik's guard, but I've used that trick one time too many. He jumps away from my fist.

It doesn't matter. I haven't beaten larger opponents because I'm strong. I've beaten them because I'm quick.

I spin on my hip and drive my foot into the crook of Horik's knee. As his leg buckles, I scramble behind him. I wrap my legs around his torso and my arms around his thick, corded neck. His large hands clamp on my arms to pry me off. I'm tempted to bite him, but I'm not that far gone yet. I just squeeze. Horik tries to shake me off, but I cling like a tick on a dog.

It's not until the impact of the ground shocks the air from my lungs and Horik's huge weight is lifting from me that I realize he's slammed me into the ground. Black spots dance through my vision.

Horik stands over me, his wide grin distorting the blue tattoos that peek above the edge of his beard. With his blunt nose and heavy jaw, he's not a handsome man, but I like his face anyway. Maybe it's his eyes always dancing with humor. Maybe it's because he doesn't mind that his chin is smudged with dirt and that the Runish braid that usually keeps his dark hair out of his face has pieces pulled loose. Maybe it's because he's not so much the king's champion that he can't wrestle in the dirt like some stable boy, like some uncivilized churl. Like me.

"Had enough yet?" inquires a smooth voice from behind Horik.

I push myself to a sitting position with a very unladylike grunt. I glare at Bran as he stops beside Horik, who edges away from him, grumbling something about "stuffy Earthmakers."

Bran gives him a look of deep patience that makes Horik curl his lip. If my head weren't spinning, I might grin. At least I'm not the only one who gets annoyed with that Earthmaker calm and disdain.

I'm being unfair, I know, because Bran is one of the least disdainful Earthmakers I've met, and I know he's here—at least in part—because he's worried about me, but it's easier to be annoyed with him.

"What do you want?" I grumble, pushing hair out of my eyes. "Can't you see I'm busy?"

As I start to shove to my feet, Horik's hand clamps under my elbow, lifting me powerfully. He looks a question at me, asking if I want him to stay.

I hesitate, but Bran waits quietly, and my conscience pricks me with guilt.

Horik must see the fight go out of me. He dips his chin and says my name with sudden formality, "Astarti," as he turns to walk away.

"Thanks," I call after him.

He pauses. "The Firstborn can always call on me."

"Don't call me that," I remind him irritably. I hate that Horik accords me some special place because I'm his king's oldest child. Doesn't he realize that Heborian himself offers me no such regard, that even before I was born I was nothing to my father but a bargaining piece?

Horik only shrugs, refusing once again to obey my request. Huh. Some respect.

I watch Horik's retreat for as long as I can, avoiding Bran's eyes. I know what he must be thinking: everyone else is sick of fighting after the battle with Belos, mere days ago. Haven't I had enough violence?

When Bran doesn't say this, I snap, "I know what you're thinking."

"I doubt that."

I snort.

"Walk with me. Unless you want to clean up first?"

I glance down at the grass stained front of my white shirt and the scuffed knees of my leather breeches. I shake some grass from my long, messy braid. Even though a faint heat creeps up my neck as I eye Bran's clean tunic and the red-gold hair tied neatly at the nape of his neck, I mutter, "Like I care."

"Come on then." Bran jerks his chin toward the open gateway, and I follow him with an irritated sigh.

I shouldn't be so selfish. Of course Bran wants to know the outcome of my discussion with Heborian. Of course he wants to know whether Heborian will give me what I need to free—

I cut myself off. I can't say his name, not even in my head, or I will break down. I can't allow myself that weakness, especially in front of Bran, not when he is so strong. I focus on the pain in my shoulder and thigh, where stitches strain to hold together flesh that I will not allow to rest. I grind the palm of my hand into my hip, where an arrow grazed me. I use the pain to center myself, to tear my mind from the horrible image of eyes that should have been a gorgeous swirl of green, blue, and gold flooded instead with oily blackness.

Bran and I pass through the arching gateway to emerge into the narrow alley between the wood-sided barracks. Laughter rises from within, soldiers celebrating their victory and the escape from death. I feel annoyed with their good humor until I see one soldier, a man not much older than I am, emerge from one of the low buildings. His stiff smile fades the moment he's out of sight of his companions. His shoulders droop as he hurries away.

"Everyone deals with things in their own way," Bran says when he see me watching the soldier.

I give him a sharp look. "I suppose you mean me, beating the crap out of Horik."

Bran's face remains expressionless. "It looked like he was 'beating the crap' out of you."

"He was not. I had everything—"

"It looked like that's what you wanted." His serene blue eyes show too much understanding.

I grit my teeth. I'm so edgy, so angry. I don't know what to do with myself.

We leave the barracks behind and emerge into the huge, walled courtyard. The castle, with its smooth stone walls and turrets that pierce the spring sky, towers grandly to our right. The clear morning light pricks jewel-bright colors from the stained-glass windows. It's beautiful, yes, but the smooth cobbles under my feet still feel like bare skulls.

"Where are we going?" I demand, hating how churlish I sound. Bran doesn't deserve my anger, but he takes it so well that I can't stop myself. How can he be so calm when Logan—

I exhale slowly and force my mind to clear.

"I thought we'd go into town and get a bite to eat."

"It's not yet midday."

Bran shrugs.

"I'm not hungry."

"So I've gathered. Your lady's maid told me you've not eaten for two days."

I sniff at the mention of Clara, always fussing, but I feel the truth of Bran's words in my light head and the inward clenching of my body. Even so, I meant it: I'm not hungry.

I glare at Bran to throw away his concern. "Why do you care?"

His eyes search my face, and I sense there's something he won't say. Then, "You won't help him by destroying yourself. You need to make yourself stronger, not weaker."

I hate that he's right, yet I say bitterly, "It doesn't matter. Heborian—"

"You can tell me after you've eaten."

I fume silently, embarrassed by Bran's caring, as we pass through the towering castle gates and cross the sweeping bridge into Tornelaine.

The mood in the streets reflects the same, almost manic glee I've seen in the soldiers. No one can quite believe that Tornelaine stood firm against the combined might of Belos, his Seven, and the army of Count Martel. If they really knew how very close it was they would be more frightened than giddy.

Even now stonemasons work day and night to repair the city wall, which was split nearly in half. Only those of us who stood on the wall realize it was one blow away from crumbling, one blow away from total disaster.

Bran leads me to a pub whose brightly painted wooden sign above the door declares the place The Brimming Mug. Realizing how directly he led me, I ask, "You know this place?"

"Not all Earthmakers stay hidden in Avydos. I've been to Tornelaine before."

My eyebrows jump in surprise. Bran, with his scholarly bent, seems the type to stay cloistered in some Earthmaker library, not the type to seek out pubs in a human city like Tornelaine. I'm reminded that I don't know him very well.

With its scrubbed tables and serving girls modestly clad in neat dresses and aprons, the place is one of the cleaner pubs in the city, and clearly prosperous. Even though it's early, several patrons sit scattered at tables or hover along the bar, where a heavyset, keen-eyed man dries a pottery mug with a clean white towel. Bran motions me toward the fire while he goes to the bar. When the heat washes against my legs, I realize how chilled I am. My hands respond stiffly as I spread them before the flames. I didn't even know I was cold. Except for the pain that I use to ground myself, I feel so separated from my body, so detached. Nothing is quite real right now.

Bran carries two mugs to a nearby table, and I leave the fire reluctantly. When I plunk down in a chair, Bran pushes a mug toward me. I peer skeptically at the steaming, amber-gold liquid I don't drink much beer, but I know it's not usually serve warm.

"Just try it."

I take a cautious sip and taste spiced apple. Ah, cider. I wra my chilled hands around the mug and hover my nose over letting the steam wash my face. The scent of cinnamon eas me until I catch another scent beneath it: clove. The smell sparks memories of Straton, with his sly condescension, his too-neat appearance, his scent of clove oil meant to mask the dusty smell of the Dry Land. I push the mug away.

I can't take Bran's silence, so I try to break the news. "So I said to him—"

"Ah," Bran interrupts. "Our stew."

A pretty blonde serving girl with an innocent face sets down two bowls of thick brown stew, each with a hunk of bread resting on top. She says sweetly, "Anything else?"

Annoyed by her light manner, by her obliviousness to all that is wrong in the world, I don't trust myself not to give a surly reply, so I let Bran answer politely, "No, thank you."

Bran stares pointedly at my bowl until I take up my spoon. The smell of food turns my already queasy stomach, but I take a bite to please him. I set the spoon down but cup my hands around the warm bowl.

"Stronger," Bran reminds me, "not weaker."

Grimly, I pick up the spoon and work on the stew. Halfway through the meal, my appetite finally awakens and before I've finished wiping up the last of the stew with my bread, another steaming bowl appears under my nose. When I finish the second bowl and my shrunken belly presses uncomfortably against the band of my pants, I force myself to meet Bran's eyes.

I expect him to make some snotty comment like, "Better?" but he only takes a sip of his ale.

I don't have Bran's restraint. I say tartly, "Am I allowed to speak now?"

"So what happened?"

"What do you think? He refused. He won't give it to me."

Bran folds his hands around his mug, staring blindly at them. "Tell me again what he said the knife can do."

"You already know."

"Let's just think through it once more."

I place a mocking finger across my lips. "Well, let's see. We know it can cut a Leash because it cut mine, and, hmm, isn't that exactly what we need it to do?"

I don't realize my voice has risen until Bran looks over his shoulder to see if anyone is listening to us. The barkeep has gone still, watching for trouble.

I force myself to go on more calmly, in a low voice. "The knife can cut through barriers. Yes, I understand that makes it dangerous—"

"Very dangerous. Belos could drift right into Heborian's castle."

"And by that same token I could drift right into Belos's, cut Logan free, and be gone before Belos knew I was there."

"That's the idea, yes."

"What do you mean, 'that's the idea'? Don't tell me you don't want me to try to get Logan out of there? Do you realize what Belos is probably doing to him? Do you *know*—"

I grip the edge of the table to still my shaking hands. My words are cruel, unfair, and I hate myself for them. Of course Bran wants Logan out. The pain in his eyes reproaches me as words could not.

"I'm sorry, Bran."

Bran is silent at first, putting away his pain, then he says, "We will get Logan back, Astarti."

His gentleness breaks something loose inside me, and I feel tears threaten. Before I can dissolve, I force my mind to empty.

Bran adds, "We will have to get him back to Heborian, then free him."

I shake my head. Without the knife, unable to cut through Belos's barriers and get in and out quickly, I will be seen. At long last I understand why Belos built his fortress as he did, high on a plateau overlooking flat, open land. Because no one can drift through the barriers, anyone who approaches must drift to the Dry Land, and risk being seen in the Drift, then leave the Drift to pass the points of the barriers in the physical world, and risk being seen there. I consider the hidden stair, which leads around the back of the fortress to Belos's study, but even there the barrier exists. Even if I somehow managed to reach the edge of it without being seen in the Drift, I would still have to somehow break the Drift-lock on the physical door, get all the way through Belos's study and past his sleeping chambers, and make my way down to the dungeon.

No. All but impossible. Why should I take such absurd risks, endangering the whole rescue mission, when I could just slip in and out with the knife? Yes, of course I could still be seen in the Drift, but I could be so quick. It is the best way, the only way.

I say despairingly, "I *must* have the knife."

For a moment, I feel hollowed out, empty, my anger washed away by this one bleak fact. Then that very bleakness, that very simplicity clears away the debris of my thoughts. I must get that knife, period. There is no time for persuasion or permission. I must make it happen, by any means necessary.

"Astarti?" Bran asks warily, "What are you thinking?"

Even if Bran could help, which he can't, I won't drag him into this. This is *my* mess; *I* will clean it up.

"Nothing, Bran, nothing."

The stillness of his body suggests he doesn't believe me, so I resolve to act quickly, before he figures it out. Tonight. I will get that knife tonight.

Chapter 2

I pace my room, waiting for the moon to go down. I don't need the darkness, but I do need to be sure everyone has long since gone to bed, especially Heborian. My feet ache from hours of this restless movement, and I swear I must have worn a path in the woven rug that spans the stone floor. Finally, the white disk sinks in the west, withdrawing its cold light and plunging my room into darkness. I ease along my mooring into the Drift.

The complex structure of the castle fades into the background, and I pick out hundreds of sleeping forms. The number of people needed to make this place run astounds me after a lifetime in Belos's fortress, manned only by the Seven and a handful of servants. I drift toward the wing that houses Heborian and Rood—I still can't think of him as even my *half*-brother—but they are both asleep. I keep my distance, but even so I can make out the turbulence in Heborian's energy. He always seems so untouched by everything; I wonder what troubles his dreams. Rood, on the other hand, sleeps peacefully. Would I sleep that soundly had I grown up in the safety of this castle, as he did? It's a bitter question, and I force myself to move on.

I search for the barrier that guards Heborian's secret tower. I find it easily enough, a bright twisting of lighted threads. It's much like the barrier that sweeps around the castle itself, preventing the passage of anyone through the Drift, but this barrier is smaller and tighter. I don't know how to get through it, but I must try.

I drift to the barrier, passing through ghostly stone walls. I circle the sphere of energy, its glowing threads silent like everything in the Drift. Even so, they seem to hum through my own lighted form. As I draw near, the barrier constricts. I wonder as I have so often before: how can a barrier sense me? It's almost like it's alive.

I circle again, searching for a weak point, but everywhere I go the barrier tightens. I withdraw for a better perspective. Within the sphere, the knife glows brightly. How did Heborian trap Drift-energy into dry bone to make such a tool? Even while I'm angry with him, I am struck by his brilliance. Beside the knife, another item burns with equal power, though this one is ancient. My energy shivers at the sight of Heborian's Shackle. He insists it's only a tool, like the knife, one designed originally for teaching young Drifters to control their power, but I can't be so objective. I glance involuntarily at the region of my heart, as though the Leash I once bore might somehow reappear in the Shackle's presence.

Now Logan is the one Leashed. Bound, controlled by Belos to a degree even I never suffered. During the battle, in a moment of lucidity, Logan begged me to kill him, but I couldn't. I was weak and selfish, and I couldn't do it. Now, because of me, the gods alone—if they even exist—know what Belos must be doing to Logan. I *must* get that knife.

I shape my spear and flood it with silvery-gold energy until I am reeling with emptiness. I spin the spear like a staff, forcing it to greater speed as I deepen my concentration. When all my thought, all my will throbs in the point of my spear, the weapon ready, focused on this one need, I slash into the pulsing light of the barrier.

Pain explodes through my energies. Light flares, engulfing me. I am spinning, flying, blinded by light. I scream, my whole being echoing with it, but there is no sound.

When I finally shudder to a stop and the Drift settles around me, I shakily look myself over. I expect some black gash through my silvery-white energies, but I am whole. Whole, yes, but the threads of gold, blue, and pink that usually run strongly through me glow more faintly. I prickle with fear. I hope that's not permanent.

Slow with weariness, my thoughts scattered and slippery, I drift toward the barrier again. Circling like a fish, I wrench my fuzzy thoughts into better focus and study the writhing mass of energy. I want to poke it, but the way it blasted me makes me cautious. I'm so focused on the puzzle that I don't see the bright form until it's almost upon me.

I whirl to find Heborian, his silvery-gold energy teeming with fury, swooping toward me. I try to shape my spear and feel only a sluggish pulse. I'm as weak as a child her first time in the Drift. I try to dart away, but Heborian catches me easily. Hands bright with power, their tattoos glowing, clamp onto my arms. I wrench out of his grasp, but he grabs me again. His face contorts with rage, energy ripping through him, sparking in gold and blue. I do the only thing I can to escape: I slip through my mooring.

Entering the physical world, I am swallowed by cold, damp darkness. My foot wobbles on some ledge. My arms spin automatically to save my balance, but I slip. My other foot catches briefly on another lip of stone, but it's not enough. My stomach soars into my throat as I fall. My shoulder smacks against stone, then my knee hits, then my elbow. I slam to a stop when my back and head crack against something solid with the dull sound of wood. My body curls instinctively from the pain.

Bluish Drift-light flares above me, revealing that I am in a closed stairwell, the one that leads to Heborian's locked and barred tower room—and the knife. So close but still impossibly far from my reach. Heborian's Drift-light dims, withdrawing into a small globe that hovers over his shoulder.

I stagger to my feet as he tromps down the stairs, bare feet slapping on stone. The Drift-light glows whitish-blue across his handsome, furious face, highlighting the tattoo that hooks around his right eye and spikes down his cheek toward a neatly-trimmed dark beard. His hair, free of its Runish braiding for the night, hangs in unruly waves to his shoulders. He wears only loose sleeping pants, and the Drift-light shivers over his muscled torso, thickened with age but still lean and fit. An ugly scar threads from his ribs to his hip. Despite his state of undress, he looks every inch a king.

"What did I tell you?" he barks as he stops halfway down the stairs.

I brace against the door behind me as I push to my feet. My head spins, my legs tremble, and I can't stop my hand from covering the pain of torn stitches in my shoulder. My linen shirt is wet with blood.

"How—" I clear my throat and try again. "How did you know?"

His eyes narrow, and the tattoo hooking his eye seems to sharpen. I cringe, hating that he towers above me on the steps, that I'm backed into a corner. Why am I always made to feel so small?

"I could throw you in the cells for this."

I snort with false bravado. "And how would you keep me there?"

His silence looms, and a chill washes through my body. He couldn't, could he?

"I should do it, for your own good."

"Oh, and we both know how keen you are on my own good."

His jaw tightens, but he doesn't rise to my bait.

Since he doesn't seem inclined to seize me, I venture a question. "How does the barrier work? It fought me. How it that possible? What is it?"

His nostrils flare dangerously. "I'm surprised Belos never told you."

I lean wearily against the door, deflated by this reminder. "With so much else he didn't tell me, this surprises you?"

He grunts, offering no other acknowledgement of the deal he made with Belos, how he traded me to him as an infant in exchange for help in his conquest of Kelda. Oh, he has his justifications. The fact that they are even a *teeny* bit legitimate only vexes me more. I wish I could just hate him, plain and simple.

I shove these thoughts away. Only one thing matters right now. I force my body straight and stare up at Heborian. "I *need* that knife."

The Drift-light flares above his shoulder, but he gives no other sign of emotion. "I won't tell you again, Astarti. That knife will never leave my keeping."

"But if I—"

"No."

"Listen to me!"

"I will not! I don't care how much you love him. I don't care how much he is suffering. You will not take that knife anywhere near Belos."

"But I won't be near—"

Heborian thunders down the stairs. He slams me against the heavy door, dark eyes boring into mine. "I make no claims over you as your father, nor as your king. But this is *my* castle, and that is *my* knife, and I will never let you take it out of here."

My body trembles with rage. I long to shape my spear and settle this with him, but weakness deadens me.

I make a final, desperate attempt to move him. "You owe me *something.*"

He says harshly, "Yes, that's true. But you can't have this."

Unbidden, a tear wells in the corner of my eye. I never cry, but I am so exhausted, so angry, so beaten by my failure that I cannot will it away.

Heborian's face softens. For a moment, I see regret, pain, and some longing I don't understand. His hand lifts like he might touch me, but he lets it drop.

"I *cannot*, Astarti. I can*not.*"

He brushes me roughly aside and grabs for the door handle, Drift-light flaring as he unlocks it. The door flies open to crash against the wall, and he storms out.

I want to scream at his retreating back, but I don't want to wake anyone and attract attention, so I choke down the sound, all but gagging on it as Heborian's Drift-light disappears around a corner.

ॐ ॐ

I limp-shuffle to my rooms, making my way more by instinct than by conscious thought. I'm light-headed with pain and despair.

I stumble through my outer room, banging my shin against a chair, and grope my way to the bedroom. When I reach the bed, I grab a pillow and press my face into it. Finally, finally, I can scream. My body clenches with the force of it. I scream and scream until I am empty.

ℵ ℵ

Logan prowls the battlefield, his shirt hanging in ragged, bloody strips. His eyes, which should be a gorgeous swirl of color, are oily black. His face is hard, cruel, not his own at all.

I recoil from him, scrambling away over stiff, slippery bodies, my hands sticky with blood.

He watches me, and for a moment, his expression clears, and he is my Logan again. "Please," he begs, "please."

A bow appears in my hands.

I aim at his heart, but my hands shake. I want to tell him that I can't, that I'm sorry, but no sound comes.

His jaw hardens, his eyes blacken, and suddenly it's not Logan stalking toward me, but Belos. He laughs, sneering. A Shackle dangles from one hand, the links of pale bone gleaming, the two cuffs clicking softly against one another.

Chapter 3

LOGAN

I shift to ease the pressure on my right shoulder. I suspect it's dislocated again, but there's nothing I can do about it with my hands chained above me. I would stand for a while, but I doubt my leg can take it. I don't know how badly I'm hurt. My back is on fire from the last lashing, but I'm too tired to hold myself away from the wall. My shoulder feels huge with pain, but it's the leg that worries me. I can still feel my toes, but I can't bend my knee.

I'm glad it's dark, for so many reasons. One, I can't see the damage to my body, and two, they leave me alone at night—as long as I don't try to escape again. I should sleep and recover my strength, but this is the only time my mind is my own. Oh, I can still feel him, that oily, alien presence sleeping inside me. But at least my mind is not being violated; at least I can recognize my own thoughts.

The temptation to unlock my earthmagic, to rip this cell apart and seize freedom for even a moment, eats away at me.

But I know the moment he senses my power stir, he'll be down here like last time. I hate myself for a coward, but the pain in my leg warns me off. He's too fast and too strong.

As the sky lightens, making a pale square of the iron grate overhead, dread coils in my stomach. It won't be long.

༺ ༻

I recognize the light, excited tread of Koricus's feet on the stairs leading down to my cell, and my muscles tighten with anticipation. I force myself to my feet. A pointless defiance, I know, but I can't quite bring myself to meet him sitting down. I swallow a horrible taste as my torn back scrapes against the wall. My left leg blazes with such pain that blackness crowds the edges of my vision.

Koricus whistles as a faint glow of Drift-work unlocks the gate. When he steps into the cell, I marvel that he comes from the blood of my people. It's his manic energy, the way his wiry body seems to crackle with it. True, he has blue Earthmaker eyes, but that's all I see in him that speaks of Avydos, and even those look wrong—darting, electric, too eager. I wonder: is that how I look to my people? I know they think I'm not one of them, and maybe it's true, but I hope I don't look as crazy to them as Koricus looks to me.

"Morning, sunshine," he says brightly.

I refuse to follow his delighted eyes down the bruised and bloody mess of my bare torso to the filthy, blood-stained trousers.

His eyes rove back to my face. "Protect that other eye today." He mockingly holds a hand in front of one eye and fakes a few defensive maneuvers. "Getting pretty ugly."

Surprised by his words, I try to open my left eye. I didn't even realize it was swollen shut.

He draws near, a fist under his chin as though in thought. "What shall we decorate today? Most of this canvas is already painted. Feet, maybe? Hands?"

A chill spreads from my belly, and I can't stop my feet and hands from curling. I try to block out his voice, knowing how he loves to taunt me, but it slides into my consciousness.

"Some of this is still all right."

I flinch when he touches my belly, which makes him smile with cruel pleasure.

What sickens me most, however, is not my own situation. What eats away at me, day and night, is the thought that Astarti grew up here, with the likes of Koricus and the others. Seventeen years she spent here, *seventeen years.* I can't decide whom I hate most: Belos for enslaving her, or her father for selling her to him.

"Koricus!" booms a voice from the stairs, making me and Koricus both cringe.

I force myself to straighten as the gate crashes open and Belos storms into the cell, that sly-faced Straton close on his heels. Despite my efforts, a shudder wracks my body at the sight of Belos, clad as usual in his black leather pants and vest. Harsh blue eyes rake over me, assessing, strangely bright in his gaunt, tanned face. Blond hair curls damply behind his ears. If my face didn't hurt so much, my eyebrows might jump in surprise to think of Belos doing anything as ordinary as bathing. Somehow, this helps undercut my fear. I take a deep, resolving breath. He is just a man. I can endure this.

Koricus drops to one knee, head bowed. "I didn't touch him, my lord."

"Did I not say to wait for me? What use is he to me if your…eagerness renders him dead or unconscious?"

"Of course, my lord, I only came down to—"

Belos waves him away.

Koricus pops to his feet and slides behind his master, hands twitching with anticipation.

"Sleep well?" Belos inquires politely.

Everyone, it seems, is in a mocking mood today.

When I only stare back at him, Belos drops the pretense. He takes four careful steps, his boots thudding dully across the stone floor. He stops just out of arms reach and studies me with the detachment of a farmer looking over a damaged plow. "You don't have to make this so hard, you know. There was never any need for pain."

"I would think you know me better by now." My voice rasps through my dry throat.

The corner of his mouth lifts. "Oh, I do. I know *so* much about you, more perhaps than you know about yourself. Just what do you think you are, Loganos, son of Gaiana?"

I don't miss the fact that he leaves out my father. Father? Arathos acknowledged me as his own, but was I his? I hate that Belos's words stir all the doubts I've kept buried deep for so many years. Who was my father, really? *What* was he?

Nausea assails me, and my eyes jerk to Belos, his gaunt face still with concentration as he draws on the Leash between us. Are these thoughts even my own, or is he putting them in my head?

"Oh, those are your thoughts, Loganos, your doubts, your fears. I don't need to give them to you."

I grit my teeth at his intrusion into my mind. I clamp down on my thoughts, willing my mind to close.

"Don't fight me," he warns.

I try to spit at him, but my mouth is too dry. "Stay out of my head."

"But I like it here. It's so dark and turbulent; I feel very comfortable. Just what are you, Primo Loganos?" His eyes light with pleasure at my growl. "Does that touch a nerve? Is it the question of what you are? Or the question of whether you have the right to call yourself Primo? Surely a bastard has no claim to royalty?"

He waits for me to rise to his various baits. He knows very well there are no royals among the Earthmakers. Rulers, yes, like my brother, Aron, the Arcon, but it's not the same as royalty.

"Oh, Logan, Logan, Logan. Are you really fooled by that? Do you really think your brother views himself as a leader only?"

"Yes." I don't trust myself with more words.

"I must say I disagree," Belos counters in a would-be reasonable tone. "I remember him, even when his father was Arcon. What a little prince he thought he was."

I can't help it: he's opened the door for me to taunt him back. "Was that when you came back to Avydos to show off how you'd perverted yourself with Drift-power?" This only makes his mouth quirk, so I try again. "After my mother had already married Arathos instead of you?"

My back flares with pain as he slams me against the wall. His hand squeezes my throat, cutting off air. Blackness, beautiful blackness, crowds the edges of my vision. Let it take me—*please*, let it take me.

"I think not."

When Belos lets go, I can't stop myself from falling. I cry out as my injured leg buckles, as the chains jerk my hands up, wrenching my damaged shoulder.

"You always make this so hard," Belos grits out.

Distracted by pain, I'm unprepared for the flood of his mind into mine. My whole being fills with his oily slickness. It slides through my gut, poisoning me with his anger and madness. I scream with the horror of it, grasping at the shreds of my thoughts as he probes into my mind, as I sink beneath the oily surface of his will.

ꕥ ꕥ

Harsh sun beats down on us. We stand on a flat plain, the dry earth bleached pale yellow by the light. Our Seven flank us, ready to serve. When we sway from the damaged leg, one of the Seven steadies us. Theron. We curl a lip. Of all the Seven, he's the softest. But he still serves. It's Straton we don't trust, with his sly eyes, always hiding his thoughts in some dark corner, as though he would withhold himself from us. Fool. What could he or the others possibly do to threaten us, or even to draw away from us? We are part of them, melded into their very essences. We shaped them as the Old Ones shaped the earth. We made them our own. Our energies hum with the branching power of that network, which has made us immortal, which has made us into a *god.*

We falter, questioning. What "us"?

Confusion swirls through us. Us? We? Wait! Not we—*I*!

Oily blackness consumes us, and the confusion is gone. Everything is simple again. We stare across the barren landscape, worn to flatness except for the fortress behind us and the fingers of stone on the horizon where the Broken City continues to crumble. The place intrigues us. What happened there?

Focus!

What is that place?

Submit yourself!

Our gaze drifts away.

We try to calm our mind, to sense the deep, sleeping power of the earth. Our task is simple: rip it open.

The earth lies quiet, untouched.

"Why doesn't this work?" says the Other.

The Other?

He? We? Us?

"Whip him!"

Crack! Pain flares across our back.

No! We cannot give in. This is not who we are. This is not *what* we are. No one can make us. Close it off, close it off, close it off.

"Again!"

Crack!

"Again!"

Crack!

Our mind splinters. We scream with rage and plunge into the sleeping, angry heart of the earth, which understands us so well. It rumbles, wakening. Elation floods us. Freedom!

Boom! Snap!

The earth trembles, eager now to move, to change. It splits before us, lets itself break and crumble in relief. We are unloosed, flying on this freedom we have so long denied ourself. Such release! Why did we resist this?

Greedy and eager, we grab for air—so still and sluggish here!—but we find it. We draw, draw, draw, and whip it into a frenzy. It wants to move, to change, to be alive again. It only needs direction. It needs a will to shape it.

We let it take us.

Freedom! Ecstasy! We *are* wind. We whip across the dry earth, snagging stones, even boulders, whirling them, flinging them, dizzy with our power and freedom. The great plateau of the fortress rises before us, and we whip toward it, eager to batter it, to change it.

No! Not there!

We hesitate. The voice came from both within and from beyond us.

Away from that!

Who—

Away!

We? He. *He.*

No, no, no. He's done it again. The Other has taken us. Not us—me. Me! I am Logan!

I scream with fury, knowing myself all at once, feeling the oily taint of him inside me. I will kill him for this!

He and the Seven are dark blots on the yellow-brown plain. I will blow this place clean of them.

Something jerks in the core of my being. I falter, sickened, weakened. I gather my strength and rage, blowing harder, darkening the sky with dirt, but that something jerks again.

And again.

I churn with nausea as my body collects and separates itself from the wind.

I make a last, feeble attempt to pull away from him, the Other, but that *thing*, that *Leash* wrenches me from within. I fall to dry earth, retching.

Dust eddies around me. I cough, but my throat is so dry that the effort wracks my whole body. When a boot slams into my ribs, pain explodes, and the air is shocked from my lungs. Another kick lands in my gut, and I retch again, but there's nothing in my stomach to expel.

Someone—*he*—screams with rage, and this saves me, reminds me that he hasn't won. I can hold on. For a little longer, I can hold on. I stagger up and lunge at him, hands grabbing at his vest. He cries out as I brush the ugly wound that Astarti dealt him. Fresh blood coats my fingers. Triumph bursts inside me, then pain explodes in the back of my head, and the world goes black.

ꕤ

I swim up from the blackness. Before I can even open my one good eye, I smell the cool dryness and know I'm in my cell and that it's night. It hurts even to breathe, and I don't dare try to move my leg. The pain radiates all the way through my hip and into my belly.

I will the blackness to take me again, but the tread of boots on the stairs yanks me into consciousness. Light bleeds through my right eyelid, and I open it reluctantly. Everything is fuzzy at first, and I have to blink several times before I can force the dark blob in front of me to take shape. Green tunic, narrow face, sharp chin. Theron. He crouches, and the torturous scents of bread and some unidentifiable meat waft toward me. But it's the cup of water that nearly makes me moan.

He tears off a chunk of bread. "Here," he says roughly.

"Water," I rasp.

He lifts the cup to my lips but allows only a few drops to slide into my mouth. Even that nearly chokes me, and the cough that jerks my lungs tortures damaged ribs.

He chides, "Slowly."

We go through the same ritual each night, and throughout the long, degrading process of accepting food from another man's hand, I hate myself. This repulses me more than the beatings, more even than the violation of my mind, because *this* I want. My body simply takes over.

When the food is gone, Theron pushes to his feet. I ask him again, as I did the first night, "Why?"

He stiffens, just as he did before, and gives me the same answer, "If you die, even if it's his own fault, who do you think will pay for it?"

I don't entirely believe him. His face is different from the others'. His eyes are different.

"What were you, before him?"

For the briefest moment, pain crosses his face, then his expression hardens, and he says sharply, "Mind yourself."

When the gate clicks shut behind him, my thoughts, held together with such effort, drift again. In my dreams, she comes to me, dark-haired, beautiful, blue eyes sparkling with humor. She laughs, and the sound nearly breaks my heart. Then she says, "Logan. Logan. *Logan.*"

My good eye pops open, and I stare, stunned, bewildered.

She is here, crouching before me.

Astarti.

CHAPTER 4

LOGAN

I blink in the Drift-light that hovers over her shoulder, limning her delicate jaw with bluish light. Her long braid hangs in a messy tangle, nearly invisible against her dark clothes. I am still dreaming. This cannot be real.

Slender fingers reach for my face, and I know those short, blunt nails. She touches me gently. "What have they done to you?"

I have gone mad. I swear I can even feel the light pressure of her fingers. I want to lose myself in this hallucination, but some shred of sanity makes me say, "You aren't real."

Her eyes cloud with worry. "I will *kill* him for this."

She stands, stepping between my splayed legs, careful not to bump me. She leans near, her thigh almost brushing me. She smells like the Dry Land instead of like herself, but I forget this oddity when Drift-work glows faintly above me. The biting pain of the shackle vanishes, and her gentle fingers circle my right wrist. She lowers it slowly, carefully, but the pain of my damaged shoulder makes me grunt. *That* is no hallucination.

My heart lurches. My body jolts, and I jerk toward her, catching against the other shackle. "Astarti! It's really—"

"Yes." She kneels between my legs, her expression a confusion of pain and joy and, oddly, a sort of giddy eagerness. "It's really me. I'm getting you out of here."

I stare at her, at this face I love, at this impossibility, and for the first time since Belos brought me to this place, I weep. Her arms circle my neck, and she leans her cheek against my temple. Her tenderness breaks me, and I am all but sobbing with exhaustion, with disbelief, with joy.

Sudden terror seizes me, and I jerk back. "You shouldn't have come here!" I strain to keep my voice low. "If he catches you—"

Her jaw sets. "He won't, Logan, and I won't leave without you."

"But—"

"Just be quiet."

My Astarti. So stubborn. So determined.

She rises to work on the remaining shackle, and I gasp with relief as she lowers my other arm.

She kneels again between my spread legs. "How badly are you hurt?"

"My leg is pretty messed up."

Her eyebrows lower as she glances at it. "What about the rest of you?" Her fingers begin a light exploration of my body, skimming over my chest and ribs. Her lips thin when I wince, but I try to reassure her, "Just cracked, I think."

Her fingers brush over my belly, down to my hips. When she grazes the band of my pants, her touch stirs my desire. It surprises me to feel it through so much pain and exhaustion, but I'm so glad to see her, and there's so much I should have said, so much I should have done while I had the chance.

"I love you, Astarti."

Her hands freeze and she looks up at me. There is delight in her face, and even if it's a strangely greedy, triumphant look, I don't care. She's here.

She crushes her lips to mine. I'm startled by her aggression because it doesn't seem like her, but all that matters is that she's here. I reach for her with my good arm. My head is light and dizzy as I grip her waist, as my hand skims over her hip and up to her small, firm breasts. Suddenly, she draws a sharp, pained breath.

"Are you hurt? What happened?" I tug at the neck of her shirt to see the wound.

It's half healed. And familiar. Freshly ripped open. Foreboding seeps through my gut even before she smiles against my neck.

I jerk away, slamming my torn back against the stone wall.

She rocks back on her heels. Her grin is cruel and every bit as familiar as that wound. "You just had to ruin it. You, with your groping hands."

I'm shaking my head, delirious with horror and revulsion. I hold understanding at a distance. No, no, no.

When Drift-light surrounds her—*him*—I close my good eye so I won't see the transformation. I cannot bear to watch her face broaden and harden, to see her dissolve into him.

When I open my eye, Belos is still crouched in front of me. "What's the matter?" he says, voice deep again. "You don't like this face as well? Am I not pretty enough for you?"

He hooks a finger in the band of my pants, and I jerk away.

"You didn't mind a minute ago."

"Get away from me!"

"Oh, come on now. Don't deny you enjoyed it."

Disgust rolls through me, and my punch sends him tumbling back.

"Koricus!" he bellows, climbing to his feet, wiping a bloody lip with the back of his wrist.

Koricus comes flying into the cell.

"Chain him!"

I don't even try to fight. I am dead, hollowed by self-disgust. How could I have let him fool me? How could I not have known? How could I have touched him or responded to him with desire? What is wrong with me?

Only when Koricus wrenches my right arm up does pain drive me out of my thoughts and into the physical reality of the cell. Another of the Seven, Ludos, approaches with a steaming cup.

"Make him drink it *all*," snarls Belos.

I clamp my jaw. Even from three feet away I can smell something wrong with that drink. Koricus tries to pry my mouth open, and when that doesn't work, he hits me. My head cracks against the wall, sparking lights in my vision, and suddenly the hot, foul, sharp-tasting liquid is in my mouth. I gag and try to spit it out, but someone holds my mouth shut and pinches my nose until I swallow.

I'm still hacking, couching, trying to retch when Belos says, "We'll make a believer out of you yet."

ꕥ

My mind is a whirlpool. I rise to the surface for brief moments, straining for clarity, but I'm quickly sucked under again.

Astarti comes back. I don't know if it's her, but it feels like it. She talks to me. Sometimes she touches me, but I don't feel anything, which irritates her. I don't like when she's mad at me, but I can never focus enough to make things right.

I vanish into the pool.

It's when Arathos visits that I feel most dead inside. He asks me why I didn't save him, why I let Belos kill him. He asks me if I know that his head rotted on a pike in Belos's hall until no one could stand the smell. He asks me if I know he's not my father. He asks me who my father is. I tell him I don't know, but he doesn't believe me.

"Your mother must have said *something*. Was he a Drifter? Something else? Where did she find him?" His face isn't quite as I remember it, a little too gray, edged with decay, but my mind is too hazy to make sense of it.

"I don't know. I'm sorry, father."

"Don't call me that."

Occasionally, I am aware of *him*, the Other, out there somewhere. Or rather, in *here* somewhere. In my mind, my body. A dark, oily presence.

Once, I hear him say, "If the drink doesn't work, I'll have to do it."

Someone answers, "Why does it matter so much? You said you would not do that again, that it was too dangerous. That's why you didn't do it to her."

He says, "I *must* know, by any means necessary."

I don't understand what they're talking about, but I know it's not good, so I try to draw away. Immediately, there's more of that hot, bitter liquid in my mouth, gagging me, and I spin through the whirlpool once more.

Others come and go. The Ancorites, pale and hairless, with their hard, cruel fingers. I can't help but cringe when they come. Their questions grow ever more impatient.

"What did I tell you?" Dioklesus demands. "Where does your power come from? What are you?"

I cringe at his rusty, scraping voice. My mind goes blank.

His hands curl like claws. "What are my brothers and I doing in the tower? What is our purpose? You must remember!"

The words he spoke to me so long ago rise through the fog of my memory: "Keeping the balance."

Dioklesus screeches, "What does that mean?"

Why is he asking these questions? Why doesn't he know?

Dioklesus closes his ancient, watery eyes in frustration.

I brace for the whip, but it doesn't come.

I wait for Astarti to return. When she does, she asks me to use my earthmagic for her. I say I will, even though I'm not sure I say the words out loud. It doesn't seem to matter. She understands.

I try for her, I really do, but I can't quite rid myself of this nagging doubt that something's not right. It's only when she hits me and cries and says she would rather be with Belos than with me that I feel myself break, feel my power spin away from me, and I am grateful to have another take control of it.

Chapter 5

I'm on the beach, as far as I can get from the towering walls of Heborian's castle in a morning's much-needed walk, when movement catches my eye. I look to the distant bluff shielding my stretch of beach and spot an approaching figure. I slide into the Drift and sweep toward the energy form, confirming my suspicion that it's Bran. He stops, gazing in the direction where he must have seen me moments ago.

He stares around for a good long while before turning back the way he came. I detect no particular strain in his energies, so I assume there's no emergency. Besides, if anyone needed me urgently, Heborian would send a Drifter.

I wait until he's safely away before returning to my beach. What could I say to him except that I cannot save his brother?

Part of me reasons that I should ask for his help. I can't get to that knife through the Drift. I don't understand the barrier, and Heborian, somehow, knows when anyone tries to breach it. My only hope is to use earthmagic, to tear that tower apart and snatch the knife from its ruins.

But Bran has tried to teach me earthmagic over the last few weeks, and it's never worked for me like he describes. I don't need any witnesses to my failure, nor any false encouragements.

I stare out across the wide blue expanse, where the waves roll and crash in their endless rhythm, oblivious to my will. I try again to open myself as Bran has instructed, try to surrender to the waves' push and pull, but I feel nothing. I pick up a stone and hurl it into the water. The rush of the waves swallows the feeble plink. A seagull struts by, and I pick up a second stone. I almost aim for the bird, but it takes off into screeching flight.

I have found the other elements no more responsive than water. How is it that I wrought such destruction during the battle when I can't shift a grain of sand now?

I think I know the answer; I just don't like it. Every time I have entered the elements, I've done so as I was trying to reach the Drift. But I nearly lost myself in something far more powerful than I am.

I still my trembling hands. It doesn't matter. Trying to control the elements from outside them is not working. I have no choice.

I start my slide into the Drift. I force myself to hover at the edge and grope for the deep, buried power of the earth, trying to sense the veins and cracks deep below the surface.

Nothing.

No, wait.

A faint throb. Pressure in the earth's old, heavy bones.

An image asserts itself in my mind: a ten foot deep trench cut through the battlefield. Broken bodies half buried in stone and soil. Dark blood, white bone, yellow entrails. Another image, this one imagined but no less real: Heborian's tower ripping apart, showering stones, crushing people as they thunder to the ground.

Just how many am I willing to kill to save Logan?

Part of me screams, *I don't care!*

Another part insists, *Stop*.

I try to ignore these voices, reaching again for the power of earth, but it's gone. I grope through the Drift, empty now of the elements. There is only me, powerless.

I slide out of the Drift and am surrounded again by the lifeless sand, the oblivious water, and the unfeeling sky with its heartless sun. I press my face into my hands and scream.

I try again.

ꕥ ꕥ

I hunch on the footstool before my sitting room fire, staring into the flames. Even the plush cushion of the footstool reproaches me. Here I am, comfortable, safe, warm. I know all too well that Logan is none of those things.

My mind, relentless, will not let go of the questions that have haunted me all through this fruitless, wasted day: do I risk harming others to save Logan? Do I let him keep suffering because of something that *might* happen? And, of course, what if I destroy the knife in my attempt to get to it?

I drag fingers through my hair, further ruining my braid. Annoyed, I strip the tie off its end and claw through the tangles until my hair hangs loose and dark around my shoulders.

When someone knocks at my door, I gruffly tell them to go away.

Bran calls through the wood, "It's me."

I repeat, "Go away."

"Please, Astarti."

I try to wait him out, listening for the sound of retreating footsteps, but guilt at having avoided him all day sends me to the door. I pull it open, but that's the only courtesy I can muster. Without a word to Bran, I return to my footstool.

He joins me by the fire, repositioning a chair before he sits. I expect him to say something about having seen me on the beach, but he doesn't.

Instead, he says, "I know you tried to steal that knife last night. Because you couldn't get to it through the Drift, you want to try with earthmagic."

I say nothing.

"I want to help."

"And how will you help me, Bran? If I go after the knife, I could kill dozens, hundreds even, if I can't control the elements well enough, which you know I cannot. Should I risk that?"

Bran arranges the folds of his cloak neatly over his knees, as though putting the cloth in order will bring the rest of the world in line. "Your control may not be fine enough, but mine is. Earth is not my strongest element, but I can break the tower more safely than you. Then you can get the knife."

Hope unfurls within me, and with it, shame. Why didn't I think of this? I am not accustomed to looking for help, so I stood on the beach alone, like a fool, while my only chance of success walked away. I squeeze my eyes shut at the horror of lost time.

I say, holding off the full blooming of hope, not ready yet to believe, "You will make an enemy of Heborian, not only for yourself, but for your people also. You understand that, right?"

"I have a condition."

His tone makes me wary. "What's your condition?"

"I'm coming with you."

"But you can't. You can't enter the Drift."

His eyes latch onto mine, and I shrink from his determination, his certainty, his challenge.

"I can if you Leash me."

I stare at him blankly. I did not just hear that.

"I want you to Leash me, Astarti, and take me with you."

He starts to get up, hands reaching for me, and I recoil, lunging up from the stool. It pitches over, clattering, snaring my feet. I am stumbling, tripping, kicking free of it like it's the Shackle itself. I scramble across the room, away, away, away.

I thud into a table, which bangs against the wall, making the picture hung behind it wobble on its nail.

Bran is on his feet. The fire burns behind him, leaving his face in shadow but outlining all the determined lines of his body. "I want you to do it."

I clutch the table ledge behind me and lean away. He cannot be serious. My head swings in denial.

"I want you to Leash me and take me with you."

"Stop saying that!"

"I mean it, Astarti."

"You have no *idea* what you're asking! I will *never* do that."

His hands clench, backlit by the fire, and when I see that, another image asserts itself over his.

Belos stalks near, hands clenching, the Shackle dangling from his grip. "You will *do it."*

I back away, shaking with horror.

"You must learn. You must stop being a child."

The man chained to the dungeon wall jerks, rattling the chains. The gag in his mouth muffles his screams.

Belos's lip curls. "I can *make you. I will."*

I collapse, banging my head against the table. I try to tear away from the hands holding me until I smell clean linen and pine. Bran is shouting my name.

I take a choking breath and will the images to blackness, forcing my mind to empty. The panic recedes from my limbs, settling into a chill in my heart.

"What happened?" Bran's hands flutter over me, not touching. "Are you all right?"

I scramble to my feet and shove past him. I stalk to the fire on trembling legs. I feel Bran hovering a few feet behind.

"You don't understand what you're asking." I can't force my voice above a whisper. "I could never do that."

But you did, sneers a nasty voice inside me. I shut it up, drive it deep down.

"Astarti, listen—"

"Get out."

"Listen to me—"

"Get *out*!"

When Bran doesn't move, I snarl, "I *can* make you."

Bran's voice goes gentle, and his tone, as much as his words, freezes me. "Do you know what they did to Logan, when he was a child? Do you know how they tried to teach him to control his power?"

I close my eyes, picturing the lash scars across Logan's back. I say miserably, "What do you want from me?"

"I want you to understand."

I fall onto the stool, head in my hands. This is the story I've wanted, the one I've needed: to *know* what happened to Logan. Resentment burns dimly inside me. Nothing else Bran might have said would have caused me to let him stay. I'm sure he knows that.

Bran begins softly, standing somewhere behind me, like this story is spoken straight out of the past. "My father sent Logan away, to the Ancorites, when he was ten. You've probably never even heard of them. They're a group of ascetics who live in a tower on the remotest of the Outer Islands. They have little contact with the rest of us. They are powerful, isolated, ancient. No one seems to know their origin, and they are rarely spoken of.

"When my father made this decision, I argued with him but not hard enough. He reminded me that when Logan was five, he had killed two people. Accidentally, of course, but it was still awful. He reminded me that in the years since, Logan's control had scarcely improved, that he was danger to himself and to others. At that time, Logan was barely even speaking anymore. It was like he had closed himself off from the world, almost like he was dead. But, on occasion, he would erupt, and his earthmagic would come pouring out.

"One day, Logan was teased by another boy. Even Earthmaker children can be rough and cruel before they've learned restraint. Logan was used to being teased and was used to ignoring it, but on this day, he had had enough. He split the earth under the boy's feet. The boy fell deep into the crevice and broke his leg. It was hard to argue with my father in the wake of that. What if Logan had killed that boy? I bowed to my father's logic and reason.

"I accompanied my father when he took Logan to the tower of the Ancorites. Logan did not cry or beg us to take him home as another child might have done. The only time I saw even a flicker of fear in him was when the Ancorite appeared out of the air before us. I sensed others hovering, invisible. I do not know how they did that or what they even were. All I know is that the Ancorite who appeared had the oldest, maddest eyes I'd ever seen. He was pale and hairless, with skeletal hands. Logan barely came up to his ribcage." Bran swallows audibly. "The Ancorite did not even speak to my father, though my father was the Arcon. He did not even look at us. He latched onto Logan, and they both vanished."

Bran falls silent, and I squeeze my eyes shut. Horror washes through me as I imagine Logan, *my* Logan, as a child, ripped away from all he knows by some ancient, terrifying creature.

I can't stop myself from asking, "What did they do to him?"

"I don't know. He doesn't speak of it. The physical force is obvious. He certainly didn't have *whipping scars* when we took him there. I don't know what else may have happened."

"But they let him go?"

Bran hesitates, as though uncertain. "I don't think so. I think he escaped. About a year later, a fisherman in one of the smaller towns on Avydos found him in the water, half-drowned. Logan was with the fisherman's family for several months because they didn't know who he was. He didn't speak. Only when Polemarc Clitus went recruiting in that village and spotted him was he returned to us."

"And the Ancorites never came for him?"

"No. I don't know this for certain, but I've always suspected they could not stray so far from their tower. There was something strange about that place, Astarti, something that made my skin crawl across my bones."

At those words, my own skin crawls, my body sensing a mystery that my mind cannot begin to unravel.

"When Logan returned, he still did not speak. His earthmagic never erupted again, at least not until many years later, when our father was killed." He adds bitterly, "I guess they did teach him to control himself. But at what cost? He came back to us more ruined than when we'd taken him. Only when Clitus began to train him as a Warden, to teach him the sword, did he speak again."

Bran shakes his head, and his tone changes. "Do you understand now? I let my father take Logan to them. I *went with him*! I have to get him back this time, as I did not before." When I don't respond, he begs, "Astarti, please."

I force my hands to unclench. I am sick, shaking with the horror of this story. Because my horror has no other outlet, I lash out at Bran. "You told me once that what was done to Logan helped. You acted like it was necessary."

He doesn't answer at first, then, softly, "We all lie to ourselves sometimes. I'm not asking for pardon."

Because I understand Bran's guilt, his need to make it right even at my expense, most importantly because I could give in to his need, I try another tactic, "You realize that if you died while Leashed to me, your energy would become mine. Your lifeforce, soul, whatever you want to call it would be trapped in me." Bran's mouth sets stubbornly, so I add, "And if Belos managed to Leash me again, you would be Leashed to him by proxy."

For the first time, doubt clouds his face. He stares into the fire. "It's worth the risk."

I say angrily, "You would make me into Belos."

"You aren't Belos, Astarti."

I force my heart to stop booming, force myself to think. Hearing Bran's story, I am more desperate than ever to free Logan. I am sick to imagine him once more being terrified, forced into submission. I must free him, by any means necessary—well, almost any. I may not be Belos himself, but I am his creature, and I have learned to use what advantages present themselves. How, then, can I use this? I see two boons: Bran's offer of help, and his trust. Clarity stills me. I will take one and betray the other. I will never Leash Bran, but I can let him believe that I will, right up to the moment the knife is in my hands and I leave him behind. It is betrayal, yes, but surely of all the evils before me, it is the least?

I know better than to agree too suddenly. It would only raise Bran's suspicions. I rise from my stool to pace up and down the chamber, not having to feign my agitation.

Bran, his hands clenched on the back of a chair, watches me. I shake my head, as though in denial. This is my real skill, the thing that made me useful to Belos—and sometimes kept me safe from him—I am a very good actor. Or, as Belos might rightly say, a liar.

I snap, "We will cut the Leash the minute—the *second*—we get back. Is that clear?"

"Yes."

"I hate you for this, Bran, I hate you."

"I know. But I take full responsibility."

I wheel on him, allowing my anger to be real. This is the key to lying: make yourself feel what you would feel if it were true. "How can you take responsibility? *I* will be in control. *I* will be the one *holding your Leash.* Do you get that, Bran?" I stalk near and jab a finger into his chest. "Do you understand what that means?"

Bran tries to take my hand, but I wrench it from his grasp and pace again.

"I trust you, Astarti."

I snort. Even what I'm doing in this moment shows him for a fool. "Have you lost your mind, Branos?"

"No."

I pace away and back to him, pointing an accusing finger. "Don't you dare die. Don't you *dare* die while Leashed to me." I let the horror of this idea fill me, and it's not difficult because this is the very reason I will never do it.

Bran's blue eyes are calm, sympathetic. "Why are you agreeing to this?"

I don't trust myself with a complex lie, so I snap, "You know why," and let him draw his own conclusions. Because I care more about Logan than about Bran. Because, like Bran, I cannot stomach the idea of leaving Logan in the hands of someone so cruel, not again.

Bran's body language tells me he has more questions. I need to end this before something gives me away.

When a knock sounds at the door, Bran and I both jump. I frantically try to decide how loud my voice has been. Could I have been overheard?

"Aren't you going to answer that?"

I call roughly, "Who is it?"

"It's Clara, my lady."

My teeth go on edge. My lady's maid, what a joke. She is, more accurately, the woman Heborian assigned to me as a lady's maid, but whom I send away every time she comes. I don't like being waited on, especially by someone who fusses over my hair and clothes, who tries desperately to make me into something I'm not.

I stalk to the door and wrench it open. Clara, young and prim, dressed for dinner in an elegant taffeta gown, draws back, frightened. She is a low-ranking nobleman's daughter, soft and ignorant, sent to court, ostensibly, to serve as a lady's maid, but she's really here to find a husband. She told me as much, back when she suffered under the delusion that I would enjoy chatting about men. I swiftly disabused of that notion.

Clara dips a curtsey. "I'm sorry, my lady, but His Majesty has requested your presence at dinner."

I ignore her use of "my lady." I've tried to get her to stop calling me that, but she's as stubborn as Horik. "Tell him I'll eat in my rooms, as usual."

Clara's thin fingers twist together. "He was most insistent."

"Why?"

Clara's eyes fall to the toes of her velvet slippers, which stick out at the hem of her shimmery gown. "I'm not privy to such things, my lady."

I shift guiltily. I shouldn't be so mean to her. She's just trying to do her job, and, unlike some of the others at court, she's never sneered at me. Besides, this will get me away from Bran and his scrutiny. I should be grateful for her sudden appearance.

"Tell him I'll be there shortly."

"Shall I come back and attend your hair?"

When my lip curls involuntarily, Clara dips a hasty curtsey and scurries away.

Chapter 6

After Bran leaves to wash up for dinner—it seems I won't be able to avoid him after all—I pace my rooms. Perhaps I should ignore Heborian's summons and avoid both him and Bran. Bran and I have a basic plan now, hastily agreed upon before I shooed him out. We will get that knife tonight, after everyone is asleep. My body goes jittery at the thought.

I must not raise anyone's suspicions, especially Heborian's. If he was so insistent that I come to dinner, he will no doubt seek me out if I don't. It will be easier to lie in the crowded dining hall than in the privacy of my rooms; there will be a limit to the questions he can ask there. The most important thing will be for me to maintain my anger with him. If I appear at ease, he'll suspect I have a plan, and he'll watch me like the wolf he is. But this act will be simple and easy: I need only remember that Logan would already be free if Heborian had let me take that knife. Oh, my anger is very real indeed.

When I enter Heborian's dining hall, I automatically crane my neck to see the crystal and gold chandelier that blazes with such a heady mix of warm yellow candlelight and cool blue Drift-light. The crystals catch and recast the light everywhere, laying it in slashes and swathes across the domed ceiling, the crowded ranks of tables, the tiled floor, and the tapestry-hung walls. I've eaten in here before, but I don't like it. Too many people.

I see status in the seating arrangements, the plain-clothed men and women, probably petitioners, taking up the tables at the far end. The clothes grow finer, the mannerisms more confident, the speech more boisterous, as the tables stretch nearer the raised dais, where the king and his company sit.

Heborian's chair is like any other on the dais, sturdy and handsomely carved, but it's no throne. He is such a strange mix of pride—even ostentation if the Drift-light is any indication—and unexpected restraint.

The dais itself, a raised platform of dark-veined marble, looks old, and I'm sure it was built long before Heborian took Tornelaine. Other things also speak of age: the fine porcelain plates, the gold cups, the polished silverware. Some details are distinctly Keldan, such as the woven tapestries depicting long-ago battles and kings. And yet, while Heborian has left these reminders that this is indeed Kelda, he himself bears symbols of his homeland. His long dark hair, distinctively braided away from his face on one side, and his blue tattoos, highly visible on face and hands, speak loudly of Rune. Why leave Keldan details and Runish ones together? Is it a reminder to all that he's a conqueror? Or is it an effort to blend two cultures?

Indeed, that blending is most obvious among the seated folk, where light brown, occasionally blond Keldan hair mixes with dark. The faces of some folk under twenty show the marks of both cultures. My eye catches on one girl, no more than five, whose dark-haired father lays a tender hand on her strawberry blonde head, looking over her to smile at a red-headed woman in a distinctly Keldan dress. My heart pricks at that. Could that ever have been me, seated between Heborian and Sibyl?

My jaw tightens. Of course not. That possibility was thrown away before I was born, before I was even conceived.

Heborian's eye catches mine as I hover in the arching doorway. The chair to his left is empty, the plate untouched. His eyes slide to it in…invitation? Command? It annoys me to sit beside the king, as though I have some place at his side. The barb only deepens when I see Rood, the child he kept, at his other hand. What stupid pretense for me to be here. Worse, though, is the fact that Bran is seated to the left of my empty spot. I will be surrounded by everyone I want to avoid.

Clara, seated at one of the tables near the dais, starts to get up, looking a question at me. I shake my head and make my way around the perimeter of tables to the dais.

"Finally," Heborian says by way of greeting when I drop into the chair beside him.

"I had to get ready."

He eyes my rumpled linen shirt, but I only stare back defiantly. I let my lie become truth: just because I've found another way to get the knife doesn't mean I've forgiven him. I won't jump and run at his command; he can wait.

Bran, seated on my left, has a half-cleared plate, so he's been here a while. He, unsurprisingly, is not prone to the disrespect that I am, even though he also plans to steal from Heborian within a few hours. Fortunately, Bran is busy with his fork, pushing meat from one side of his plate to the other before taking a small bite. I almost shake my head at his obvious discomfort. Does he want to give us away?

Heborian drawls, "Frankly, I'm surprised you came at all." I turn to see his dark eyes narrowed on me, suspicion evident.

I put a snap into my voice. "And why is it important for me to be here tonight? You know I prefer to eat in my rooms."

His dark eyes rove over my face, the suspicion fading, replaced by a softer expression. I draw back warily—what's going on?

Abruptly, Heborian tears his eyes away. He raises his wine cup to his lips and says, voice muffled by the cup, "It's your birthday."

I gape at him.

His throat moves on a huge swallow of wine and he slams the cup down, empty. "Figured you didn't know."

A serving man hustles along the table and tips a silver pitcher to refill Heborian's cup.

My birthday. I've never even thought about it before. I press my hands into my lap to still their trembling. "How old am I?"

Heborian, who has raised his cup again, chokes on his wine and has to wipe his chin with a white napkin. When he lays it next to his plate, the wine stain reminds me of blood. "Eighteen."

I nod. The number agrees with what Belos has told me, but it's nice to know for sure. Oddly, I feel grounded by this knowledge, the definitiveness of it. I came from a particular place on a particular day. I can't help wondering why it should mean so much to know one's origins.

Because I won't let Heborian see how this affects me, I harden myself with sarcasm. "Is that why I'm given this place of honor tonight?" I gesture grandly to my chair.

"That will always be your place, should you desire it."

I can't help but notice that my place is on his left, where Rood sits at his right. Stupid that I should care; stupid that I should even notice. My question was a joke. Why am I taking myself seriously?

Rood leans around Heborian to look at me, knife and fork held properly in a trained balance. He's younger than I am, about Korinna's age, but I feel like a child when he stares at me, the prince in his embroidered doublet, with his fine court manners. What does he want? What is he thinking? I know he doesn't like me, but there are so many possible reasons for that I cannot begin to guess which one is his. At least his face lacks the open hostility of Wulstan's, who sits on Rood's other side. Because I won't let Wulfstan see me squirm, I raise my gold cup in mock salute, which makes him scowl and sit back. Something eases in my chest. There. Now I feel better.

I turn my attention to my plate, which a serving man has mounded with tender beef and carrots drenched in white sauce. I reach for my fork. What Bran said yesterday was true: I need to make myself strong. Tonight Bran will help me get that knife. Tonight I will free Logan. My heart thumps with anticipation, and it's an effort to keep my hands steady and my mouth chewing. I cannot taste anything, but it doesn't matter. I'm eating not for pleasure but for purpose. Not even Heborian's revelation can be allowed to distract me from that.

Beside me, Heborian drains his wine cup once more, then reaches inside his velvet doublet. He pulls out a sparkling silver bracelet.

"Here," he says roughly, pushing the bracelet at me. "Your birthday present."

My temper flares. Does he think to buy me off with gifts, make me as soft and complacent as the likes of Clara? Just last night he prevented me for taking the knife, consigning Logan to another day of torment. There is nothing he could give me, nothing he could do or say, to earn the smallest amount of forgiveness from me. What does he want, a hug, a smile? I shove his hand away.

Heborian's fingers tighten protectively on the bracelet. "It was your mother's."

That strikes me dumb, freezes my hands. I've never before seen anything of my mother's, any physical evidence of her existence, as though she has always been only an idea. Why must he do this to me tonight of all nights? I want so very badly to know about her, but not right now.

Heborian pushes the glittering bracelet at me again. My fingers tremble as they graze it, warm with Heborian's body heat. He drapes it over my fingers and withdraws, watching me.

The bracelet is made of tiny, delicate links of bright silver. I half expect it to make a tinkling sound, but all it does is shine. My eyes start to prickle. This was my mother's. She touched this, wore it.

"Put it on," Heborian says roughly.

I shake my head. This is too fine for me. *She* is too fine for me. How awful it would be for her, had she lived to know what I became. No doubt as she carried her daughter in her womb, she imagined a princess in pretty dresses, a girl, perhaps, like Clara. I'm sure she never pictured me, a coarse, rude young woman with blood on her hands, a woman who lies even to her friends.

I set the bracelet down. No, I could never wear it.

"She would want you to have it."

I push it back toward Heborian. How can he not understand?

"Astarti, take it." He nudges it back my way, and the tiny links slide over one another in fine, delicate movement.

I shove back from the table, my chair making an ugly screech against the marble. "I don't want it," I hiss, panic closing over me as I reject this thing of my mother's, this thing I want so desperately to touch, to have. I will only profane it. Better that she never know me, better that none of my darkness come over any memory or memento of her. Better that she be an idea only, that I be separate from her.

Emotion—anger? sadness?—rolls through Heborian's dark eyes as his hand closes protectively over the bracelet again.

ꕥ ꕥ

Heborian finds me on the castle's battlements, where I am looking out over the moonlit roofs of Tornelaine. Of course I can't hide from him, not when he can step into the Drift and identify me so easily. I had hoped, though, that he would leave me alone.

I keep my back to him when I say, "What do you want?"

"You and I need to have a conversation."

My throat tightens. "No, we don't."

"About the knife."

My heart gives an anxious thump. I was afraid he would want to talk about my mother, but this is even worse. I must remember my lies; I must not let him suspect me. "I believe we've had that conversation already. Several times. It always ends the same."

"Not this time." Heborian's voice is harsh.

"How do you figure? You'll tell me the knife is too dangerous; I'll say I don't care. You'll make it clear that I can't ever have it. I'll accuse you of not caring about what Belos is doing to Logan—"

"It's not that."

"—you'll say, 'It's not that'"—I mock his voice—"I'll say—"

"Astarti, *heed me.*" The sudden intensity of his words shuts me up. "The knife cuts energy, *links* in energy, the link between one person and another, like a Leash, like a barrier."

That takes a moment to sink in, then I spin to face him. He's so close that he breathes the smell of wine into my face. Moonlight washes his cheeks pale, shows the tight set of his mouth. I can't have heard him right. I ask warily, "What did you say?"

He shoves past me to brace himself on the stone teeth of the crenellation. His body is so tense, his energy so primed that I half expect him to tear the stones free with his bare hands. He says tightly, "Belos would know the instant you cut through his barrier, just as I knew the instant you tried to breach mine."

Gooseflesh rises on my arms and legs. "How—"

"A barrier is like a Leash, Astarti. It is energy, harnessed through a Shackle, bound to the one who made it. You cannot cut through a barrier without the creator's knowledge. Belos would be on you in an instant."

Horror washes at my feet like a tide, threatening. I hold it off a moment longer, refusing to believe what he's saying. "Whose energy forms the barrier?"

"As I said, girl, it's like a Leash."

"You'd better explain that."

Heborian's fingers tighten on the stone. "A barrier is a necessary evil. Without mine, Belos would take Tornelaine. A little evil to ensure a greater good."

"Whose energy forms your barrier, Heborian?"

He hesitates. "A small portion of it is my own, of course, but mostly it's that of others."

The horror I've held back washes over me as the truth becomes undeniable. "You have Leashed them."

Heborian says tightly, "In a manner of speaking."

Understanding hits me. "That's why you can't drift through a barrier, isn't it? Because the barrier is a *person*."

"Yes, or several people. The threads are drawn out, twisted together. It's a complex process, but in essence, you're right, the barrier is a person, and you cannot drift *through* a person. But. The knife can *cut* through. I've never tested this theory, but the knife may also be able to sever a mooring, to kill someone who is not even within the Drift."

I sink to my knees, weighed down by horror. "How could you do such a thing?"

Heborian's voice comes to me from above, gruff, unapologetic. "I do what is needful, always, no matter how distasteful."

"Evil," I correct him sharply.

He accepts this. "No matter how evil."

"And when do we stop doing evil and telling ourselves that it's good? Even Belos can tell himself such lies."

Heborian doesn't answer me, so I am left with the question myself. Am I not about to do the same thing? To take the knife into Belos's reach to save Logan? If Belos gets that knife, nothing will be able to stop him. Can I accept that evil to do a little good? Or rather, to try, because if the barrier is bound to Belos and he knows the moment I cut it, I will never even get to Logan anyway. I close my eyes at this bleak reality.

I say, deadened by the failure that awaits me, "I'm still going after him, even without the knife. I can't just leave him there."

"You must. You will only get yourself killed and do him no good. You must leave him to his fate."

I ask bitterly, "As you left me to mine?"

"Yes. As I left you to yours."

"I would rather die than do as you did."

"Why can you not let him go?" Heborian makes a harsh, cutting gesture. "He's gone, he's done."

I scramble to my feet. "Don't you say that!"

I don't realize I've shaped my Drift-spear until Heborian's eyes travel its length.

"You won't let this go, will you? You'll run off and get yourself killed, even though you know it's pointless. Won't you?"

I snarl, "At last, you're starting to understand me."

"*Gods*," he mutters furiously and turns away, staring out over the city. He shakes his head, muttering to himself.

I wait him out. I've made myself clear; I have nothing more to say.

"If you're so determined, you'll need more than your spear to get into that fortress."

My hand tightens on the familiar smooth length of it. "What do you mean?"

Heborian looks over his shoulder at me. "Belos never taught you to hide yourself in the Drift, did he?" At my blank look, he goes on, "I'm not surprised. The only things that served his purposes were for you to fight and to lie."

My heart sinks at the truth of that. That is what I am: a fighter and a liar. I don't know how to be anything else.

"If you give me time, I'll teach you."

"There is no time! I won't leave him there any longer."

"If you go now, with nothing more to serve you than your spear and your determination, you will die, and Logan will not be freed. Give me one week, and I will teach you Drift-work such as you have never imagined. Wouldn't you rather have *some* hope of success?"

"I can't wait a whole week."

"Give me five days, then. These things take time to learn."

"Two."

Heborian only grunts.

"Let's start now."

He pushes wearily away from the crenellation. "In the morning."

"Right now!"

"I'm tired, I'm half-drunk. We'll begin at dawn. Get some sleep."

With that, Heborian vanishes into the Drift, and I am left alone on the battlements, clutching my spear with no one to fight and no one to lie to but myself.

Chapter 7

It's still dark when I arrive at the door to Heborian's chambers. Light from the bracketed sconce draws highlights on the guard leaning beside it, glowing bright in the fur edging of his cloak and gleaming across the Runish tattoo spiking from behind his left ear. Other than Horik and Wulfstan, I haven't paid much attention to Heborian's other Drifters, but I think this one is named Jarl. He stood near me on the wall as Belos's army crested the hills.

When he sees me tense to enter the Drift, he says, "Don't even think about it."

"Think about what?" I ask innocently.

He shoots me a don't-give-me-that-bullshit look.

"Fine," I grumble and wander off to sit by the fountain in the middle of the huge foyer. Dawn, Heborian said. I'll wait until the first rays of light peek through the high windows but not a moment longer. If he doesn't want a surprise visit from me while he's still in his nightclothes, he'll be out here on time.

Unfortunately, waiting here is no easier than waiting in my chambers was. I still can't stop picturing Bran's face when I told him why we couldn't take the knife. He understood and he agreed, but…

Bran didn't say it, but the way he turned away like Logan was already dead spoke loudly enough of his doubt in this new plan. I get up and pace around the fountain. Beside the king's door, Jarl stiffens at the loud clap of my boots on the tiles.

When a scullery maid scurries through the foyer bearing a hamper of wood, I follow her to the door. Jarl eases the door open for her. She slips through, and he pulls the door shut again.

I scowl. "Why does she get to go in?"

"Because she won't wake him. It's rare enough he sleeps. I won't let you disturb him."

"Aren't you the good guard dog?"

"Yes," he says simply, ignoring my jab.

I can't help but wonder what makes Heborian inspire such loyalty. Do these people know the things he's done?

When the scullery maid comes back out, darting an anxious look at me—I don't want to even imagine the stories she's heard—I catch a glimpse of firelight and the shape of someone moving within the chamber. Before Jarl can get the door closed, I shout over his shoulder, "Good morning!"

Jarl snaps the door shut, throwing me a dirty look, but opens it again at the sound of Heborian's voice. He ducks his head through, and I watch his shoulders droop. He swings the door wide without a word to me. I sniff loudly and march through. The door clips the side of my boot as Jarl shuts it impatiently behind me.

"You're up early," Heborian's sleep-roughened voice rumbles from the shadowed depths of an upholstered chair.

The budding firelight flickers over his bare feet and the legs of his sleeping pants but fades to darkness around his knees.

I give my arms a swing and slap my hands together. "When do we start?"

"Have a seat."

"I'm fine here."

"Gods, you're stubborn."

I cross my arms in agreement. "I must have gotten that from you."

Heborian grunts.

"Tell me how to conceal myself in the Drift."

"Have a seat." He makes it both invitation and warning.

I bristle at his play for dominance; I want to snarl at him, clench my fists, refuse, but I gain nothing by walking away. He knows things I don't, things I need to know, and he's forcing me to acknowledge it. I am, it seems, to be a student again. I force my feet to move and plunk myself into the chair beside him.

Just so he won't think me soft and compliant, I study his chamber with cynical eyes. The massive stone fireplace gives way to wood-paneled walls, which stretch barrenly to distant corners. The firelight dies well before reaching the room's dark edges, but I still pick out an armor stand, heavily hung with chainmail and Heborian's golden breastplate. A chilly draft slips in from the farthest—and by my calculation of direction, seaside—wall.

"Cozy in here," I drawl.

"In Rune, the king—or chieftain, rather—does not live so removed from his men. A ruler's hall has a huge central hearth, completely open up to the smoke vent in the roof. The 'court' is smaller and more personal. The king lives *with* his people."

"I suppose you prefer this high and mighty Keldan approach to things."

The firelight, stronger now, brushes over the weary lines of his face, but the dark eyes studying me so impassively indicate I haven't even come close to pricking his pride. He wears a dark dressing robe, though it hangs open, exposing his scarred torso. His body language as he leans back into the chair's cushioning is confident, untroubled. The man who tried to give me my mother's bracelet last night is gone, and the man who conquered Kelda sits in his place. Even tired, and perhaps a little hungover, he's unshakable.

He says, "You didn't sleep."

I prickle at his observation. I hate when people notice things about me, hate even more when they comment on them. I say, using my sharp tone to remind him of why we're here, "Don't waste my time, Heborian." It's the first time I've addressed him by his name, and it feels awkward in my mouth.

Heborian leans forward in his chair, elbows on his knees. The blue tattoo that winds around his right wrist and up his forearm looks black in the firelight. He twines his fingers together. I detect a slight tremble, but that could be from fatigue or from the lingering effects of too much wine.

I've long been curious about his tattoos, and though I tell myself this is only a distraction, I gesture at his hands, "What do they mean?"

He brushes his left hand over the markings on his right. His fist closes powerfully. "Strength, steadiness, resolve in all things." He traces a finger along the tattoo hooking his right eye. "Clear sight."

I think of such marks glowing within the Drift, and I know they are more than ink. "They have true power."

Heborian looks at me steadily. "Yes."

Hair rises on the back of my neck, prickling through the Griever's Mark, a symbol of protection in the face of certain death.

I don't mention my Mark, and neither does Heborian. It hangs in the air between, serving both to drive us apart and bind us together.

Heborian shakes his head, shattering the moment. He says gruffly, "Tell me about Belos's fortress. Describe every entrance."

For a second, I'm disoriented by this abrupt return to the business at hand. I clear my throat.

"The main entrance requires you to walk up a long sloping ledge to an open courtyard. From there you pass through the front doors. It's very exposed."

"Where is the barrier?"

"It starts around the outside of the plateau."

"What's to prevent you from drifting to the edge of the barrier, walking past the point of it in the physical world, then reentering the Drift just inside it? That would be easiest."

I shake my head. "The barrier is a tangle of threads that extends from the foot of the slope to the top. I'd have to walk to the top, then enter the Drift from the courtyard. Belos doesn't always keep a guard on the door, but I'd bet anything there's one there now, since Belos knows I'll come for Logan. He's probably counting on it. I'd be seen at once."

Heborian rubs at his dark beard. "Is there any other way to enter?"

I take a deep breath because what I'm about to describe represents my only chance of getting in, and I don't see how it can work. "Just one. I'm not supposed to know about it, but there's a hidden stair on the back side. It leads to a door that opens into Belos's study. But the barrier is the same. I would have to drift to the bottom of the stairs, climb them, and get through the door before I could reenter the Drift."

"But will this door be watched?"

"It never has been before—that would kind of give it away—but who knows what level of paranoia Belos has reached? Besides, Belos's chambers are on the other side of that door. His sleeping chamber adjoins the study."

"Hmm. How is this door so well hidden that Belos would believe you don't know of it?"

"There's some kind of illusion over it—I don't know how it's done. The eye sees only the smooth face of the plateau."

Heborian's eyes narrow. "Then how did you find it?"

"By accident. I was young. Belos and the others were gone. I was playing and fell into it."

"Playing?" he says, as though the word is foreign to him.

I stare him down. I refuse to reveal that I was playing a game of chase with an imaginary friend. Pathetic, I know.

"Do you know how the door is locked?"

I shake my head. "I climbed the stairs once, but I couldn't open the door. There was some kind of Drift-work used to lock it, like you have locking the door to your tower room. How do you do that? You must have somehow tied off Drift-energy. I asked Belos about it once—not about the door, of course—but he only said it was beyond my abilities."

"Rubbish," Heborian growls. "Beyond your abilities? Why on earth did you believe him?"

My face heats. There are so many things I believed from him that seem foolish, even obvious, now. It took me years to start questioning Belos, and even then I only questioned his actions. I never thought to doubt what he told me about myself. All of it seemed to ring true. I had no trouble believing that my mother had abandoned me—why wouldn't she have? I had no trouble believing my power was small—Belos proved it to me again and again.

"Belos tried to teach me, and I couldn't do it."

Heborian flicks this away with an impatient hand. "Just one more illusion of his. Do you know what I saw when I cut your Leash?"

My nostrils flare. He's doing this on purpose. Just like Belos, just like all of them, he wants me to be uncomfortable, embarrassed, forever reminded of my own degradation.

"When I cut it, your energy flared."

I hiss, "So?"

"Astarti, I think he was siphoning off your energy. I can't be sure, but I believe he was putting limits on your power. Testing you, forcing you to fail, to believe yourself weaker than he, so you would not challenge him." Heborian shakes his head in disgust, though I can't tell whether it's with me or with Belos. "He wanted you because of your power, but once he got it, it scared him."

That makes my eyebrows jump.

Heborian goes on, "Belos wanted you, and your power, fully under his control. I suspect that the limits he once placed on you were very real, while you were Leashed, but now they are only in your mind." He taps his temple. "Like a horse that's been trained to be tied. When he's young you have to tie him with strong rope, but by the time he's older, once he's already learned that fighting is pointless, you can tie him with a string. The restraint is all in his head."

I don't like the comparison, but Heborian, of course, doesn't give me time to work up a good reply before he moves on to other questions. "If you never got through the door, how do you know it leads to Belos's study?"

I say tightly, still offended by his horse analogy, "Because I found it from the inside, behind a tapestry."

His half-smile looks approving. "Good girl."

I am torn between two annoyances: one, that he thinks I need his praise, and two, that it feels good to hear it.

He waves everything away anyway. “We’ll work on the door later. First you need to learn to conceal yourself in the Drift. If no one’s watching there, it won’t matter, of course, but you can’t count on that. You need to be able to approach the fortress and identify everyone’s location before you run any risks of being detected.”

“So teach me,” I say, anxious to end this conversation.

“I don’t do Drift-work on an empty stomach, and neither should you. The energies of the body feed the energies of the Drift. I trust you understand that at least?”

I hate the way he phrases things, making any response I might give sound childish. Will he always leap back and forth between faint praise and embarrassing criticism? I remind myself sternly that I am not here to win his approval or acceptance. He is nothing to me but a source of knowledge, and that knowledge will help me free Logan.

When the door eases open and Jarl sticks his head through, Heborian mutters, “Finally.”

“Will you break your fast, Sire?”

“Send her in.”

A young maid, different from the scullery girl who came to light the fire, enters bearing a silver tray. So many servants. Heborian acknowledges her with a nod but says nothing as she sets the tray on the table between his chair and mine and slips away.

Once we’ve eaten a much-too-big breakfast of eggs, buttery croissants, and seared venison tenderloin, Heborian disappears into an adjoining room to change. I take the opportunity to inspect the chamber better, especially now that dawn has bled pale light through the glass-paned windows. Because there’s very little to look at in the room beyond its yawning fireplace and finely-joined wood floor, I wander over to the massive tapestry. It’s a typical hunting scene, complete with horses, hounds, and men with bows, but their prey surprises me. An elegant white creature, like a cross between a horse and a deer, flees through the woods. A twisting white horn protrudes from its forehead. When I reach out to touch the strange image, my fingers make a hollow thump on the wall behind.

I lift the heavy tapestry and feel a definite draft slipping through the wood paneling of the wall. I thump on it again.

A door opens, and Heborian says drily, "I see now how you found Belos's door."

I step away from the wall and let the tapestry slide back into place. Humor lights Heborian's dark eyes. He's exchanged the dressing gown for woolen trousers and a loose linen shirt, eerily similar to something I might wear. I'm glad I chose a gray sweater and tight black leggings this morning—we can't go around looking like twins. Or like father and daughter.

"What's back there?"

The humor fades from his eyes. "It used to be open. It's a balustrade. It looks out to the ocean."

I raise an eyebrow. I haven't seen anything like that anywhere in this castle. In fact, I haven't seen anything like that anywhere but Avydos. Sudden understanding fills me and I open my mouth to venture my guess.

Heborian anticipates me with, "Yes. Your mother." He adds gruffly, "I should just wall it off properly. This room is freezing in the winter." Something in the way his eyes unfocus when he says that tells me he won't.

I shift with the same discomfort I felt last night when he tried to give me the bracelet. My mother stood in this room, probably in this very spot. I step away from the wall, as eager as Heborian to abandon the subject.

"So," he says, "concealment. There are a few basic principles to keep in mind. First, the very nature of Drift-work. What is the Drift, Astarti?"

I bristle at this tone of lecture. I learned these things when I was a child. "Energy. The energy world. I know this. Why are we—"

"And how do you control that energy?"

My nostrils flare, but Heborian lifts an expectant eyebrow.

I grind out, "Force of will, concentration."

"And whose energy can you control?"

"My own." I can't help giving him a dirty look when I add, "Unless I Shackle someone, of course."

Heborian ignores this. "Your ability to manipulate your own energies is limited only by your imagination. The Drift is limitless. Remember that."

"But—"

"Do not allow yourself to be the horse, tied only by a string."

I force my breathing to ease. I expected this, his condescension. I remind myself that I endured it for years with Belos; it's not like I can't handle it.

"Shape your spear," he commands.

When I do as he says, tugging on my energies through my mooring and shaping them into the familiar smooth length of my spear, he reaches out and grabs it farther down the shaft.

"Why is it real, why can I touch it? It's just energy."

"I am creating its existence through my mind. It's real because I make it so. I've reshaped—recycled?—my own energies into it, just as a huge tree grows from a tiny seed; one thing is made into another. That's how Theron explained it anyway. The seed takes the energies of the elements and uses them to create itself. I make my spear the same way."

Heborian frowns thoughtfully at this, then says, "Set it down."

I lay my spear carefully on the floor.

Heborian says, "You are no longer touching it, but it's still there. Why?"

"I'm still willing my energies into its shape."

Heborian's hand is so fast that I don't see the slap coming. I reel back from the sting on my cheek. "What the—"

"Why is the spear gone now?"

I follow his eyes to the empty space of floor where my spear lay only a moment ago. "You broke my concentration."

"And how did your teachers explain that?"

"Theron said that if you cut the tree off from its sources of energy—light, air, and water—it would die. The spear's source of energy is me, maintained by will and concentration. When you slapped me, you cut the spear off from its source of energy, and it died. What's your point? I already know these things."

"It never hurts to remember the basics."

"Could you possibly be any more patronizing?"

His brief grin tells me that, indeed, he could be, then his face is serious once more. He clasps his hands behind his back. "Why does our energy express itself as light within the Drift?"

My eyebrows jump. "I don't know. I never thought about that."

Heborian tries again, "Why is the purposeful shaping of a Drift-light the first thing children are taught?"

"Because it's the easiest to learn."

"Why?"

"Because you don't have to concentrate, don't have to hold a shape. You just let the energy bleed through your mooring into the physical world."

Heborian nods and starts pacing, his stride eating up the chamber. "And when you see *unintentional* light around a Drifter, what does that signify?"

"Wasted energy, lack of focus."

Heborian halts at the tapestry. "Precisely."

"What are you getting at?"

He turns to face me but only crosses his arms, waiting for me to put it together.

I venture, "So you're saying that our light within the Drift is wasted, unfocused."

He nods for me to continue.

"So if we could somehow focus that energy, it wouldn't waste itself as light, it wouldn't show?"

His face breaks into a wide grin. "There's my smart girl."

I search his face for any hint of condescension or insincerity and am surprised to find none. "Surely you're not suggesting that I can make my Drift-form vanish by simply willing it? That seems too easy."

"Oh, it's not easy. Don't expect to master it today." Heborian starts to pace again, moving toward the fireplace. "But you understand the principle. Drift-light is wasted, unfocused energy. Now, I want you to flood this room with Drift-light. Don't focus it, don't shape it, just let it out as you might have done as a child. While you're doing that, pay close attention to what you feel."

I let energy flow through my mooring. As the room fills with cool blue light, I understand Heborian's point. This is energy that is not controlled, not used for any purpose.

"Now," Heborian says, "draw it together, pull it into a ball, and pay attention to what you feel happening. Do it slowly."

I pull the energy toward me, forcing myself to slow the process instead of doing it quickly and automatically like I normally would. The light draws tighter and tighter, forming the globe I am used to shaping. Heborian has moved back my way, and the lighted orb hanging between us paints his face an otherworldly blue.

"Now tell me: are you forcing the energy to be light, or are you *allowing* it to be light?"

I consider. "Allowing."

"Then *force* it to be something else."

I grin. "With pleasure."

Heborian's eyes widen with understanding in the moment before I tighten my Drift-light into a blast that takes him straight in the chest. He flies back, landing on the wood floor with a heavy thud of boot heels, elbows, and head.

Jarl comes bursting into the room, Drift-sword in hand, his expression furious. He rushes to Heborian, who is climbing to his feet, rubbing an elbow.

"It's all right, Jarl. Leave us."

Jarl hovers uncertainly, Drift-sword in hand. He casts me a wary look. I smile brightly.

When Jarl has left, snapping the door shut behind him, Heborian resumes his questions. "And what was that? It had no shape—it wasn't a spear, nor a sword—but it was still energy. How did you make use of it?"

I blow out my cheeks, considering. "I directed it, then let go."

Heborian holds up a finger. "Exactly. That's why it's a focused blow, and that's why the energy is gone once it hits its mark—like lightning, it's been sent out with no strings to pull it back. But this is a little off track. The point is that the light vanished—there were traces of it, but they were faint—once you began to use the energy for a different purpose. Instead of blasting me in the chest, you could have used that energy to shape a weapon, to lift an object, to bind me—any number of things."

"I understand, but how does this apply to my Drift-form? Are you suggesting that I shape my energy into something else?" I blink. I don't need Heborian's grin to tell me that this is exactly what he's suggesting. Of course. This is how Belos changes his own shape, which I have seen him do on occasion, and how he hid the stair, though that would also require tying off. This is how I will make my lighted form vanish. The energy itself cannot vanish, but it can be transformed, reshaped into something else. This, I realize with sudden clarity, is how I blended myself with the elements: I simply reshaped, reused my energy.

Heborian stays silent, letting me process this. I wander to the wall and lean against it.

Eventually, Heborian says, "The key to doing almost anything, and I'm not just talking about the Drift, is to understand the basic, underlying principles. Most people forget those. They make things too complicated, get sidetracked by detail, and therefore fail to reach clarity."

Even though it's off topic, I ask, "Why can't other Drifters blend with the elements? If it's simply a matter of reshaping one's energy, they should be able to do it. Right?"

Heborian takes a deep breath. "That's a bigger topic than you realize. Sibyl and I had many long conversations about it. Trust me, that's not something you want to delve into right now. Focus on the Drift."

I reluctantly tuck my questions away—so much for simplicity and clarity. "So I will need to reshape my energy in the Drift, use it for something?"

"Kind of. Your energy will still be there, of course, it will still be *you*, but you cannot let that energy be expressed, wasted as light. Force the light to recede, to be held in that same kind of nebulous ball that you used to hit me. But. Unlike the blast, this you will not let go, this you *cannot* let go. You must simply allow it—you, yourself—to travel. It will take constant focus. Even a moment of inattention and the light will flood out, just as your spear vanished when I slapped you. Are you ready to try?"

I grin. This I will enjoy.

I spend all morning and well into the afternoon working with Heborian. What sounded easy in principle is difficult in practice, for it takes absolute concentration to will my energy to hold itself in what I come to think of as a kind of knot. When I explain my knot analogy to Heborian, he tells me to use it, to weave my energy into it, letting no filament escape.

Even harder than containing the wasted light of my energy is moving through the Drift while in this state. I have to focus on two equally important things: containment and movement. I move through the castle and its grounds in fits and starts, playing a kind of hide and seek with Heborian. Every time my light bleeds out, he races toward me and the game is up.

Finally, I successfully sneak up on him as he lurks in the stable near the quiet shapes of dozing horses. When my light floods out to show him my success, he nods approval then jerks his head, indicating for me to follow him out of the Drift.

When I step into the physical world of the stable, the smells of hay and horses wash over me. A groom nearly drops the saddle he's carrying. He hurries away, the saddle's stirrups clanking as they swing.

Heborian reaches over a stall door, scratching the neck of a big dapple gray horse. The horse's lip twitches, and he leans into the scratching.

I rest my elbows on the door. "We scared the groom, but why aren't the horses startled?"

"You do like to ask the big questions, don't you? That was another theory of Sibyl's. Animals, she said, live in a better balance of the physical world and the Drift. Even in the physical world, they never lose their awareness of the Drift. That was her idea, anyway."

The idea tickles my memory. I recall the first time I met Logan, how he seemed to sense me within the Drift. Could he, like the animals, sense the Drift even from outside it?

When a blonde head emerges from the adjoining stall, I blink in surprise at Korinna. I was so focused on Heborian that I didn't notice her from within the Drift.

I have not spoken with Korinna since before I learned she is my cousin. My mother, Sibyl, was her aunt, though Sibyl was Stricken, cast out of Avydos, before Korinna was born.

After the battle, Korinna went back to Avydos for Healing, but she returned to Tornelaine almost at once. I'd like to know why, but I've been avoiding her. What could she feel other than disgust knowing she is related to a half-Drifter, one raised by Belos, her people's enemy?

Korinna is wearing her leather Warden's vest, embossed with a branching tree and laced down the side. Her intricate braid of bright blonde hair hangs over one shoulder. She's so beautiful, with her high, Earthmaker cheekbones and delicate chin. I feel almost as coarse and messy in her presence as I do in Prima Gaiana's. I resist the urge to tuck a few loose stands into my own braid.

Because I feel awkward, I'm rude. "What are you doing here?"

She doesn't seem to take offense. "I like horses."

"I'll leave you," Heborian says, pushing away from the stall. "Tomorrow, we'll start on unlocking."

I'd like to protest that I don't want to wait, but the truth is that I'm exhausted, and I don't think I could possibly learn anything more right now. Even so, I'm surprised to not be more tired. We spent all day in the Drift, and learning new things is always tiring. I should be passing out, not just leaning on the stall door. I wonder if Heborian is right that Belos was siphoning off my energy. I shudder inwardly.

Heborian says, "I didn't think you'd be able to learn that in one day. Even I didn't master it so quickly."

This doesn't seem to invite me to say anything, so I just shrug.

"Come to my chambers in the morning. *After* breakfast." With that Heborian strides out of the stable.

"What was the king saying about…Sibyl?" Korinna stumbles over the Stricken name, which she is not actually supposed to say. "Something about animals?"

"He said Sibyl had a theory that animals could sense the Drift."

Because leaving would be too cowardly, I unlatch the door and slip into the stall where Korinna is brushing a chestnut horse.

"Huh." Korinna looks thoughtful as she goes back to making vigorous brush strokes across the horse's rump. I cough and pull my sweater over my nose as dust and loose winter hair dance through the air. Korinna chuckles.

The horse's sides expand with a deep sigh, and I reach for the thick, hairy neck. I pat gently, unsure how to touch a horse.

Korinna leans over the horse's back, brush dangling. "She's a horse, not a fragile human infant." She gives the animal's broad rump a firm pat to demonstrate.

I rub the horse's neck more firmly, making my way to the powerful, curving jaw. She leans into my hand, the way I saw the other horse do with Heborian. I scratch harder and she stretches out her neck, her lips contorting ridiculously.

Korinna laughs, and I feel a smile tugging my own mouth. Korinna does not seem to hate me. Perhaps I should have given her a chance.

When my arm gets tired, I cease my scratching and idly run my fingers through the coarse mane. "So why are you here anyway?"

"I told you, I like horses. The stable master lets me come and brush them."

"I mean, why are you in Tornelaine?"

Korinna brushes the horse's side fiercely. "Bran is here also."

"Yes, but Bran is Logan's brother."

She says angrily, "Do you want me to leave or something?"

"No," I say quickly. Is that what it sounded like?

Korinna pauses in her brushing, still not looking at me. "I don't want to be in Avydos right now."

"Why not?"

Her mouth tightens like she won't tell me, and she starts brushing again, sending loose hair flying. Finally she admits, "There are some there who don't want me to be a Warden."

That stuns me. "You'll be a great Warden. What's the problem?"

"It's complicated."

Her manner tells me she doesn't want to say anything more, and I have to respect that. I don't like when people push me for more than I want to say, so I don't push her, but I wish she would tell me. I know I'm not the kind of person that others confide in, but still.

I force myself to say, "I understand."

"The more people who know, the worse—"

"You don't owe me an explanation."

She stares at the horse's back.

I can't take the tension. "I have to go." She looks hurt, so I add, "I'm not mad at you."

She nods but doesn't look at me. She starts brushing again, and I slide into the Drift.

I hover uncertainly for a moment, studying Korinna's energy form, which is so much brighter than that of most Earthmakers. She lays her face on the horse's back. I can't tell if she's crying, but I know I shouldn't spy on her, so I drift back to my chambers. For once, I'm looking forward to crawling into bed, even though it's still early. For once, I feel like I could sleep without dreaming.

But rest, it seems, will have to wait. Someone is in my chamber.

Chapter 8

I recognize Horik by his size and distinctive Runish tattoos long before I reach my sitting room. When I slide into the physical world, he jumps in surprise. He looks huge and out of place among the fine furnishings.

"Did you let yourself in?" I ask, half-teasing, half-annoyed.

He flashes me a broad grin.

"And what if I had been in the bathtub?" I ask pointedly.

His grin only widens, so I punch him lightly in the shoulder.

"So what do you want?"

He crosses his huge arms, and his expression is suddenly serious, challenging. "I'm going with you. To the Dry Land."

I blink. "Why?"

"You are the Firstborn, and—"

"Ah, Horik," I mutter as I flop into a chair.

"You may need my help," he argues. "What if he's hurt too badly to walk? Can you carry him?"

My throat constricts at the thought of Logan being hurt that badly, but Horik has a point. That is a possibility. "Heborian will never let you go on a fool's errand like this."

"He's already granted permission." Horik turns to go. "I just wanted you to know that you would not be alone."

"Horik," I call.

I don't want to get him killed for nothing, and the thought of being responsible for such a thing presses down on me with invisible weight. At the same time, I desperately want him to come. He would be a great asset, and having the possibility of his help dangle before me makes my heart leap with hope.

Even so, I force myself to discourage him by admitting, "We might not make it back. Any of us."

Horik flashes me a grin that says he doesn't care about the horrible death that might await him should we fail.

When the door closes behind him, I lean back in my chair, stunned by this unexpected gift.

ꟹ ꟹ

I don't know if it's because I'm exhausted from my lesson with Heborian or if it's because Horik's promise of help eases my mind, but I sleep like a stone, dreamless. When I wake to the light of full sun, I wrench myself from the bed, nearly falling as my foot tangles in the sheets. I stumble to the wardrobe, scrubbing at my sleep-puffy face. I fumble with the latch. As I shrug on the gray sweater that I threw into the bottom of the wardrobe last night, I almost wish I hadn't slept so hard—I hate feeling groggy. I pull on the same tight leggings I wore yesterday because I don't have the clarity of thought needed to make fresh clothing decisions.

Having heard Clara in the adjoining sitting room, I am unsurprised to find breakfast and a pot of steaming tea waiting for me. I want to tell her I don't have time to eat, but the tea beckons me with its curls of steam. We never had tea in the Dry Land. Heborian imports it, just as Aron does to Avydos, and whatever's in the stuff makes my nerves tingle. I could use the wakeup now, so I accept the cup that Clara holds out to me.

When I sit on the footstool to drink, Clara goes to work on my hair, jerking my head back every time I almost get my lips to the cup.

"Take it easy, will you? I almost spilled. What are you doing anyway?"

"Sorry." She pauses, lets me down the tea, then goes right back at it.

"Clara, you know how I feel about this sort of thing."

"Yes, but you looked disoriented this morning, so I thought I'd untangle this mess before you got your wits about you."

I bark a laugh. Glancing over my shoulder, I see her crack a smile.

By the time I finish breakfast, Clara has my hair in a tight, crown to tip, no-nonsense braid.

"Wow," I say, running a finger over the even bumps. "You're good."

"See what you've been missing? It's severe for my tastes, but it should keep the tangles to a minimum. And it does highlight your fine jaw from the side, I'll give it that."

When I see her eyeing my clothes with her bottom lip crushed between her teeth, I mutter, "Don't push it."

Once I've escaped Clara's ministrations, a guard—not Jarl today—lets me into the king's chamber, where Heborian and Horik stand with that awkward look of a conversation hastily abandoned. Hmm.

Something more significant, however, diverts my attention from whatever they didn't want me to hear.

A large silver and bronze chest etched with Runish symbols sits on the floor in the center of the room's open space.

"What is that doing here?"

Heborian says, "You will practice unlocking. Or, one might say, unweaving."

"But the knife's in that. You took it out of the tower?"

"Just for today. For practice." His tone is too light. Something is off, and I'll have to be on my guard until I figure out what it is. Surely Heborian could create a different weave for me to unravel? No, he's brought the chest and knife on purpose.

Horik only shrugs like it's no big deal, though I don't buy it, especially with the remains of his argument with the king still showing in the downward set of his mouth.

They will give more away if they don't realize I'm onto them, so I school my expression to mildness. "So how does this work?"

Heborian's dark eyes linger on me a moment, weighing something, before he takes the deep breath that signals an oncoming lecture.

"Tying off," he begins, "is extremely difficult. I will not even try to teach you how to do it today, but you should understand the basic idea. In essence, you create a weaving of energy. It could be an object, or a binding, such as the lock I have on this chest, or an illusion, such as the one you described hiding Belos's back stair. Of course, creating each of those things requires particular skills, but to tie off the energy and make the thing sustain itself separate from the maker requires something more. Basically, the Drifter shapes energy then casts it away from himself, much like throwing a blast at someone. Consider the lightning analogy from yesterday. The energy separates from its source."

I wrinkle my forehead. "Yes, but when the lightning or the Drift-blast hits its target, it vanishes."

"Energy," Heborian says significantly, "cannot be destroyed."

"What do you mean?"

"It can be transformed, reshaped, recycled. But it never, ever disappears."

"But once lightning strikes, it vanishes."

Heborian, arms crossed and one finger raised to make a point, starts pacing. "Sibyl claimed that that was not precisely true. I oversimplified yesterday to illustrate a particular point, but the truth, according to Sibyl, was that the lightning itself—what we can *see*—vanishes, but its energy is absorbed into the air and earth, into whatever is around it. Occasionally, the energy of lightning can cause fire. Does that not tell you that the energy of one element is simply bleeding into another?"

I shrug, not disagreeing with the logic but still not quite following his point. Horik is listening with an interested expression. Apparently, this theory is new to him also. Feeling better about not being the only student here, I gesture for Heborian to continue.

"When you hit me with that blast yesterday, the energy transformed itself as soon as it struck me. It caused me to fly off my feet; it made my body tingle for almost half an hour afterwards. That is energy, still moving, still affecting what it touched. Eventually, my body absorbed that energy, much like it absorbs and changes food for its own purposes."

"Okay, I think I get the idea, but I still don't see how you can tie off energy. How do you stop it from transforming? How do you make it hold one shape?"

"Much as you make a house out of wood or a castle out of stone. You build its shape, bind it together, then you step back and let go."

"But why doesn't it vanish like the spear did when you slapped me?"

"Because you never let go of the spear—it was still part of you. Its energy went back into you once it vanished."

"But how could you possibly sever the energy from yourself? I wouldn't know how to begin."

"And you don't need to today. I can teach you that another time, after you've returned from your mission."

Horik, for some reason, stiffens at this. I look at him to see if he'll meet my eyes. He does, but there's something unhappy in his expression.

Heborian, casting a warning look at Horik, continues, "I only want you to understand the principle. You must recognize that the tied-off energy is simply a shape, simply the current form of that energy. Like a house that can be burned, a castle that can be broken, you can take the energy apart. A better example, though, might be your sweater."

I glance down, wishing I had taken the time to dig out a fresh garment. Several conspicuous coppery horse hairs cling to the fibers of the wool.

"If you know where the end of the string is and you know how the string is bound into the body of the sweater, you can unravel that whole sweater and have a long piece of yarn to knit into something else, right?"

"True."

"And with the right tools, you could pry up every piece of this floor and use the boards for something else, couldn't you?"

"Yes, I get it."

"A weaving of Drift energy is no different. You must figure out how it's put together and simply take it apart."

"Somehow, I bet it's harder than you're making it sound."

Heborian grins wolfish agreement, though he says, "But we start always with basic, underlying principles."

Horik is nodding along in agreement.

Heborian strides purposefully to the chest. "Step into the Drift with me and study the weaving around this chest. I want you to point to the joinings if you see them."

I ease along my mooring, and the room resolves itself into it bare, dim energies. Horik and Heborian are in the Drift with me, both of them crouching beside the chest. The chest itself is dull and lifeless, and I am struck by the irony that things of great value in the physical world—that chest is worth more than most people's farms or vineyards—are nothing in the Drift. Energy is the only currency here.

I crouch between Horik and Heborian to study the faint glow of bluish-white energy surrounding the chest. Within, the knife and Heborian's Shackle glow bright white. I repress a shudder at the sight of the Shackle. I could never have used that on Bran, never, ever, ever.

I place a hand on what would be the chest's lid in the physical world. Here in the Drift it has no substance, but the energy of Heborian's weaving humming gently under my hand creates a surface as firm as the metal lid. Peering closely, I see that the energy surrounding the chest is, indeed, a kind of weave, though it looks as tangled as any barrier. I study its subtle motion. If I pull back and squint, trying not to look too hard, I detect a kind of rhythm in its movement, but that's all I can see.

I look at Heborian, who is studying me as I studied the weaving, and shrug apologetically. He nods to Horik, who extends a finger, pointing at a spot in the weaving. Squinting again, I can see that this is the point of origin for the pattern of movement and that it's slightly thicker. I touch it, feeling the increased hum through the point, but I cannot begin to guess how I would break the connection. Heborian jerks his chin for us to follow him out of the Drift.

"So you saw the joining," Horik says.

"Only once you pointed it out. But how could you cut it? I thought only the knife could cut energy."

"Ah, but you're not going to cut it," Heborian points out. "You're going to unravel it."

"If energy can be unraveled, why can't you unravel a Leash or a barrier? Never mind," I say, shaking my head as I realize the answer. "Those energies are bound to a person, blended and anchored within the maker. But how do I unravel this…weaving, as you called it?"

"If I asked you to unravel that sweater, how would you do it?"

I sigh, "You do like to answer questions with questions. Do you realize how exhausting that is? Personally, I'd hand it to Clara. I don't knit."

"And *you* like to be a smartass. Things are always best understood when the student answers her own questions. Now tell me: how would you unravel the sweater?"

"All right, all right. I'd find where it's tied off, then I'd take a needle or something thin and work the end of the thread loose. Then I'd work it free of each little loop. It would take forever, hence Clara."

Heborian pinches the bridge of his nose. "It's pretty sad if I know more about knitting than you do. Once you got past the binding edge, you could just pull the string and the whole thing would come undone."

"Oh."

"But you get the point. Next question: how would you unlock an ordinary lock, not a Drift-lock, using Drift-work?"

This one's easier. "I would manipulate the internal mechanism, make it move as a key would."

"Right. You could do the same thing to unravel that sweater. You're a Drifter, you don't need a needle or any other tool. If you honed the energy to a fine enough point, you could pick the thread loose without ever touching it with your hands. The binding on the chest is no different. Horik, show her."

We all slide into the Drift again, and Horik kneels in front of the chest. A faint glow of energy extends from his finger. I peer closely but can still barely see the fine thread as it slips in and through the joining in Heborian's weave. Slowly it begins to slide free, then suddenly, the whole thing unravels, snapping and sliding until the energy of the weaving dissipates into the Drift. Faint traces of wind slip around me, and I prickle with anticipation—that feels like the Hounding.

Horik and I step back as Heborian weaves a new binding around the chest so quickly that I can't follow the logic of the weave or see how he's secured it. The wind dies away.

Heborian nods to me, and I crouch in front of the weaving. Unsurprisingly, Heborian did not put the joining in the same place, and I have to hunt for it. It's a slow process that sends me creeping around the box again and again. I glance up once or twice to see if Horik and Heborian are growing impatient, but Horik only nods encouragingly and Heborian waits without expression. At last I find the slight thickening. I let a filament of energy extend from my finger, trying to match Horik's fine control. I pick at the joining, trying to make my thread slip through, but I'm only groping clumsily. Finally, Heborian taps my shoulder, and I follow him from the Drift.

"You're too heavy-handed," says Heborian.

"Yes, well, I've never had to do such fine work. Why can't I just let Horik take care of this part anyway?"

Heborian's voice drops low. "And what if he's killed before you reach the top of the stairs?"

That sends a shiver through me. "Don't say that."

Horik, however, is nodding agreement. How can he be so nonchalant?

"Let's try something different that will help you refine your control. Horik, sit on the chest."

Horik obediently takes a seat, dwarfing the chest with his huge body. I look a question at Heborian, and he clasps his hands behind his back and rocks back on his heels. Oh, no. He's delighted about something, which means I'm not going to like this. Even Horik starts to look worried.

Heborian announces, "Using only Drift-work, Astarti, you will cut one hair from Horik's head."

"Absolutely not!"

Heborian raises an eyebrow.

"But—*no.* What if I accidently cut him? No. Find me some string or something. I'll even use my sweater. I am *not* cutting around his head."

"Cutting on your sweater will not motivate you to control your power."

"This is insane!"

"It's all right, Astarti," Horik says, straightening on the chest and looking resolutely forward. "I trust you."

I step away from him. "Then *you're* insane!"

"Astarti." Heborian's voice drops to a warning. "Do you want to free Logan or not?"

"That's not fair. If I could just—"

Horik rises to his feet and steps near, towering over me. Huge hands clamp on my shoulders. "Stop this. I've seen you do things I thought impossible. You have beaten me in the training yard more than once, which I also thought impossible. This?" He shakes his head. "Nothing. Be the Drifter I know you are, not this girl so full of doubt."

He lets go of my shoulders and takes his seat again. He's nicked my pride, as he meant to, but he's also told me in no uncertain terms that he believes I can do this.

Casting a final, dirty look at Heborian, I draw near to Horik. Even seated his head reaches almost to my shoulder. His dark hair is braided back on the right side, the braid curving above his ear and disappearing into the hair that hangs around his shoulders. I shift to his left side, where the hair is loose.

I draw energy through my mooring, and use a fine thread of it to lift a single hair.

"That's cheating," says Heborian. "You can't do that with the binding, so you can't do that here. And don't try shaping a knife either. That's not the point of the exercise."

Grumbling, I let the hair drop. I close my eyes briefly to steady myself, then I draw energy through my mooring again. Essentially, I will have to tighten the energy to such a fine point that it breaks through whatever it touches, like the blast with which I hit Heborian yesterday but impossibly tiny.

I focus all my attention on a single dark hair. My awareness of all else recedes. I draw a thread of energy through my mooring. I can do this. I let out a slow breath then—*thump, thump, thump.*

I jerk back with a startled cry at the sound of someone knocking on the door. I watch in horror as a thick lock of dark hair floats to the ground beside Horik's left foot. He stares at it with a detached expression until the door opens and the guard's head appears.

"The prince, Sire," the guard announces.

Heborian looks from Horik to the guard and back to Horik. His eyes rise to meet mine. I have a hand clamped over my mouth, and Heborian's lips are twitching.

"Send him in," he tells the guard.

"I am *so* sorry," I mumble through my fingers, staring at the shorn spot above Horik's ear.

"Well, you didn't cut him," Heborian says drily.

"What's going on in here?" Rood asks as he sweeps into the chamber, eyes pinning Heborian, Horik, and me each in turn. His eyes drop to the lock of hair resting between Horik's feet and mine. The corner of his mouth tugs upward. "Ah," he says knowingly.

Horik explores the shorn patch with his fingers. "Huh."

"Oh, gods." I cover my face with my hands.

"What is it, Rood?" asks Heborian.

"The Valdaran ambassador wants to finalize the shipping agreement."

"Is everything as we discussed?"

"All in order."

Heborian works his heavy signet ring from his right index finger and tosses it to his son. Rood snatches it from the air, fist closed possessively around it. He looks pointedly at me, though I have no idea why. His eyes narrow at my blank expression. Heborian clears his throat. The two of them look some kind of challenge at one another—again, something I don't understand—then Rood slides the ring onto his own finger and sweeps from the chamber.

When the door clicks shut, my hands flutter toward Horik's shorn hair, but I draw them back, not sure what to do. "Gods, Horik, I'm so sorry."

"It's, uh, it's all right."

"Try again," Heborian says.

"Don't you think I've done quite enough damage already?"

Heborian shrugs. "I don't see how it could get much worse."

"Oh, you don't, do you? It could be his ear next time!"

Horik feels gingerly along the top of his ear, as though to make sure it's still there.

Heborian quips, "You know what they say: get back on the horse."

I groan, "What does that even mean?"

"Try again."

I smile wickedly. "Why don't I try on you this time?"

"Why does a king have a champion if not to throw him in the path of danger instead of himself?"

"Oh, thanks for that," I mutter, but Horik only laughs. I shake my head at this absurdity.

It takes me a while to get focused, but I am eventually able to stop listening for the door and concentrate on slipping a thread of energy along my mooring. I slide the thread, humming with tiny, focused power near Horik's head. He sits perfectly still, though I don't know whether it's from trust or fear. I hone in on a single strand of hair and slice through its fragile structure with the humming thread of energy. The hair falls to Horik's shoulder and I pick it up.

"Satisfied?" I demand of Heborian.

"Yes."

Horik lets out a breath.

"Now," says Heborian, "the binding."

The work in the Drift takes the rest of the morning as I pick clumsily at the joining, refining my thread again and again until it's fine enough, focused enough to slip into the joining and work it loose. My energy form flares with relief and excitement as the binding unravels, whipping free and dissipating into the Drift. That's when it strikes me: the knife is right here by my hand. I could grab it and flee right now. I stare at its glowing white length, at the promise of what it can do for Logan. Almost, I grab for it, almost.

I close my eyes, knowing deep down that what Heborian has told me of the knife and of barriers is true. Belos would know if I cut through his barrier. With the Seven at his side, he would wrest the knife from me. Even if I got Logan free first, the ensuing destruction would be irreparable, and it would be my doing. There is enough on my conscience already.

When I step back from the knife, I see Heborian watching me. His eyes, gold and silver here in the Drift, appraise me. This, I realize, is why he brought the chest and the knife. He was testing me. I am upset that the test indicates that he still doesn't trust me, even though I know he would only have done this if he thought I would pass his test. My energy hums angrily, glowing bright from my heart to my hands.

Heborian suddenly tenses. A moment later, I feel it too. Threads of energy spool from Heborian's hands as the Hounding sweeps around us. Heborian binds the chest closed, and the Hounding shrieks past him. Horik grabs my arm and indicates for me to leave the Drift.

We wait tensely in the chamber, hovering near the chest. I breathe a sigh of relief when Heborian appears.

"Why is the Hounding drawn to the knife?" I demand.

Heborian smoothes his ruffled hair. "I don't know." I look at him skeptically until he insists, "I really don't."

"Good work," says Horik, looking slightly ridiculous with a clump of spiky hair above his ear.

I blink in surprise. "Oh. Yeah. I did it."

"Now," says Heborian, "let's see if you can get faster."

CHAPTER 9

LOGAN

Sun blazing overhead, we walk across the hot, parched earth. Everything is easier now. We don't have to fight. Pain still slows us; the left leg has to be dragged, and the right arm hangs all wrong. But it's not so bad. We can deal with pain as long as we don't have to think.

Our power is more controlled now. We don't vanish into the elements like before. Sometimes they tempt us, tug us, try to lure us, but then something clamps down on our mind, quelling the temptation. The hot, foul-tasting liquid burns our throat. We are calm again.

Today we are experimenting. We approach the fragmented spires of stone. The ruins spread far and wide, the remains of a great, ancient city. When curiosity stirs inside us, someone kicks our leg, which explodes with pain, and we fall, sick and dizzy.

A voice says, "He can't take much more of that. It's infected."

"Don't be so soft," someone else sneers.

"He's an asset. Do you want him to die? What use would he be then?"

We're shoved onto our back and someone touches the leg, setting it on fire again. We yell and try to tear away.

"See?"

Grumbling, arguing.

We're hauled to our feet, and the leg blazes so hot it's surreal, like it's something foreign, not part of us at all. Someone's hand clamps under our elbow, steadying us.

We look again to the spires, like twisted fingers of yellow-gray stone. We open ourself to the earth, call to its deep power. We want so badly to plunge into it, to vanish, but we hold back, focused on our purpose. We reach also for air, stirring it from its apathy, forcing it into submission.

We send a tremor into the tip of one spire and snap it off. We catch the fragment with air, crumble it to dust.

"Oh," someone breathes.

As the dust floats around us, an image swirls in its wake. A green valley, trees. The image shimmers and vanishes, a mirage.

Curiosity stirs. We stare into the wasted plain, trying to see the image again.

Focus.

The voice freezes us. We begin to see him again, the Other, and horror chokes us. He is not part of us at all. He has taken us. Not us.

Me.

I stagger away from the hands on my body, yelling, screaming, aware of myself again. No, no, no!

I am Logan. I am myself.

His will floods me, denying this, and confusion pummels my thoughts until nothing makes sense. I know I am mad.

Yes, agrees this other will. *Mad. But that's all right. Let go. Relax. Let go.*

I hover at the edge of temptation. I'm so tired, so very tired.

Yes, tired. Let go.

But the dust is all around me, confusing me. I see again the green valley, imposing itself over the waste. I see a colossal figure that I first mistook for a boulder, rise from the ground. Is he a man? Is he the earth? He looks across the broad sweep of blue sky. The image shimmers, vanishing.

I step forward, trying to call it back, and then I am aware of the Other trying to take me, his black will rolling through me.

I am screaming, screaming, screaming until pain explodes across the back of my head.

Lights spark through my vision.

The sky spins.

I fall.

My cheek presses to the hot, dry earth. Dust swirls through my nostrils, filling me with its deadness. The green valley is almost gone from my memory, fading like a dream.

Blackness crawls at the edges of my vision, into my mind, but *his* voice holds my awareness a moment longer: "What *is* he?"

"What was he seeing?" asks another voice.

The Other says, "It doesn't matter. He's still fighting. It's time for the final measure."

ꕥ ꕥ

I wake to pain and the sense of being held down. I struggle automatically. Only my legs are held, and I twist my upper body away. I tip off some ledge and feel the rest of my body slide over. I crash, not to stone, but to a faded orange-red carpet. Dust explodes from it on my impact. Coughing, blinking through dust, I have time only to register sunlight and coarse stone walls before rough hands grab me.

"I told you we should have strapped him down," complains Straton's sly voice.

I'm tumbled back onto what I now realize is a stone table. I wrench away from the hands until Belos lays two fingers, dangerous in their gentleness, their understated threat, across my throat. My pulse throbs against his fingers, and his sharp, too-bright eyes stare down into mine.

"Be still," he says. "Unless you want to lose that leg?"

Belos lets me raise my head just enough to peer down the length of my prone body to where a scrawny man hunches over my damaged leg. Thin, oily locks of hair hang in front of his face, obscuring most of it until he darts a look at me. His cheeks are sunken, his eyes bulging, his nose purpling with broken veins. His shirt is about the same color as the dust here, and the only clean part of him is his thin hands, which hold a steaming cloth dripping with water and blood. He turns his attention to my leg, where the trousers have been cut open to expose swollen, bleeding flesh threaded white with infection.

The man's fingers twitch nervously on the cloth. He quietly clears his throat and raises timid eyes only as high as Belos's shoulder. "My great lord," he says, voice barely above a whisper, "he may need to be held now that he's awake."

Belos pins my left shoulder and wrist, Straton my right. I grunt as Straton grinds the dislocated joint. Someone else grips my ankles, and I catch a glimpse of the huge shoulders and thick neck of Rhode before Belos and Straton slam me back onto the stone table.

When cold fingers grip my leg above and below the infection, I know what's coming. I stare into the pitted surface of the grayish-yellow ceiling. I focus on the dust floating in the shaft of sunlight that slashes the air above me. I grit my teeth, bracing. Even so, I am unprepared for the explosion of pain when the scrawny man starts squeezing out the infection. The pain roars from my leg, down to my toes and up through my hip and belly, until even my scalp feels a thousand pricking needles. I grunt, clamp my teeth, drive a scream back down my throat. My body arches off the table, but hands like iron bands keep my shoulders and feet pinned. Finally, darkness obliterates it all.

᪥ ᪥

I jerk awake from a terrible, terrible dream, surprised to see moonlight falling in squares through the iron grate above. My cell. I sigh with relief only to feel a horrible ache in my chest. I glance down, but the moonlight glows on unblemished skin. I want to rub at the soreness, but my hands are chained above me. Frustrated, I let my head fall back against the familiar stone wall. When my head thumps, I realize suddenly that my thoughts are my own, my mind clear.

Nightmare images slide through me: the Drift, Belos, the Leash, black with his will. An explosion in my chest, nausea. I shake my head to clear it. Just a small nightmare within a larger one.

What happened last? The hot compress on my leg reminds me. Ah, yes. But what happened after? I must have passed out.

Why is my mind clear?

Have I beaten him at last, outwilled him? His thoughts are far away, and the fortress around me is silent. But this brief, foolish sense of victory fades as quickly as it came. I know, even if I can't see it, that I am still Leashed. My chest aches with it. I don't know how much longer I can fight him.

Chapter 10

I stand with Heborian and Horik on the bridge outside the castle gates. The moon is down, and night has drenched the castle and city in deep shadow. Heborian's cool blue Drift-light hovers above us, painting eerie highlights across our faces and catching on the buckles of my black leather jacket. The blades I carry, though, are well-hidden from the light, strapped to forearms and thighs, with one even slid down the calf of my boot. Heborian pressed these on me this afternoon. He's right that they're a wise precaution, but I don't like what they imply. I could soon be Leashed to Belos again and might have no ability to shape a Drift-weapon, though I might, just might, have the chance to use one of the blades in a final effort.

Horik, similarly dressed in black and nearly invisible in the darkness, says, "We will return to this spot and bring him through the gates."

"I'll be ready with the knife."

Heborian leaves his condition unstated, for he made it clear enough this afternoon: if Belos or any of the Seven are trailing us, we are not to return to the castle and endanger the knife in any way. Without that promise, Heborian was not willing to bring the knife out of the tower, even though it would still be within his barrier sweeping the wall. His second condition was that he will wait on the wall only until the sun clears the horizon. He didn't say it, but the implication was clear enough. If we haven't returned by then, we are dead. Or Leashed.

Heborian and Horik share a look that makes Horik's jaw tighten. I know they've made some further agreement that has not been shared with me. If I didn't need Horik's help so badly, I might have left without him, because I can't trust any secret deal Heborian has made with him. I know they've both helped to prepare me, that the primary goal is success, but there is still something here I don't like and can't trust. I don't really expect Horik to betray me to Belos—that would not serve Heborian's interests in any way—but there is something they don't trust me to know, and that makes me wary.

As Heborian extracts a silent promise from him, Horik runs a nervous hand over his freshly shorn head, a gesture that has become common with him since he cut his hair short this afternoon. The shorn style looks strange on him, especially with his beard. It will take a while for me to look at him without cringing.

Heborian turns to me. "There is more I could teach you, but…" He trails off, anticipating my response before I give it.

"You know I won't wait any longer."

"You learned more quickly than I thought possible. Don't forget: basic principles. Strength of will, clarity of purpose, a calm and steady mind."

I'm antsy, ready to go, and my eyes flick from Heborian to the gates looming above us. In the wavering light of the guards' torches, I glimpse Bran, watching silently. When he came to my chamber door this evening, I ignored him. It wasn't that I didn't *want* to see him but that I couldn't. I knew what I'd see in his face: a goodbye. He doesn't expect us to succeed, and I don't need his doubt right now. I have enough of my own.

Even so, I'm jittery with expectation. Succeed or fail, there will be no more waiting. I bounce on the balls of my feet and raise expectant eyebrows at Horik. He ducks his chin in acknowledgement and clasps elbows with his king.

Heborian says something in the harsh-sounding language of Rune, which Horik responds to in kind. It has the sound of often-repeated phrasing, something traditional that I do not understand and can't be part of.

"Go with the gods," Heborian says to me.

"Yes, well, I'd rather go with Horik."

Horik grins, excited by the coming danger. I like him. I wish I could trust him.

I turn instinctively in the direction of the Dry Land, somewhere south and east but so far away no one knows its physical location or even if it is truly part of this world. Horik's grin is gone, replaced by the focus needed to conceal himself within the Drift.

I endure the familiar sensation of compression, then feel my energies expand with relief as the Drift renders the world simple and clear. As I practiced with Heborian, I gather my energies into a kind of knot, weaving myself inward to rid myself of light. Because Horik has never been to the Dry Land and would not know how to find the hidden stair, I let out a tiny speck, no bigger than a fly, for him to follow. It's a risk to leave anything exposed, but there is no other way to lead Horik.

The journey is difficult for me, a constant battle to detach myself from my feelings. Dread and eagerness churn through me, and I feel the occasional tap from Horik, telling me I'm losing focus and letting myself be seen.

I force my emotions to float away, as I am so practiced at doing, and by the time I've picked up the faint threads of energy that lead to the Dry Land, I am under control.

Belos's barrier blazes in the distance. As we draw near, I force myself to ignore the twisting threads, to not notice how frantically they move and contort themselves. I feel certain that the energies are somehow sentient, aware of their condition. But I cannot help them. I am here only for Logan.

I count the forms within the fortress. The Seven, in their chambers, unmoving. All asleep, all outside the Drift. Several dimmer shapes, each with a white Leash, dot the grounds, some sleeping, some guarding the courtyard. All those white strands flow to a single point: Belos's sleeping chamber. Like the Seven, he is outside the Drift, unmoving. Asleep? Could we be so lucky? I trace the thickest Leash to the dungeon and the bright form there.

My energies leap with joy to see him alive, causing my light to flood out. I'm lucky no one but Horik is in the Drift to see.

I wish I could rush straight to him, and I'm anxious and frustrated to have to slide free of the Drift at the bottom of the hidden stair, knowing there are so many steps in this plan before I can see his face.

The dry air sucks moisture from my skin. It's cold, as nights usually are in the Dry Land. Horik shifts beside me. I feel more than see it because the moon is down and the stars are dim and far away. What little light comes from them is eaten up by the plateau rearing above us.

"So dark," Horik whispers uncomfortably.

"We'll need some light to climb the stairs."

Horik produces a soft Drift-light as I feel my way along the rough stone of the plateau, groping for the foot of the stairs. I wince at every scuff of Horik's boots. Big-bodied, used to tasks requiring more strength than stealth, he's not exactly good at creeping.

When my toe thumps into something solid, I grope in front of me to feel the clean-cut edges of the stairs. I take a tentative step into what looks like empty air. Horik's Drift-light glows dimly, and my stomach turns to see nothing under my feet.

"Maybe the light wasn't such a good idea," I say, but Horik doesn't respond.

One hand planted on the wall to ground myself, I glance over my shoulder at him. He's close behind me, eyes wide with that particular look people get when they're about to be sick.

"Horik?"

The Drift-light vanishes.

"Grab onto my belt."

"What if I fall?" he whispers. "I don't want to take you with me."

"Don't you dare fall."

Horik's fingers grope down my back until they find my belt. He slips one finger behind the leather.

"Ready?"

"Gods, I hate this."

If the situation weren't so serious, I might find it funny. Horik, King's Champion, fearless in the face of battle, doesn't like heights, or at least unseen ones. I don't really blame him. It *is* creepy. But I can't afford to be sympathetic.

"Pull yourself together."

I give him three seconds to steady himself, then I start my slow climb. He keeps pace, but his boots scuff constantly on rough stone as he shuffles his way up. Halfway to the top, I want to kill him.

"You have *got* to be quiet," I hiss.

"Sorry," he whispers miserably.

We continue with less noise. I wouldn't call it silence, but it's as close as I think Horik can get.

When the hand I've kept on the wall to ground myself slides from rough stone to smooth wood, my heart leaps.

"We're at the top."

"Thank the gods," mutters Horik.

I grope with one toe for the edge of the landing. Even though I know there's an edge, my heart leaps into my throat when my toe slides off. I scoot to the edge, and Horik steps carefully onto the landing, squeezing next to me. This is the only pocket in the barrier, the only place from which we can unweave the lock on the door.

I find Horik's sweaty hand in the dark and squeeze. We slide into the Drift.

The barrier flares into sight around us. We are in a bubble within it, unable to drift into the fortress. We must unweave the lock on the door, exit the Drift, and physically walk into Belos's study. Belos is no fool. It will take a miracle for us to get through this without alerting him.

I count eight sleeping forms within the fortress and sag with relief. Maybe Horik wasn't as noisy as I thought.

Horik and I study the weave. It's thick and complex, twice the intensity of the weave surrounding Heborian's chest. I unfocus my eyes, try to follow the pattern of movement, but it just looks like chaos. Every line I trace branches and circles back on itself. I look hopefully at Horik, but his lighted face is scrunched in thought as he hunts for the pattern and the joining.

From the corner of my eye, I see it, a slight thickening near the foot of the door. I crouch down. Just as I practiced all day, I slip an impossibly small thread of energy into the joining and work it loose. It slides free slowly at first, then it whips and snaps as the weave unravels. Horik and I slide out of the Drift.

Horik teeters beside me on the landing. I grab onto him, and he steadies himself.

I grope across the smooth surface of the door to the latch. I half expect it to still be locked, but the door swings open silently on well-oiled hinges. So secretive. I wonder if even the Seven know of this door. The tapestry concealing the door from inside prevents the door from opening fully, so I slip through the crack and into the study, quietly shifting the tapestry aside to allow the door to open for Horik's larger body.

Once he's inside, I ease the door shut and let the tapestry fall into place. Though I know Belos is asleep, I still listen intently for any sound coming from his sleeping chamber. Horik lays a hand on my shoulder and squeezes to say, *Let's go.*

I shrug him off. There's something I have to do. I spent part of the day convincing myself not to do this very thing, and I thought I had succeeded, thought I had bullied myself into sense. But now that I'm here, I know I can't let it go.

The Shackle is in this room. If I take it, Belos will not be able to Leash anyone again.

Ignoring Horik's hiss of irritation, I creep through the room. The dusty rug aids me in my silent hunt. I bump into the stone table and grope across its surface. I frown when my fingers find something sticky. I sniff. Blood.

I turn from the stone table to the pedestal table, the only other place I've ever seen the Shackle resting. When my fingers brush the smooth links of bone, the hair rises on the back of my neck. Swallowing nausea, I lift the Shackle, clutching the two cuffs and the chain connecting them to keep them from clicking noisily. I slide them around behind me, carefully slipping the chain through my belt. I dart a glance in the direction of Belos's sleeping chamber door, then creep back to Horik.

He's breathing angrily. This wasn't part of the plan. I don't care. I can't leave the thing here, not when it's right in front of me.

Horik sighs. With eyes adjusted to the darkness, I can almost see him shaking his head. He vanishes into the Drift.

When the Drift comes to life around me once more, I check on Belos and the Seven again. The Seven haven't moved, but Belos, I am disturbed to see, is now shifting restlessly. Surely he didn't sense me picking up the Shackle?

Wasting no more time, Horik and I start our drift down to the dungeon and the lighted form there. Even from a distance I can see he's not as bright as he should be, and interruptions in the flow of his energy indicate injury and pain.

I push for speed.

Chapter 11

I slide into the physical reality of the cell, stunned by sudden darkness. I hastily shape a Drift-light. When my bluish light reveals the cell and its occupant, I nearly choke.

"Gods," Horik mutters behind me.

Logan slumps against a wall. His wrists are chained above him, hands limp. His head hangs low, face obscured by bloody, filthy hair. His torso is even leaner than I remember, the muscles etched, every trace of fat gone. The bruising across his ribs and stomach is layered with new purple over old yellow. His pants are torn and stained with blood.

Time plays tricks with me as I make my frantic way to him. It seems to take forever to reach him, then suddenly, with no recollection of dropping to my knees, I am beside him. With trembling fingers I brush hair away from his face to reveal horrible bruising, his face a map of purple and blue pain. Several weeks of golden beard growth shadows his jaw, but I can see bruising even through the beard. One eye is swollen shut, the other closed.

"Look what they've done to him!"

Horik crouches on Logan's other side and presses two fingers to Logan's neck. Logan jerks awake, wrenching away from us. Horik backs away, giving Logan space, but I can't. My hands flutter uselessly, and I say Logan's name over and over.

He looks at me through the slit of his right eye, which the Drift-light shows to be dull blue.

The world seems to stop when he says, in a dry, raspy voice, "Just. Go. *Away.*"

I look over my shoulder at Horik, but his expression is as baffled as mine must be. I turn back to Logan.

"We're here to get you out."

His head hangs, swinging side to side in denial.

I hear myself muttering, "Oh gods, oh gods," as though they would help us, as though they even exist.

Horik says, "He's delirious."

"Logan, it's me. Astarti."

Horribly, he starts to laugh, a dry, scratching sound.

"What's wrong with him?" I hiss at Horik, as if he would have the answer. But I can answer my own question: Belos has done something to him, something horrible that my eyes can't see.

Logan feigns surprise. "What's this? No drink? And tears." He nods as though impressed. "Very good. That's new."

I feel my cheek, surprised to find it wet. Then something registers. "Drink? What did they give you?"

"This is an admirable performance, but frankly I don't see the point."

He's acting like this has happened before, like I've been here before. Sudden understanding chills me. "Oh, no. No, no."

Logan scowls. "*Enough* already."

His kick to my gut sends me tumbling into Horik's legs. I grab at Horik's boot as he looms threateningly over Logan.

"Stop," I gasp. "He thinks I'm Belos."

Logan is braced for punishment. When it doesn't come, doubt clouds his face. I push myself to my knees, begging him with my eyes to believe me. I know what Belos is capable of. The Deceiver. The Liar. He's been in Logan's head, messing with his thoughts, with his hopes and fears. He did it to me once, briefly. I know how convincing he can be.

When the faintest tinge of hope lights Logan's one good eye, it renders him vulnerable, and I see the fear in him. He knows I see his hope, and he expects me to exploit it, to use it against him.

"Horik, unchain him."

Horik moves cautiously to Logan's left side. I hear the screech of metal as the cuff opens. Logan groans as Horik slowly lowers the arm. His wrist is red and raw.

When Horik moves to Logan's right, I eye Logan's bruised shoulder with concern. His shoulder was dislocated even before Belos took him. The damage now is far worse.

"Careful," I warn.

Horik slowly lowers the arm, and Logan's face contorts with pain as the joint grinds.

"Is it out of joint?" I ask Horik.

"I don't think so, but it has been recently."

Logan is still staring at me with suspicion. I harden myself. We don't have much time. We have to get out of here.

But when Logan says hesitantly, "Is it…?" all my hardness bursts, and the tears come streaming.

Green swirls through his open eye, then gold chases after it.

I lay a hand on his bruised cheek. "Gods, I've missed that."

"Astarti." He savors my name, like he never expected to say it again.

Shyly, I lean my face against his neck, reveling in the warmth of him. He's shaking, and his teeth start to chatter.

He growls, "You foolish girl, what are you doing here? You shouldn't have come."

His left arm slides around me. He stiffens suddenly as his fingers find the Shackle hanging from my belt. I pull back, reading the doubt that's returned to his eyes. He's bracing again, wondering if I am Belos after all.

"I couldn't leave it. I don't want *him* to have it."

Logan's body seems to melt. He lets out a shuddering breath.

"Hate to interrupt," grumbles Horik, "but we really do need to go."

I peer with concern at Logan's leg. I shift the compress tied there, nearly gagging at a mere glimpse of the torn, inflamed flesh. "Can you stand?"

"He'll have to," Horik says brusquely. He grips Logan under the left elbow, avoiding the damaged shoulder, and draws Logan to his feet.

Logan grunts as his back scrapes the wall, and I look behind him to see a crisscrossed mess of bleeding lacerations. My fists tighten.

"I will *kill* him for this."

Logan tenses briefly at my words, something setting off his suspicions again. There's only one way to prove to him beyond any doubt that I am not Belos. I grab his hand and pull him into the Drift.

As the Drift flares to life around us, Logan stares at me. His fingers lift to the region of my heart, free of any Leash. He presses lightly, and I shiver at the touch. Beside us, Horik shifts impatiently.

Logan follows my eyes down to his own chest, which I can't help staring at in horror. Black threads start to snake along his Leash, and I trace its path to Belos's study, where that bright, familiar form is already moving.

Chapter 12

Axe glowing silver and gold in the Drift, Horik grabs Logan and heads for the courtyard, putting our contingency plan into motion. I skim along behind, shaping my spear. The black taint thickens along Logan's Leash, and he's starting to struggle against Horik.

We reach the courtyard and the edge of the barrier. Horik drags Logan from the Drift. When I slide into the physical world behind them, Horik is already half carrying, half dragging Logan to the sloping path. Their long shadows surge ahead of them as the blazing light of torches and braziers around the entrance flares against their backs. Voices shout behind us. Belos's servants, guarding the entrance, and Belos himself.

I rush to help Horik as Logan wrenches away from him, amazingly strong, given his injuries. Horik clunks Logan in the head with a fist, and Logan crumples.

"Run!" Horik shouts at me as he slings Logan over his shoulder and starts down the slope.

I know better. I spin to meet Belos's attack.

Belos, though, is still standing at the top of the fortress steps.

Suddenly, the earth crumbles under Horik's feet. He falls, disappearing to his torso in a narrow crevice, and Logan tumbles from his grip. Conscious now, Logan tries to catch himself. He skids to a stop and staggers to his feet. Horik, trying to jerk free of the tight crevice, yells at me to run, but I'm not leaving either of them.

Logan limps up the slope, stepping around Horik. Horik lunges for Logan's leg and trips him, but Logan wrenches free. He staggers to his feet once more and continues on without reaction.

I know what I'll see when he steps into the light, but I call out anyway, "Logan, listen to me!"

He stalks my way, emerging from the dark slope into the lighted courtyard. Gooseflesh rises on my arms as the firelight paints his face yellow and gleams in the black pool of his single working eye.

When I whip my spear around to hit him with the butt of it, a blast of air sends me flying. I land hard on my elbow. I spin on my hip, swiping at Logan's legs. With his leg so damaged, he goes down easily. I leap on top of him and pin his chest with my spear shaft. I don't allow myself to consider his injuries or what further damage I might be doing. I have to stop him.

He stops struggling, and the black fades from his eye. I ease the pressure on my spear and shift back so he can sit up. He's panting, bewildered. It is so painful to watch his confusion, and it makes me sloppy and unprepared. Logan's face twists, then the oily blackness floods into his open eye again.

I'm scrambling away when my hands clamp to my sides and I tip over like a statue. Panic suffuses my stiff and useless body. I recognize the suffocating constriction of Belos's binding. Logan gropes along my arms and legs, ripping my knives free and tossing them away. He digs into my boot for the one hidden there. Logan would not know where to seek my knives, but Belos would. He reaches behind me and tears the Shackle from my belt.

Mindless, Logan staggers to his feet, clutching the Shackle in one hand and dragging me by my jacket with the other. He limps toward Belos, still waiting calmly on the steps, certain of his control.

This is the end. He will Leash me again. Panic closes my throat, and, like a fool, I wrench against the binding, wasting energy.

When I hear Horik shout, I work my head around just enough to see him charging up the slope, free of the crevice, his axe raised to throw. I gauge his aim and realize that he's aiming too low for Logan. He's aiming at me.

At the last moment, his arm shifts, rising, and the axe goes spinning end over end toward Logan.

I scream in terror, and my body electrifies with the surge of Drift-energy that I rip through my mooring. I burst free of Belos's bonds and send a blast of energy at Horik's axe, catching it just before it reaches Logan's back. The weapon spins and clatters away across the stony courtyard.

Horik vanishes into the Drift only to appear beside me. My legs feel boneless and wobbly as Horik hauls me to my feet, tearing me out of Logan's grasp. He deals Logan a kick to the hip that makes his bad leg buckle.

"Ruuu-ahhh!" Horik's yell turns into a strangled cry as Belos's glowing lash whips around his neck. Belos yanks, and Horik goes flying back.

Belos stalks down the fortress steps. I don't remember shaping my spear, but it's in my hands, and I run, lunging for Belos's neck. He vanishes.

He reappears beside Logan and rips the Shackle from Logan's grasp. He slides one cuff over his hand and turns to me. At the sight of him with that confident set to his mouth and the Shackle waiting for me, I recoil.

I slide into the Drift.

Seven waiting figures converge on me.

I dart away, but I'm trapped within the barrier. There is no escape, not from Belos, not from the Seven. I shape my spear to fight, but bindings loop around me from every direction. They don't even try to engage me.

I am hauled from the Drift.

I scrabble for purchase against the stony ground, but the bindings squeeze until I can't breathe. They drag me to Belos's feet.

He crouches down, studying me. He sighs, taking his time, brushing hair from my face. I wrench my head away.

"You do look like your mother, you know. I see the resemblance particularly with you bound here before me, as she was before she died."

Somewhere behind me, Horik gives a muffled shout.

I choke on my own horror. Belos's lip twitch with amusement.

"It was almost in this very spot. Do you know, the last thing she ever saw was me lifting you into my arms?" He slips the Shackle's cuff over my pinned hand and says with satisfaction, "You must have always known it would come to this."

I am screaming, screaming, screaming until my head must surely burst. Something rumbles deep in the earth, something angry and powerful. I can't hear it above my own screaming, but I feel it tremble through my body.

A hand—Logan's, glowing with bluish light—clamps on the bone chain connecting my cuff to Belos's. The Shackle hums and trembles with power. The chain bursts, and the explosion sends me flying back amid a spray of bone fragments. I try to get to my feet, but the earth quakes and bucks.

With an earsplitting crack, the fortress fractures up the middle, and one half slumps, crumbling, falling inward. I hear angry, panicked shouts and see flashes of Drift-work.

Horik scrambles to my side, but I can't hear his shout over the tumbling stone. Wind whips over me, tearing at my hair and driving dirt into my eyes. I stagger to my feet. Dark figures stumble around me, and I careen into someone as the earth shudders. Instinctively, I tear away, but in the glow of frantic Drift-work I catch sight of a bruised and bloody torso.

"Logan!"

His hand closes on mine. He lunges for Horik. I feel my body dissolve into weightlessness as Logan blends us into the wind.

Chapter 13

LOGAN

I tear across the face of this dead land. Part of me remembers that I am carrying two people and yearns to return to Astarti, but a more primal part of me wins out, reveling in simple freedom. The Other is far away. I can still feel traces of him—inside me, outside me—but I just keep going.

I want to blow across the surface of this place until there is nothing left of me, but I'm not alone. Astarti hovers at the edge of my awareness. Her companion is more distant to me, but I feel him too.

With my senses dissolved in wind, I feel more than see the world around me. The temperature drops with the predawn chill, and moisture rises. We've reached the ocean.

I tear across its surface, frothing the waves, leaving a mad churn in my wake. I don't know where I'm going, just that I'm moving away from *him*.

Eventually, exhaustion weighs on me. I cannot hold this form much longer. I press onward, desperate to reach land.

When a rocky cliff looms in the distance, I surge toward it. Just a little farther. When the edges of my wind eddy in the pockets of the cliff's uneven surface, I force myself to slow, to calm.

I withdraw from the wind, reshaping myself and the others. I register cool predawn air and the tang of the sea before the return to my body brings waves of pain: the shock of bruised and torn flesh, cracked bones, utter exhaustion. My mind breaks apart. My body begins to convulse. I feel hands on me. I hear Astarti's voice. Then everything is gone.

Chapter 14

I try to slow Logan's fall, but he's thrashing too hard and we collapse onto cold, rocky ground. Horik and I try to hold Logan still, to keep him from hurting himself further. His muscles strain and twist, and I grip his head against my lap to prevent him from cracking it against the rocks that dig into my knees. With a final wrench his body freezes, every muscle etched with tension, then he goes limp.

I hear a sound like, "meh, meh, meh," and realize it's coming from my own mouth.

Horik lays a hand on Logan's chest, making sure he's still breathing, then his fingers work themselves into my tight grip, loosening my hold on Logan's jaw. I release, pained to see red finger marks where I've dug into Logan's flesh. I cradle him, rocking his unconscious body, trying to still the shaking of my own.

My hands unconsciously stroke Logan's chest, running again and again over the old, curving scar that arcs across his left pectoral down to his bruised ribs. I want so badly to see his eyes and crooked grin, to hear the deep rumble of his laugh.

I find my voice. "He needs a Healer. Now."

Horik pushes unsteadily to his feet. "We don't even know where we are."

I follow Horik's sweeping gaze. The predawn sky is light enough to reveal the rocky expanse of a dim cliff that rises behind us, giving way at the top to spiky trees. In all other directions beyond our rocky outcropping there is only the ocean.

"It doesn't matter," I say sharply. "Help me."

Horik crouches at Logan's leg. He carefully lifts an edge of the bloody poultice and grimaces.

"It's been treated, but it's still infected. He's lost a lot of blood, and not just from this."

"Do you think I can't see that?"

"I'm not a physician."

I'm shaking, my teeth chattering as the horror of the last twenty minutes still courses through me. "You were going to kill him."

Horik slowly raises his dark eyes to mine. "And he would have thanked me for it, had he been taken again."

There's a lump in my throat that I can't swallow. I know he's right, that he was only doing what I should have done myself during the battle in Tornelaine. But now, with Logan here in my arms, I'm glad I failed, and that Horik failed.

I say more softly, "You were going to kill me, but you changed your mind."

Horik runs a hand over his close-cropped hair, scratches the back of his head. "I should have. I was supposed to. Imagine if Belos had managed to Leash you again. It was close, Astarti, so close, and I would be responsible, and an oath-breaker."

Understanding slaps me. "That was the deal you made with Heborian."

"You knew about that?"

"I didn't know what your agreement was, but I could tell that there was one. You're not a very good liar, Horik."

The corner of his mouth twitches, then tugs down. "It was the price of the king's permission."

I sit back a little. "I see."

"He meant it as a protection for you."

"I'm not angry about the agreement."

"You're not?" Horik sounds skeptical.

"I'm angry that he—and you—kept it from me."

Horik has the grace to look shame-faced. "I'm sorry."

Unable to accept the apology, I circle back to an earlier point. "You say it was the price of his permission. Then it was your idea. Why? Surely not that Firstborn bullshit. If Heborian doesn't care about me, I don't see why you should."

Horik shifts uncomfortably. Despite his intimidating size, his words are soft, begging me to understand. "The king wasn't against it. He was only exploiting the opportunity to get that oath from me. I would have given the oath anyway, because it was the right thing to do, and the king would have let me come with you anyway, because it was the right thing to do. That doesn't mean either of us were happy about the situation."

I glare at him, refusing to let him or Heborian off the hook just yet.

Horik plows on. "And it isn't that you're the Firstborn."

"Oh? What is it then?"

"It's stupid. Just drop it. It doesn't matter."

"*What?*"

Horik's heavy jaw grinds with refusal, but he gives in when I keep staring at him. "You remind me of someone."

That surprises me. "Who?"

"Brigga. My little sister."

That makes me grin. I had no idea Horik was so sentimental. I have to tease him, if for no other reason than to break the awkwardness. "So she's an ass-kicking Drifter like me?"

"She was." He says it brusquely, with finality.

Was.

I freeze with uncertainty. Is he implying that she's dead? Should I ask?

Horik releases me from my discomfort, sort of, when he acknowledges, "Yes, she's dead."

"Horik, I—"

He waves off whatever I was going to say, which I hadn't even figured out for myself, so I'm glad. He clearly doesn't want to discuss it further. He probably regrets saying anything.

Horik turns his attention to Logan's injured leg again, feeling around his knee. "At least it's not broken."

I move my hand from Logan's neck, where I've been feeling his pulse, a rhythmic assurance of life. I gently probe along his bruised ribs to feel for the edges of broken bone. Thankfully, I find nothing jagged.

I wish I had water to wash him; I hate seeing him like this. "We have to get him back to Tornelaine. He's still Leashed."

"I know that, but I'm not sure it's safe to take him into the Drift in this condition."

He's right, of course. Neither of us knows enough about medicine to truly determine the extent of Logan's injuries. With him unconscious and unprepared, the stress of entry could be too much. And yet, what choice do we have?

Logan stirs against my legs, and his one good eye slits open.

With trembling fingers, I brush a lock of blood-crusted hair from his face. "There you are," I say shakily, then I reprimand him, "Don't scare me like that." When he doesn't respond, I plead, "Say something."

He inhales deeply, then winces at the pressure it puts on his ribs.

Finally, his voice rasps out, "You should have killed me. I almost—I—" He lays a shaking hand over his eyes.

My heart wrenches. "Nothing that happened was your fault."

"I handed you over to him!"

"No, Logan. *You* didn't."

The hand covering his eyes tightens, fingers digging into his own bruised flesh. I lay my own hand over his until it eases. I don't try to peel his hand away. He needs whatever small privacy it affords him.

I lean down and press my lips to his forehead above our hands. He's shaking with repressed emotion. There is nothing I can say right now to make things right for him, so I just hold on.

I feel his efforts to stop shaking, to put himself back together. I think of what Bran told me of Logan's childhood and how he stopped speaking for a time. His whole life has been a struggle of too much emotion with too little release. But he's not a child any longer, and he's clearly learned to bury things deep in order to function. I don't know if that's good, but it helps him get through this moment. His shudders stop. He says roughly, "Help me up."

"I don't think—"

Logan rolls partway onto his side to push himself up. Scrambling to my feet beside him, I try to steady him, but he's too heavy. He wobbles. Horik's hand darts out, gripping Logan's elbow. With his other hand hooking Logan's ribcage, Horik helps him to his feet, eliciting a pained grunt.

Logan squints at Horik in the predawn light. "I don't know you."

Horik inclines his head. "Horik, son of Hornir."

Logan's one good eye narrows further. "You're Runish. One of Heborian's?"

I sense the danger in his tone, so I quickly remind him, "Horik came to help you, and to help me. At great risk to himself."

Logan's jaw unclenches. "Then thank you. But you would have done better to prevent her from endangering herself."

Horik raises a dark eyebrow. "And how should I have done that? Do you know how stubborn she is?"

Logan snorts in agreement, and some of the tension drains away.

"I *am* right here," I remind them.

Horik says, "We'll take you through the Drift to Tornelaine. Heborian is waiting there with the knife to cut your Leash."

When Logan's face darkens, I think it's the word "Leash" that bothers him, but he surprises me by saying, "I'm not going through the Drift."

Horik is nonplussed. "It's the fastest way."

"*No.*"

"What's the problem?"

Logan shifts uncomfortably. "What if—" He cuts himself off, and even in the dim light I see his face drain.

He's afraid Belos will be there.

I say gently, "If he's there, we're already done for. We're better off getting back to Tornelaine as quickly as we can."

He says stubbornly, "I don't want to enter the Drift. Ever. I can take you to Tornelaine."

"But you're already exhausted. You can barely even stand."

"I'll take you as far as I can. If I can't make it, you can take me into the Drift."

"Logan—"

"Deal?"

My skin crawls at the word, but I try to make light of it. "You know, people offer deals when they know what they're offering is unreasonable, but they also know that the other person really has no bargaining power. It's bullshit."

"I knew you'd see things my way." Logan's mouth quirks in that half-smile of his.

No matter how pleased I am to see him able to joke right now, I can't give up on this. "I *don't* see things your way, but I'm not going to force you into the Drift. But, Logan, *please* be reasonable—"

"Astarti," Horik says, "we're wasting time. I don't know how much longer we have before Belos comes after him. I'll travel the Drift. There's no need for Logan to carry both of us. You should stay with him in case he can't make it. I'll see you in Tornelaine."

With that, Horik vanishes.

Logan comments, "I like him."

I throw up my hands.

Wind stirs. Logan takes my hand. As Logan's form grows insubstantial, I feel myself begin to dissolve. My thoughts scatter, and I can cling only to my wonder. How on earth is he doing this?

CHAPTER 15

We fly over the wide blue expanse of water, disturbing the waves as we blow against their normal pattern. We falter from time to time, dipping into the spray or tumbling off course. I prepare to plunge into the water, but each time Logan falters he puts on more speed.

Eventually, fishing boats rock below us, tipping precariously, trying to find balance against wind and water. I know we've reached the harbor when the crowd of boats thickens and they start to knock against each other and the docks.

We meet the resistance of stone walls and buildings. We catch and snag on rooftops. I feel my consciousness solidify and expect to go crashing into a building at any moment. But Logan finds some last reserve of strength.

We tumble over the wall enclosing the castle grounds, and suddenly I am myself again, bumping and rolling painfully over cobblestones. Voices shout. Footsteps pound toward me. I stagger to my feet, but the early morning sky and the buildings swing dizzyingly. I fall.

Rough hands turn me over, and I squint Heborian's tattooed face into focus. I lurch up and shove past him. I stumble to where Bran and Korinna are pinning Logan down, trying to control his body as it's wracked by convulsions.

I drop to my knees beside Bran. I lay a useless hand on Logan's bruised and bloody torso, horrified by the rigidity and spasming of his muscles. Blood streams from his nose, slipping down his cheek and neck to the cobblestones.

"Korinna!" Bran shouts. "*Do* something!"

Korinna, crouched on Bran's other side, looks panicked. She places a shaking hand on Logan's head and closes her eyes. Her eyes pop open again.

"I don't know what to do!"

"Just trust your instincts!"

I stare at Korinna, barely daring to hope. Her face twists. She wrings her hands. Then, in that way of Earthmakers, she lets it all go. The tension sweeps out of her body. Her face goes still. She closes her eyes once more and lays her slim hands on either side of Logan's head.

Logan's body seizes up, arching off the cobblestones, then his muscles loosen and his body thumps to the ground.

Korinna falls back with a thud.

My eyes dart from her to Logan and back. "You…"

Bran asks, "Can you do his leg?"

Korinna drags herself toward Logan's worst wound. With trembling fingers, she peels the bandage away. She makes a face at the sight of the blood and inflammation, but she places a careful hand on the injury. Logan, returning to consciousness, groans.

Korinna's head hangs. "Nothing comes."

"It's all right," Bran assures her. "When you recover your strength."

Logan starts to pull away, struggling to get up. Bran tries to prevent him, and Logan's one good eye widens with panic at the restraint.

I tug Bran away. "Let him up." Bran, who has never been held against his will, has no idea what instinctive fear he's causing.

Horik appears from somewhere, and together we help Logan to his feet. We both stay beside him, keeping him from swaying, grounding him with something familiar as he looks around with a disoriented expression.

"Where's Heborian?" I demand.

"Right here," he says from behind me, and I jump in surprise.

I tug Heborian's sleeve, pushing him toward Logan.

Logan ties to jerk away when Heborian latches onto him, and his eyes widen as he realizes Heborian is about to take him into the Drift. They vanish.

My booming heart counts double time for the seconds they are gone.

When they reappear, Logan lunges away from Heborian. His injured leg buckles, and he falls to one knee on the cobblestones. I crouch beside him. Everyone else, thankfully, has the sense to stay back.

I tug Logan's hand away from where he's clawing at his sternum. "It's gone," I murmur, I pulling his face against my chest. "You're free of him."

His trembling eases, and he says, as though this is the first time it really sinks in, "You came for me."

ꙮ ꙮ

Heborian disperses the crowd that has gathered. Logan refuses to be carried on a litter, so I lead him slowly to the room that adjoins mine. The stairs are hard for him, and I'm annoyed with his stubbornness, but he somehow makes it into the castle and down the long sequence of hallways.

When Logan, Bran, Korinna, and I reach the room, Logan goes straight to the pitcher of water on the sideboard table. He ignores the cup and lifts the whole pitcher to his lips.

"Easy," I caution when he starts to choke.

He splutters, coughing. Water sloshes from the pitcher, and I take it from him.

"Do you want food?"

He runs the back of a hand across his mouth. Water and blood drip from his beard to trail pinkly down his chest. "I want to get *clean*." He says the last word harshly.

Troubled by the shame I hear in that word and not trusting myself to speak, I nod.

Logan's room, like mine, has an attached bathing chamber, and Bran leads Logan into it. I didn't see Heborian give any orders, but clearly he sent word ahead of us because steam rises from the huge copper tub.

I hang back. I want to stay with Logan, but this is an intimacy I have never shared with him, and it seems more appropriate for Bran to help him clean up. The door clicks shut.

A splash, thump, and muffled curse come from the bathing chamber. My hands twitch anxiously. Maybe I should have gone in anyway.

I pace to the fireplace where Korinna is sitting tiredly in one of the plush chairs. Her face is drawn.

I say, "You're a Healer."

She winces like it's an accusation.

"You probably saved his life."

"He's still hurt," she says miserably, as though she has failed somehow.

I know better. She's young, untrained. I can hardly believe she did what she did.

Understanding hits. "This is why you don't want to go back to Avydos, isn't it?"

Korinna stares into her lap. "I want to be a Warden." Her voice is defeated, as though she knows this will never happen.

"But you're so important."

She sinks deeper into the chair. "You sound like Feluvas."

I hold back my other comments. This is something for Korinna to work out, and I'm not without sympathy. It doesn't feel good to be forced into something. And yet, with only two Healers in Avydos, I'm sure they can't afford to let Korinna endanger herself as a Warden. I blink, surprised at myself. Am I so much like my father? Do I really see people in terms of their use? Part of me cries, *No*! but another part contends reasonably, *Well, yes.*

It feels like hours before the bathing chamber door finally opens and Logan limps out. His hair is dark gold, but even the dampness can't keep the waves out of it. The beard is gone, but clean and shaven he almost looks worse, all the bruising of his face more obvious, more out of place. He has a thick linen towel cinched around his waist, and his bare torso is a mess of bruises and lacerations. Blood soaks through the towel at his leg.

He moves painfully through the room, and he won't look at any of us.

"I think I have my strength back," Korinna offers shyly.

Bran nods from behind Logan.

We make our way to the bedroom. Logan eases onto the edge of the bed. I go to his side, wanting to catch his eye and see if he's all right, but he's still looking away, uncomfortable with everyone's scrutiny.

"May I?" asks Korinna, hovering beside Bran.

Logan wordlessly shifts the towel to expose the wound. Korinna and I both hiss as we see it fully for the first time. The wound is a good seven or eight inches long and at least two wide. It extends from his thigh into his knee. I can't tell if the white I see is bone or infection. He's had the wound for a while because the edges are already granulating in.

Korinna steps forward cautiously. She looks to Logan for permission, but he only braces his hands on the bed. When Korinna touches the wound, he sucks in a breath. Low, choking sounds escape him. I'm sure it hurts like hell.

When Logan's body relaxes and Korinna rocks back, I frown at Logan's leg. An ugly red scar marks the wound's former location. It's certainly far, far better than it was, but it has that look of a wound that healed poorly, an injury that will still cause pain.

"Thank you," Logan breathes.

Korinna shakes her head. "It's still not right. I could feel the remaining damage, but it wouldn't Heal."

Bran says, "Even my mother couldn't have Healed that properly. The injury was too severe, and it had gone untreated for too long. It's not your fault, Korinna."

Korinna's mouth tightens, not quite accepting this. Even though she's shaking with fatigue, she lays a light finger on Logan's shoulder, signaling him to lean down. He tenses, not wanting anyone to look at his back. I touch his arm gently, silently telling him it's all right, and he gives in after a brief hesitation, leaning forward to expose the crisscross of lacerations. He hisses as his movement makes the wounds gape. Blood slips from them to stain the edge of the towel.

My hands shake at the sight of these new wounds layered over old scars. Hatred surges through me. I *hate* Belos. I *hate* the people—these Ancorites, whoever they are—who did the same thing to Logan before Belos. I hate everyone for their cruelty.

Korinna's hands move from laceration to laceration, leaving behind a new network of scars. When the last wound closes, she collapses over Logan's shoulder. Logan gently eases her into Bran's arms.

Logan says tightly, "It was too much to ask of her."

I disagree, but I keep my mouth shut.

Korinna mumbles, "I'm not done."

"That's enough for now," Bran says gently.

Even though he should feel better, Logan is trembling.

I give him a worried look. "Logan?"

"I just…really…need everyone to leave." His voice sounds too tight.

Bran nods in understanding and guides a shaky Korinna to the door. Miserably, I follow.

When I'm almost to the door, Logan calls my name brokenly, "Star-ti."

I surge back to him, but I have to hover anxiously, because his eyes are still cast down, his body language not inviting me to touch him.

"Bran?" I say.

He looks back.

"Just keep everyone away, will you?"

When Logan and I are alone, I find him a pair of loose sleeping pants. Shyly, I turn away while he puts them on. When I hear the bed creak, I turn to him again. He's lying on his back, one arm over his eyes. I tug the heavy drapes closed to shut out the morning light and approach the bed. I'm not sure what Logan wants from me right now, so I wait. He's still for so long that I turn to leave, imagining that he wants to be alone after all, when he grabs my hand.

The pressure in my chest eases. He does want me here; he just doesn't know how to communicate right now.

I unlace my boots and shrug off my jacket. My clothes, skin, and hair are still choked with dust from the Dry Land, but I don't want to leave Logan long enough to wash up. I climb into the bed, careful not to bump him. Korinna took care of the worst of his injuries, but his ribs are still cracked, his shoulder damaged, and his bruising marking a dozen points of pain. Even so, he pulls me closer, and I lie against his body. He's shaking like he's cold, so I pull the covers over him. It doesn't help. He's twitchy and restless.

Finally, I slip out of the bed and pad through the bedroom and sitting room. I open the door to find a page boy waiting, and I send him to find the king's physician and tell him to prepare a sedative.

Renald, the balding physician, comes so quickly that I know he must have already been working on the drink. I wonder who had the foresight to know that Logan would need it.

Renald wants to come in and check on Logan, but I send him grumbling on his way. The last thing Logan wants right now is attention.

I return to the bedchamber with the steaming cup. When I lay a hand on Logan's shoulder, he jerks in surprise. His mind has been somewhere else.

I offer the cup. "Drink this."

He recoils violently, bolting up and scrambling across the bed.

My mouth pinches. I want to cry out, *What did he do to you?* but it's not the time.

I take a sip of the drink myself and hold it out again. "It will help you rest."

Logan eyes me warily, but he accepts the cup. He stares at me over the rim, waiting, perhaps, for me to turn into Belos, waiting for everything to crash down and for him to find himself once more in Belos's dungeon.

I close my eyes, imagining what he's been through. Even though a logical part of me denies it, I feel complicit in Logan's torture. For years I served the man who did this to him.

When Logan tips his head back and drinks, I silently thank him for his trust.

Chapter 16

I'm startled awake when Logan's elbow cracks into the side of my head. I lurch upright.

Logan thrashes in a tangle of sheets, his body sheened with sweat. He's making low, harsh sounds. When I gently shake his shoulder, he lunges up with a yell.

"Logan!"

His eyes snap to me.

His hand latches onto my throat. He bursts up, driving me out of the bed. I scramble for footing as he drives me backward across the room and slams me into the wall.

His face is a rictus of fury, made more horrible by the bruising and the eye that's swollen shut. His lip is curled, his teeth clenched. He's growling, and his one good eye burns vivid green.

I can't breathe, can't think. I claw at his hand.

I kick him in the shin. He winces. I kick him again. Blue threads through the green.

Suddenly, his face melts with horror. His hand springs open.

I slide down the wall, choking for breath.

Logan's hands clench in his hair. Then he reaches one hand toward me but snatches it back almost at once. He starts mumbling in a language I've never heard, something guttural and harsh. He spins away from me and back.

I use the wall to push to my feet. "Logan."

His good eye meets mine briefly. Blue and green roil through the iris in frantic motion, horror and panic barely controlled. He turns away, hunching around his stomach like he's going to be sick.

He flinches when I touch his back.

"Logan, it's all right." My voice is raspy, raw, my pulse still thundering.

He crumples, hunching around one knee. He's shaking his head, mumbling, "I'm sorry, I'm sorry, I'm sorry."

I crouch beside him. I don't allow myself to rub at the soreness of my neck. I force myself not to choke as my lungs recover. I force my hand to steady as I lay an arm across his shoulders. A silent sob wracks his body.

Now I'm crying. For his confusion, his pain, his shame. I know he didn't mean to hurt me. In that moment, with the nightmare riding him, he didn't even know who I was.

"Come here," I rasp, trying to pry him away from his knee. "It's all right. I'm fine."

He resists me for a long time, but at last he unclenches enough that I can snake an arm around his chest. His forehead rests in the joining of my shoulder and neck. Shudders course through his body.

"I'm sorry," he says, his voice muffled by my shirt.

"Shh."

"I'm sorry," he says again, and I feel his eye squeeze shut.

After I've gotten him back into bed—after stripping away the sweat-soaked sheet—I seek out another, stronger sleeping draught. It's partly because I know he needs to rest, but it's also because I don't know what else to do.

ꕥ ꕥ

In the late afternoon, Logan wakes again, this time without violence. I never got back to sleep, so I'm leaning against the headboard, fingering the waves of his hair when his good eye eases open.

"Hey," I say.

The light slipping through a crack in the drapes falls over my shoulder onto his face. The green and blue of his eye is bright in the light, so beautiful. Gods, how I've missed that. He's staring at something on my neck. His jaw clenches.

I say, to distract him from whatever he's looking at, "Are you hungry? There's food in the sitting room."

I heard someone deliver it about twenty minutes ago, and the scent of roast beef has been tormenting me ever since.

Logan must smell it too because his eye drifts away from me and he sits up.

"Do you want me to go get it?"

"I'm getting up," he says, voice rough from sleep.

I draw back my feet as he edges around me. When he slides out of bed, his left leg buckles and he has to catch himself against the bedpost. I slide out of the bed beside him. He shakes his head when I offer my hand. He takes several stiff, halting steps away from the bed before the leg loosens and he can walk. His path is not very straight. No doubt he's groggy from the sedative.

A fire plays in the hearth, and the tray of food sends waves of temptation my way. Logan halts in the doorway and I nearly run into his back.

This, I understand. After where he's been, the ordinary, comfortable room doesn't look quite real. He looks around—for enemies, for hints that this is an illusion—before proceeding cautiously into the room.

Despite the temptation of food, I have to slip away to answer the even more insistent call of my bladder. When I return to the room, Logan is sitting in one of the chairs. He hasn't even taken the lids off the plates. He looks up, staring at my neck.

While I washed up, I caught sight of myself in the mirror, and I now realize why he's been staring. Fingerprint bruises line my throat. I do my best to ignore his stare, to act like it's nothing.

I sit in the chair beside him and lift one of the silver covers to reveal a mound of tender meat and thick slices of fresh bread. The fare is simple, suited to someone who hasn't eaten well in a while. I hold out a piece of bread for Logan.

His face darkens. His pulse throbs in his neck. "I can feed myself." The words are harsh, angry. Almost immediately, his expression turns apologetic, and he buries his face in his hand.

I touch his knee. "It's all right."

I can take his anger, the sudden snaps of temper—I expect that after what he's been through—but I don't like seeing his constant self-reproach. He needs to give himself some leniency; he needs to give himself some time.

I return the bread to the plate and take the whole thing into my lap. I uncover the other plate but don't offer it to him. I begin to eat, hoping he will follow my example. He needs the food, needs to recover his strength and gain back the weight he's lost. He's still well-muscled enough that they clearly did feed him, but I don't like seeing the sharp lines of his ribs or the way his stomach look so sucked in around the notched muscles.

When I hear the other plate being lifted from the table, I don't look up. What he *doesn't* need is my scrutiny.

A few minutes later, when Logan puts the plate back on the table, I go to the sideboard to get him some water. I bring it back and set it on the table instead of handing it to him, allowing him to start recovering the sense of autonomy that's been taken from him. My jaw tightens when I see how little he's eaten, but I reason that his stomach is shrunken; it will take time.

He downs the water too fast, and I have to save the cup before he drops it. He's choking, coughing, clutching at his cracked ribs. I want to help him, but I force myself to do no more than lay light fingers at the nape of his neck.

Now that his hair is dry, the color is blond again. The streaks are lighter than they were, which isn't surprising after he's been under the harsh sun of the Dry Land. Recovered from his coughing fit, he leans back in the chair, and I let my hand drop. I take my seat again.

Abruptly, Logan says, "He wanted to know what I am."

I wait for him to continue.

"He knew I wasn't an Earthmaker. Not fully."

This seems hard to deny, after Belos took him through the Drift even before he was Leashed. I'm still hunting for words, feeling stupid and silent and useless, when Logan barks a laugh. He says bitterly, "She must know. She would have to."

He means his mother.

I offer, "We can find out, if you want."

"Oh, yes," he whispers harshly, "I have some questions for her."

"She never said anything?"

Logan doesn't answer this. His expression tells me he's moved on to another line of thought. He says woodenly, "Ironic, isn't it? They were right. All of them. When they called me a bastard."

"Logan," I say firmly. "Don't do this to yourself."

He stares upward. "Do you know what just kills me? That *Belos* was right. About so many things."

Anger simmers in my chest, at Belos and his power to manipulate all of us. "Belos is a liar. *The* Liar. I once believed him also."

Logan looks at me, his one good eye narrowing, color swirling through it. "I will kill him. For everything little thing he did to you."

I shake my head in disbelief. For what Belos did to me? I never endured a fraction of what Logan did at his hands. If it's possible to kill Belos, *I* will do it, for Logan. But I force my mouth to crook, to make light of this when I say, "You'll have to get in line."

Chapter 17

With the help of another sleeping draught, Logan gets back to sleep. I linger in the doorway, watching Logan's chest rise and fall evenly. Soon, he will have to start dealing with what happened. Better, though, for him to do it tomorrow, when he's rested, when the sun is up again and the world doesn't look so evil.

I'm wide awake and too restless to stay with him any longer. I resolve to find Bran. I'm sure Horik reported the basic facts, but I feel like I owe Bran something.

Bran isn't in his rooms, so I make my way to the royal library, the only other place I've known him to be in this huge castle. Only one lantern burns in the vast room, casting light over a young scholar and his table of open books. The light blooms over the nearest shelves, revealing volumes of every size before fading away into the dark stretches of the room. A brief curiosity stirs within me—what's in all these books?—but I push it away for another time.

"Have you seen Bran?"

The scholar looks up, squinting.

When I get no response, I add, "The Earthmaker?"

"I know who he is. He's here all the time."

"Well, have you seen him?" I can't mask my impatience.

"Not all day."

My eyebrows contract. What else would Bran have been doing?

The only other place I can imagine him being is with Heborian. I make my way to the royal chambers, passing through the foyer with its constantly spilling fountain.

I ask the guards at the door to Heborian's study, "Is Branos in there?"

One of them answers, "No, miss. I mean, my lady."

I snort at his confusion, and he blushes furiously.

"Do you have any idea where he might be?"

"No, my lady," he says, veering on the side of caution.

I'm about to leave when the study door eases open and Heborian peers out.

"Astarti. I thought I heard you. Come in."

I don't like the tone of command, so I don't move.

Heborian exhales loudly through his nose and adds a perfunctory, "Please."

When I follow him into the study, I immediately wish I hadn't. Every one of the Drifters is here: Horik, Jarl, Rood, two whose names I don't know, and Wulfstan.

Wulfstan straightens from where he's been leaning against a heavy table covered in maps. His eyes narrow at me.

I turn to leave, but Heborian snags my elbow. "Not so fast."

I slip out of Heborian's grasp. "I'll just let you gentlemen continue with your plots and schemes. I'm sure they have nothing to do with me."

Horik rises from his seat by the fire. "Astarti, please stay."

I grit my teeth. I can refuse Heborian, but I can't refuse Horik, not after he risked his life to help me. I sigh sharply and stride over to him. He's the only one I'll stand beside in this room.

Horik fills me in. "We've been discussing what happened. I've told them about the collapse of Belos's fortress. I've told them about how Logan took us into wind. I've also told them that Logan broke Belos's Shackle. We are trying to anticipate Belos's response."

Wulstan says loudly, "We don't need her."

I step toward him aggressively, leaving only enough room for my spear. "What is your problem, old man?"

Wulfstan's dark Runish eyes dance at the invitation to confront me. "You are an error we would do better to forget."

Heborian growls a warning, "Wulfstan, you will mind how you speak to my daughter."

"Then kindly tell me, Sire, what is her position here? Will you declare her your heir, in place of Rood?" Rood, standing at the other end of the table, stiffens. "Are we to endanger everything we've worked so hard to build, everything for which we have made such sacrifices?"

"Are you quite finished, uncle?" Heborian says in a low, dangerous voice.

I reel back. Uncle? They are related? Oh, gods, that means Wulfstan and *I* are related. And me, the heir? I almost gag.

Wulfstan's lined face is drawn into a scowl, his white eyebrows angled furiously.

Heborian addresses the whole room. "Astarti is here. We must accept and make use of that. We would be fools to turn her away. Rood is my heir, but you are *all* fools if you feel certain there will be a throne for him at all if we don't take care of the threat Belos poses to Kelda."

I don't like this speech. Oh, it's delivered in true Heborian style, with its unfeeling practicality, but the whole make-use-of-Astarti bit doesn't sit well with me.

Rood, chest puffed with youthful pride, publicly assured of his place, has the confidence to say, "My father is right. Can we continue?"

Wulfstan turns to the table, his back to me, pretending I don't exist. Heborian watches him with that wolfish expression of his, then comes to the hearth and leans against the mantle. Still bristling, I make my way back to Horik.

Heborian says, "Horik tells us that Logan grabbed onto the Shackle and broke it. Can you tell me how that's possible?"

I remember the Shackle thrumming with Logan's power. I remember the faint bluish light enveloping his hand. I remember being thrown back by the force of the explosion. I remember the shards of bone flying. But I won't give Heborian or his Drifters any of my information because I don't know how they might use it—or how they might try to use Logan.

I say, "How should I know? It all happened so fast. I'm not sure it even *was* Logan. Belos had a hold of it, too. Maybe he broke it."

"Why would he do that?"

"I'm not saying it was on purpose. Look, I don't know what happened. Horik doesn't know either." I shoot Horik a pointed look, which he accepts by inclining his chin.

Heborian takes a deep breath. "Then we will have to ask Logan."

I snarl, "You will leave him alone."

Heborian meets my eyes steadily. "I will give him a little time."

My nostrils flare. "You do realize that he's a Primo, that his brother is the Arcon of Avydos? You have no authority over him."

Heborian doesn't react. He moves on as though I haven't spoken. "It's clear that Logan is something more than just an Earthmaker. His power is similar to yours, so it's possible his father was a Drifter."

I tense at this suggestion. Of course, it has occurred to me also, but if it's true, and Logan's mother had a love affair with a Drifter, she would be Stricken for it.

Heborian goes on, "The way he merges himself with the elements is not unlike what I've seen you do. But the scale of his power, the chaos of it… It's not quite the same. Only the oldest stories tell of power like that."

"What are you getting at?"

"We need to know what he is."

"No, you don't. That's Logan business—"

"Belos will want him back. We need to know how Belos might be able to make use of him. We need to be prepared."

"But Belos can't Leash him again. The Shackle is broken."

"There are other Shackles, Astarti." He says it heavily, reminding me. I close my eyes at this bleak reality. There is a Shackle in this very castle.

"So what do we do?"

Heborian answers unhelpfully, "Prepare for the worst."

"And that means…?"

"I can't risk putting too much information in your head."

My temper flares at his distrust. "And why is that?"

"What if Belos recaptured you with that information in your head? Do you want to be responsible for the consequences of that?"

Annoyed, I snap, "You could always just have Horik kill me."

Horik winces. Heborian glares at him.

"Sorry, Horik," I mutter. No doubt I've gotten him in trouble with my big mouth. "Will that be all? I really just came to look for Bran, but seeing as he's not here…"

"He went to Avydos."

"What? Why?"

"He'll be back in the morning, I suspect. Come now, Astarti, don't be naïve. Branos is also a Primo, and he will report Logan's return and Horik's news of what transpired. The Earthmakers, too, must prepare for Belos's retribution."

I know he's right, but it still makes me angry with Bran. "I have to get back to Logan."

I stride for the door. Heborian catches me there and leans near to whisper. His hand barely touches my throat, brushing the fingerprint bruises. "Be careful, Astarti. He's dangerous, even if he doesn't mean to be."

I push past him.

ꟹ ꝶ

I watch Logan sleep. Enough moonlight filters through the drapes that I can see his brow furrow from time to time. Cautiously, afraid of a repeat of the morning's incident, I smooth a hand over his head until he relaxes.

Because I have nothing to do but sit and think, I torment myself with questions. What will the Earthmakers do with Logan, or to him? Like Heborian, they must realize by now that he is not fully of their blood. What will Gaiana be willing to tell him that she has not told him before? Most importantly, what will Logan do with this own questions?

He stirs again, restless, the sweat of nightmares sheening his body. I lay a hand on his chest, and he calms. My fingers, though, trace gouges in his skin, and I let out the tiniest glow of Drift-light to see. Red scrapes show where he's been clawing at his chest. My heart sinks. I have done that to myself in the past, so I know what it means. What troubles me, though, is that Logan is no longer Leashed. He should feel free of it. I did, once mine was cut. The sense of violation he's still feeling, of being trapped and controlled by that Leash, is now in his head, and that's something no simple swipe of a knife can fix.

Chapter 18

I must doze sometime after moving into a chair by Logan's bedside. A creak of wood stirs my consciousness. I open my eyes to see Logan, scarred back to me, leaning against the bedpost. He's not putting any weight on his left leg. He's breathing hard, forehead pressed to the post. As he straightens and starts to turn, I close my eyes so he won't know I've seen him struggling.

His uneven footsteps thump out into the sitting room. I wait another minute before following. He sets down the water pitcher when I enter the room.

"I didn't mean to wake you." His voice is rough with sleep.

"I'm all right."

He's staring at my neck again. I wish he would stop that.

I head for the door. "I'll call for breakfast."

"And hot water?"

"Sure."

He just bathed yesterday and he's done nothing to get dirty, but I don't question him. I tell myself he might only want to ease sore muscles, though I doubt it. He *feels* dirty.

After we eat—Logan, I'm pleased to see, has recovered some of his appetite—I ask if he wants me to call an attendant for his bath. Personally, I hate the idea of strangers attending me in the bath, but I don't want to make assumptions about his preferences. He is, as I reminded Heborian, a Primo, and the braceleted servants I saw in Avydos make clear that Earthmaker society is full of rank and delineation. His rank is high. I don't really know what he's used to.

Regardless, he makes a face at the suggestion, which makes me smile. "All right, then."

Soon after he disappears into the bathing chamber, I hear the same splash, thump, and muttered curse I heard yesterday. I go uncertainly to the door and crack it open. He's sitting in the copper tub, back to me, his elbows propped on the sides, his face in one hand. Water sloshes in the tub and sheens the tiled floor around it.

"Are you all right?"

He barks into his hand, "This *stupid* leg is pissing me off!"

"Gods, Logan, you have to give yourself some time."

He mumbles something I can't make out and probably don't want to. Because I can't leave him like this, I ease into the chamber. Uncertainly, expecting him to tell me to leave, I grab the stool which an attendant would normally use and place it behind him. He tenses, and I wait for the dismissal, but he doesn't say anything. I take a bar of lavender and mint scented soap from the wire basket beside the tub.

I reach around him to wet the soap for lathering. When my wrist brushes his shoulder and chest, he sucks in a breath. As though his sharp breath sends a signal to my own body, heat spreads from low in my belly. Frankly, I have often touched his shoulder or chest, and I can see no more of his body now than I ever have. But this is different. It's partly the knowledge that he's naked beneath the water's line, but it's also the way he is so vulnerable, the way I'm taking care of him, that makes the situation so intimate.

I work the soapy lather down his arms and across his shoulders, careful of the horribly bruised right one. As I rub the soap across his chest, with its old arcing scar, it rises and falls in time with my own breathing. After a brief hesitation, he leans forward so I can do his back. At first he flinches when I touch his lash scars, but then he relaxes, trusting me. He has so many scars, but these are the only ones that seem to shame him. I understand because I, too, have been whipped. Never as badly as he has, but I still know that to be whipped is to be shown that you are both powerless and unacceptable.

I use the nearby pitcher to pour water over his head and start on his hair. As I scrub through his thick, wavy locks, he sighs in contentment, and it occurs to me that this is one of the most beautiful things I have ever done.

When I've washed the soap from his hair, he stands in the tub. Water streams from him, and I catch a glimpse of muscled buttocks before I lower my eyes. I'm still blushing furiously when Logan steps from the tub and wraps a towel around his waist.

From the corner of my eye, I see the tension in his body. Does he feel what I feel?

He says slowly, perhaps a little reluctantly, "I'll let you get cleaned up. Do you want fresh water?"

"No need," I say quickly, embarrassed now by my feelings. How can I even think like this? He's just been tortured, brutalized. How could there be anything on his mind right now but that?

"All right."

I hear the hint of a smile in his voice as he decides to enjoy my discomfort, but I refuse to raise my eyes from my lap. Well, at least he's getting his sense of humor back.

After I've bathed, finally washing away the last traces of the Dry Land, I wrap a towel securely around myself and hurry through Logan's sitting room to the door that opens into my own rooms.

Logan, I see, is already dressed, looking more like himself in leather pants and a dark blue tunic. He's crouched before the grate, tending the dying fire. He looks up when I blaze past, and I could swear I hear him chuckling.

Clara has obviously been in my rooms because there's a set of clothes laid out on the bed. I frown at the simple, elegant dress and silver-inlaid belt. For a dress, it's reasonably functional, I'll say that for it, but it's still a dress. The girl is relentless.

I go instead to the dresser and dig out a pair of slim-fitting woolen breeches and a linen shirt. I scrape through my wet hair with a brush. I only have it half-braided when I hear voices in Logan's room. I tie a band where I've left off braiding, leaving a long wet tail, and hurry to the door.

Even before I've gotten the door open, I know whose voice I hear: Aron's. My heart thumps.

When I open the door, Logan, Aron, and Bran all stop arguing at once. Logan looks relieved, Bran drops his eyes guiltily, and Aron stares. Aron is slightly shorter than Logan and Bran. He's handsome, like his brothers, but he has a more squared jaw and his combed-back, soldierly haircut makes him look severe. His eyes drop from my face to the bruises along my throat. He doesn't say anything, but when Logan tenses at his stare, Aron gives him a sidelong look.

"Astarti." Aron makes the syllables of my name snap.

I raise an impatient, demanding eyebrow that says, *What?*

Aron surprises me when his expression suddenly softens and he breathes, "Thank you."

I blink at him.

Already dismissing me, Aron turns back to Logan, picking up where he left off. "Well? Will you come back? Mother is worried sick."

Logan's nostrils flare, but whether it's at Aron's commanding tone or at the idea of his mother, I don't know.

"Aron," Bran says in a tone that tells me he's repeating something. "Logan needs to do things in his own time. You have to understand—"

"I *do* understand."

"I don't think you do—"

"I will go," Logan cuts in. "But for my own reasons. I was planning to do it today anyway"—this is news to me—"so really all you've done is waste time coming here. And, Bran—"

"Logan, I'm sorry. I *promised* Mother I would tell her the moment—"

"I get it, Bran."

Aron says, "Where is Korinna? Mother was very clear that she is to come with us."

"And Astarti," Logan says.

Aron's face tightens. "She's done her part. That's enough."

Logan goes very still. The silent threat emanating from him fills the room. Everyone freezes, including me.

Bran breaks the silence with a hurried, "I'll go find Korinna."

"Take Aron with you," I say sharply so that Bran will know I'm not pleased with him.

Bran colors a little and Aron's jaw tightens, but when Bran nods Aron toward the door, he follows.

When they're gone, I ask, "Are you sure about this?"

Even from ten feet away I can see Logan's pulse throbbing in his neck.

Instead of answering me, he asks with sudden shyness, "Do you even want to come? I should have asked you before I said that."

I say firmly, "I'm coming with you."

His lets out a shuddering breath. I'm touched that he's relieved. He wants me there. No one has ever wanted my presence.

"Are you sure you're ready for this? You don't have to do what he says."

Logan's answer is a tight, discussion-ending, "I have questions for my mother."

When Aron and Bran return with a dejected-looking Korinna in tow, Aron says, "Korinna, please do something about Logan's face. It's awful to look at."

When Korinna steps obediently toward Logan, he backs away. "Astarti first."

My temper snaps. "Logan, will you just let it go? I'm fine! It's a bruise! Why is it *such* a big deal?"

"*Because I can't stand looking at it!*"

Without taking my eyes off Logan, I say, "Will you two give us a moment?"

Aron and Bran practically trip over each other in their haste to clear the room.

Korinna shifts uncertainly. I motion her toward me. She darts a nervous glance at Logan then recovers her concentration. Because my throat doesn't even hurt anymore, I don't feel anything but a slight warmth as the bruises vanish.

"There," I say. "All better."

"No," Logan says tightly, "it's not. I would kill another man who did that to you."

"You were having a nightmare. Did you even know it was me?"

"It makes no difference. I will never forgive myself. It will never be gone."

I grit my teeth in irritation but force myself to let it go. I recognize impossible stubbornness when I hear it.

Because Logan towers over Korinna, he takes a seat so she can reach his face. The bruises vanish, and he blinks as the eye that was swollen shut suddenly opens. I hate agreeing with Aron, but I'm also glad to have the bruises gone.

"Shoulder?" says Korinna, and Logan shifts the neck of his tunic so she can touch it.

The way his jaw loosens once it's Healed tells me how bad it was.

Logan lifts the hem of his tunic so Korinna can work on his ribs, and again I see an easing in his body as the pain vanishes. Truly, Healing is the most amazing magic I have ever seen.

"You have a gift," Logan praises Korinna as she steps away. When her head lowers resignedly, he adds, "But don't ever let anyone tell you what you have to be. Not my mother, not Aron, not anyone."

Korinna's mouth twitches with the first real smile I've seen from her in a long time.

Chapter 19

LOGAN

Because the Current cannot be accessed within the castle grounds—the few trees there have their roots cut off from the earth by buried iron containers—we take Heborian's hidden tunnel to the beach and walk to the nearest grove. It's drizzling, and water drips coldly from the ends of my hair onto my neck. Astarti shivers and shrugs her shoulders up. Her leather jacket isn't warm enough.

I don't like the way Aron keeps looking back at her, as though he has something to say. I have to keep forcing myself to take three deep breaths in, three out. I'm spoiling for a fight, eager to work out my frustrations on someone. Who better than Aron?

Astarti casts me a worried look. I try to reassure her with a smile, but I'm afraid it comes out as more of a grimace because her frown only deepens. I know I have to calm down, but I feel so ready to explode. Everything is setting me off. I almost wish I hadn't asked Astarti to come. I don't want to explode around her. I don't want her to see it, and I don't want to hurt her. By the Old Ones, how I hate myself. If I *ever* hurt her again… She brushed it off, dismissing it as an accident. It *was* an accident, but that doesn't make it excusable. *She* should not excuse it. She should expect better of me. A lump forms in my throat as I think, *she deserves better than me.* My hands start shaking, so I shove them in my jacket pockets.

By the time we reach the nearest trees, my left knee is booming with pain, and I can't hide the limp anymore. Even Aron looks concerned, but I stare at him until he looks away.

Astarti's hand is cold when I take hold of it to lead her into the Current. When I chafe her fingers to warm them, she smiles crookedly. I love that.

I place a hand on the scaly bark of a pine tree. My mind is clenched so tight to hold off everything I don't want to think about that it takes me four tries to open myself to the Current. When I finally slide into it, Bran, Aron, and Korinna are waiting, golden forms in the golden stream. The Current is beautiful, so much warmer and more alive than the Drift. I do *not* like the Drift. I do, however, recognize the similarity between it and the Current. Both are systems that connect energy. Perhaps I am simply more comfortable with the energy of trees than that of people.

The Wood blazes gold in the distance. My heart pounds anxiously, though I don't know why I'm nervous. Astarti, beautiful in her golden form, is looking at me with worry, so I try to calm myself. She relents and looks ahead. My eyes catch on the blue glow of her Griever's Mark. We have never discussed her Mark. I know she's ashamed of it because she always keeps her hair over it. Some days, I really want to kill Heborian.

The branches of the Wood snake in agitation as we approach. Astarti shrinks back, as though the Wood might fight her as it did when she was Leashed to Belos. But the Wood isn't focused on her; it's focused on me.

A golden branch lashes out, whipping at my face. I duck, but the next branch catches me in the gut. I shove Astarti out of harm's way.

Several branches snake around me, constricting, exploring. I can feel the Wood's confusion. My first horrified thought is that I'm still Leashed after all. My second, even more chilling thought is that whatever Belos did to me exposed what I really am, and the Wood is sensing that I am not, in fact, an Earthmaker, not fully. Whatever I am, it doesn't like. Golden branches shiver with agitation. I clench inwardly, instinctively trying to hide.

Slowly, uncertainly, the branches unwind and withdraw. I catch a glimpse of four pairs of wide eyes, but I lower mine, hating that everyone saw that.

When I pull Astarti from the Current into the grove of trees, I have to lean against a sturdy trunk. Rain drips through the leaves, and I hope everyone will take my shivering as coldness.

Aron's eyes are narrowed on me, Bran's are concerned, Korinna's are lowered to pretend she didn't see. Astarti, however, is not looking at me. She's staring at my brothers, daring them to say anything.

When we step from the grove into the courtyard of the House of the Arcon, Astarti stays so close to me that she keeps bumping my elbow. She gives me an apologetic look and edges away. I feel an instant sense of loss. I want her close to me. I almost reach for her hand, but I'm wound too tight for such a gesture.

Unease fills me when I see the Wardens guarding the door. Usually, guard duty is performed by the younger Wardens-in-training, a lesson in patience more than anything. I have never before seen actual Wardens at the door. Guilt edges through me, as though this is somehow my fault. It is, isn't it?

As soon as I reach the steps of the broad porch, I ask Nason, "Where is the Prima?"

Nason, who has trained with me, even on occasion laughed with me, visibly stiffens as I approach. "I don't know, Primo Loganos. My apologies."

So formal, so distant. But then, I remind myself, he probably witnessed my near-destruction of the wall at Tornelaine. I hate that I look away from him, but I do.

I try to think. It's raining, so my mother is not likely outside, but if she were in the House, her whereabouts would be known.

Aron interrupts my thoughts. "Logan, I need to speak with you first. Polemarc Clitus and I have been—"

"Later," I growl.

I know Aron needs information, that his duty is to keep Avydos secure and healthy. I don't really blame him for his impatience, but, as always, he's not someone I can be polite to. And, as always, that's a relief. I realize that I probably provoke Aron into serving this contentious purpose for me, but I've been doing it all my life. I'm not about to stop now.

"Fine," he grumbles, robbing me of my chance to argue. "But after?"

I shrug, just to needle him.

When Bran and Aron trail behind me as I start into the entrance hall, I stop dead. "No one is coming with me but Astarti."

She looks surprised. And pleased.

"I was just heading to my study," Aron says stiffly, and Bran makes a "carry on" gesture, his fingers on Aron's arm to let Astarti and me get ahead. Korinna hangs back with a look on her face like she's waiting for the headman's axe. Poor girl.

Only a few people move through the entrance hall, but I still feel crowded by every stare. I feel exposed and dirty, like they all know I don't belong. And I don't. Except for Bran, I have no friends here. Astarti finds my hand and squeezes it in understanding. Of course, she *would* understand. Before I crush her fingers in my aggravation at that thought, I pull away.

I lead Astarti down one passageway after another until we emerge into an open, four-sided courtyard where water bubbles in a stone fountain, mixing with the rain. Instinctively, I know my mother will be down in the cave. She used to take me down there when I was very young, before they sent me away. It was our secret place, where no one else ever came, where she showed me the truth of herself. It was the only place I ever felt calm and whole, the only place where all the turmoil inside me just washed away.

Astarti looks curious about where we're going but doesn't question me, for which I'm grateful. I'm not sure how to explain our destination or why I know my mother is there. I just know. I suspect, even, that my mother is there on purpose, forcing me to return to the place where I was once calm.

We reach a stairway that winds down into darkness. I eye the unlit torch resting in a nearby wall bracket. No, I don't dare attempt lighting it. I'd probably set the whole building on fire. I pause, stunned that I even considered using earthmagic. In all the years after I escaped from the Ancorites, I only used my magic twice before Belos…well, before Belos. First, when my father—that is, Arathos—was killed. And second, when I saved Astarti from Belos, after I first met her. Since then I have used it frequently under Belos's sway. Has it become so much a part of me already?

My breathing grows shallow with the edges of fear. I'm losing control. I will hurt people again. It's only a matter of time. The years vanish, and I see myself, a child, down by the docks as buildings crumble into the water. Screams echo in my ears. Astarti's fingers close on my forearm, and the vision fades. I can breathe again.

My first step down the dark stairway makes my knee scream in protest. By the fourth step, the grunt I've been trying to hold back breaks from me. I use a trick that has helped me on many occasions: I separate mind and body. The pain is outside of me, happening to someone else. Even in the dark, I sense Astarti's attention, her watchfulness, but she doesn't interfere with me.

I trace a hand along the wall to orient myself in the dark. Blue Drift-light flickers behind me. For a moment, panic spikes, but of course it's only Astarti. Given the block on Drift-work here, I'm amazed she can do even that. The light flickers and dies.

She grumbles, "Gods, I hate it here." Then, perhaps imagining this has offended me, "Sorry, but I do."

"You're not breaking my heart." Frankly, the time I've spent in the Floating Lands with Astarti is the most time I've spent here in years. There's more than one reason I wanted to become a Warden, and escape was high on the list.

When we reach the bottom of the stairs, there's still a long tunnel before us. The air grows moist and cool, the walls slick. Astarti manages to force her faint Drift-light to hold, so I catch impressions of dark stone walls. The ceiling is much lower than I remember it from my childhood, and I crouch instinctively. The strain on my knee becomes almost unbearable.

As the tunnel widens, I catch a tangy hint of the sea. A faint, greenish light blooms ahead.

We emerge into a watery underground cavern. For a second, I am a child again, filled with awe at the beauty and mystery of this place. The rough walls glisten, their wet faces reflecting the greenish glow coming from the shallow pool. My mother's slender bare shoulders and pale breasts show above the water line. She has never been modest. Her hair, pale even when wet, is slicked back to fall behind her. Her body moves gently, in a sensuous wave. Below the water's surface sweeps a powerful, beautiful tail of greenish-blue scales that begins at her slim waist, swelling over her hips and tapering toward a translucent fin.

Memories, distant as dreams, bubble up through the long stretch of years since I last saw this. I am laughing, bobbing in the water, while my mother dips and dives around me. When she says, "Oh, Bright Fish," I'm not even sure whether it's an echo from my memory or something said in the present moment.

All my plans to demand answers, all my resolve to be firm and cold with her drain away.

She glides to the water's edge, and the tail fades and splits into long, elegant legs. She steps from the pool, water streaming from her nude figure. She goes to a nearby puddle of dark blue cloth. The silken robe flows like water when she picks it up and slips it on, belting the waist. She comes to me. Tears stream down her face, blending with the sea's water.

Her slim arms slip around me, and I crush her to me. Where was she? All those times I needed her?

"Mou gios," she says, in the old language of our people, "my son."

My hands tighten desperately, but I feel how fragile she is, and I know, as I've always know, that she could never have saved me.

She leans back to see my face. Her cool fingers, wet from the sea, trace around my eyes, as they used to do.

She whispers, "What have they done to you, Bright Fish?"

I almost shake apart from the inside, almost dissolve into a child's tears. But I am too far from those simple days, and I force it down, closing off the need to have someone take all this from me. It would be a brief moment of release, an illusion of peace that would later sour in my gut and make me ashamed.

I set her back from me. "I need to know, Mother. I need to know."

She lets out a long slow breath, seeming to shrink in my hands. "I know you do."

She slips from my grasp and makes her way to a crescent of smooth sand. She sits and beckons me. When I step toward her, knee aching from the descent of the stairs, my leg almost buckles. My mother rocks toward me, hands reaching for my knee as I sink to the sand, the knee giving out in the last part of the drop.

I say, pushing her hands back, "It is beyond Healing."

"Oh, Loganos." Her voice breaks on my name. Then she asks, cautiously, "How—"

She is asking how bad my injuries were, but she doesn't really want to know, and I won't horrify her. She's not strong like Astarti; she couldn't take it.

"I'm better now. Thanks to Korinna."

My mother's eyes soften.

"And thanks to Astarti. Without her, I would not be here."

My mother looks over my shoulder, and I follow her eyes to Astarti, whom I have not forgotten. I needed that moment with my mother, and she gave it to me, not intruding. She seems always to know what I need, and she gives it freely because her heart is so big and beautiful. Sudden, deep longing for her wells inside me.

With a dazed expression and slightly gaping mouth, Astarti lurches into motion, as though the world is unstable around her. She sits cross-legged beside me, asking nothing for herself, just being there.

My mother, though, is neither unkind nor insensitive. She gives Astarti a gentle smile and offers, "Water has always been my strongest element. It was not always unusual among our people, though most look down on it now."

Astarti clears her throat. "The fountain. In the square courtyard."

At first, I don't know what she's talking about, then I remember that the stone fountain has figures like my mother carved into the base. I marvel at Astarti. She's so observant, so intelligent.

"Yes," my mother says with a slight smile.

Her expression turning grave, my mother leans around me, her hands asking Astarti to come closer. Astarti hesitates, then she leans in to accept my mother's hands on her face. My mother kisses Astarti's forehead.

"Thank you, my daughter."

Astarti stiffens in surprise.

My mother strokes a hand down Astarti's face and says, "You are very beautiful. And strong. And brave. As she was."

She means Sibyl. I barely remember Sibyl, because I was young when she was Stricken, but I know that she was my mother's closest friend. And I know what my mother is doing now, taking Astarti in, accepting her.

Because Astarti never really believes that anyone thinks well of her, she doesn't realize that is what's happening. She sits back, looking uncomfortable.

My mother says, "I wish she could have known you."

Astarti's expression turns doubtful, pained, as though she thinks this would not have been a good thing. Heat flares suddenly in my chest. Belos. Always Belos. He has made her hate herself, and for that, more than anything, I must kill him.

My mother returns her attention to me. "I cannot help you as you need me to."

I claw my way up through the fury, trying to focus. Astarti's fingers find my knee, grounding me. I let out a long breath. I register my mother's words slowly.

"What do you mean?"

"I have never told you who your father is because I do not know. I don't even know *what* he was."

My mind reels. "How can that be?"

My mother looks into the pool, speaking more to it than to me. "I can swim a very long way in my other form, far into the deeps. Just looking at that blue surface you would never guess how much life and mystery roll through the depths."

My breathing quickens with impatience as she works up to the truth. Astarti's fingers tighten on my knee.

"For many years, I had known of a strange place, where a kind of…veil…seemed to hide something. Sometimes I would be gone for days, skimming around that place, wondering. It was something I could not see, only feel, and it hummed with power, drew me with its mystery. I dreamed of it constantly, waking in the middle of the night beside my husband, longing for something that I did not understand and that he could not give me."

She falls silent and is so still that she looks frozen in time. She closes her eyes.

"One day, I gathered my courage and pressed through the veil, which strained and resisted but finally let me through. Everything that happened after I remember as one would a dream. Sometimes, I remember being in water, still in my other form. Sometimes, in my memory, the cavern is dry, and I am in this form. Sometimes, there is no cavern, only a sense of infinite space. I can no longer remember the truth, if I ever knew it. The truth, I have often suspected, was simply too huge and strange for me to understand.

"What I do recall, in every layer of memory, is an indistinct, bluish light emanating from somewhere. I followed it, reached for it for a time that stretches to infinity in my mind. The light called to me with its beauty, its mystery, and with a power that my mind could only grasp the edges of. In some of my memories, the light shapes itself into a man, big and handsome, in an elemental way. He was like the earth itself, with rocky shoulders and a voice of water and fire. In other memories, he is only light. It's as though he was both there and not, both physical and not.

"I sensed a deep yearning in him, and deep, abiding anger. Though we never spoke, at least not that I can remember, I know he was trapped, and tormented by it."

I can't hold back the question I already know is useless. "But what—"

"I'm sorry, Loganos, I don't know what he was."

I am too dizzied by all this to be angry. "Belos wanted to know what I am. He wanted to understand the nature of my power."

She looks at me sadly. "Everyone has always wanted to know that, so much so that few could even see that you were also just a boy, then a man. Arathos tried, but it was hard for him, and he knew you weren't his, though he never said so openly. But he did love you, Logan. He did not really want to take you to the Ancorites, and he regretted it always."

The name, spoken aloud, lashes through me in such a confusion of anger and fear that I am briefly speechless. And yet, in its wake is the dead feeling that what they did helped, in a way, even if helping me was not their intent.

My mother says, "I begged Arathos not to take you to them. Sibyl never trusted them, and I always trusted her. But where I would plead with him, she would argue. And, oh, she did argue." She smiles with memory. "She was always my champion. And she was right, Astarti, about so many things, even the Drift."

I dart a look at Astarti, whose face is begging my mother to go on. Partly because I want Astarti to get her answers, partly because I don't want to speak of the old, skeletal men anymore, I ask, "What did Sibyl say of the Drift?"

My mother directs her answer at Astarti. "It *is* the fifth element, as she said. It's the spirit—the soul, as some humans call it. Every Healer knows this, deep down. Though none acknowledge it, that is why Healing is difficult on Avydos and takes decades to master, even for the strongest. That is why Korinna, untrained but unrestricted by the deadening here, was able to Heal Logan, at least to a point. *Imagine* what we could do if not for that."

I stare at my mother. "I've never heard this before." I look again at Astarti, but she looks more thoughtful than surprised.

My mother says, "None speak of it. Sibyl was Stricken for it, and the Council thought to expunge her ideas along with her name."

Astarti's face looks tormented, and she draws her hand away from my knee. The spot where her fingers were feels suddenly cold and exposed.

The fifth element? A strange and uncomfortable idea. I do not like the Drift. But then, I don't really like earthmagic either. Yes, there is freedom in it. When I immerse myself in the elements, everything else vanishes, and I am pure and unfettered by fear or doubt. But it's a dangerous temptation. I lose control; I forget everything around me.

The Drift is even worse. I should not be able to enter it. I should not be able to sense it in any way. And yet, I do. All my life, I've been aware of those around me—their emotions, their…energies? Or is it their souls? I tune it out until it's nothing but a vague sense of a person. Any more than that and it would batter me to madness.

I've always been able to sense Astarti's essence, her compassion, her kindness. I knew, even when I met her, that she was not really Belos's creature, not in her heart. By the same token, I knew when I first met the Ancorites that their spirits were dark and twisted by whatever cruel purpose binds them to their tower.

I never knew where these instincts were coming from until Belos took me into the Drift, and I felt all of it magnified a hundredfold. Belos's black energy almost overwhelmed me even before I was Leashed to him. It is too much. Far, far too much. I never want to enter the Drift again.

All my life I've thought myself mad. Maybe I am, but maybe there is some reason for it beyond my own weakness. My father, whoever he is, could hold the answer. But where is he? *What* is he?

What am I?

I push awkwardly to my feet, my knee stiff from being bent so long. I don't know where I'm going, but I know I can't sit here any longer.

My mother rises smoothly and reaches for my face. I bend down into her hands, and she presses her lips to my forehead. Maybe I should be angry with her, and I thought I would be, but I'm not. I have too many other things to think about.

Astarti and I make our way to the tunnel, but my mother calls Astarti's name. Astarti goes back to my mother, who presses a kiss to her forehead. My mother whispers something in Astarti's ear that makes Astarti twitch. When she and my mother pull apart, my mother looks content, but Astarti looks troubled.

CHAPTER 20

LOGAN

When Astarti and I reach the square courtyard, Polemarc Clitus is waiting by the fountain. The rain has stopped. Clitus is dressed for the training field in his leather breastplate and greaves, though they are wet from the recent rain, and his boots squelch as he approaches us. The sword hanging at his waist makes me long for one of my own. I feel naked without the weight of one. The one I had, which Belos broke, was given to me by Clitus.

He is stocky, his hair cut short for combat. His face is serious, even grim, but he is a good man. He was the only man who was able to put aside his fear of a strange boy and give that boy something to do. He found me, when I was living with the fisherman's family, and brought me home. But that isn't the reason I love him. During a time when I could not find the will or courage to speak, he gave me action instead. He taught me the sword, taught me to do something with myself. If not for that, I might have willed myself to die. He saved my life the day he handed me a sword. More than that, he let me grow into a man, let me become a Warden when it should not have been permitted. In many ways, he was more a father to me than Arathos was.

Clitus extends his hand, and we clasp forearms.

"Thank the Old Ones," he says.

"It was not the Old Ones who saved me."

Clitus dips his chin at Astarti. Like everyone here, he is wary of Drifters, but he is also a military commander, and he knows that actions are a better gauge of a man—or woman—than anything else.

He says, "I did not get a chance to speak with you after the battle. You fought well."

Astarti, unaccustomed to praise, shifts her weight. "Thanks."

Clitus returns his attention to me. "Your brother and I would speak with you."

I know that his questions, even Aron's questions, will be valid, driven by need, but I still cringe inwardly at the thought of reporting on my captivity.

Clitus darts a look at Astarti. "It might be best if she does not come."

Astarti bristles. "And why is that?"

"I'm afraid you make the Arcon…tense. It would be best for everyone concerned if there were as few distractions from the matter at hand as possible."

Mostly because I want to spare Astarti an encounter with Aron, I tell her, "I'll find you when it's over."

She stiffens slightly. "If that's what you want."

I want to tell her it's not what I want, but it's better to let her believe that. She would not leave if she knew I asked it only to spare her. Besides, though Astarti's presence comforts me, I am neither a child nor a coward.

I'm relieved to find Bran with Aron in his study. They're arguing across Aron's desk. Arguing, that is, in the way that Bran "argues," which only means quietly speaking his mind. I hear my name, but the discussion ceases the moment Clitus and I enter the room.

Bran eases back into his chair and gestures to another beside him. My knee is so weak that I have to use my hands to lower myself into the chair.

While Aron settles himself behind the desk, Clitus drags a chair to the side of it, positioning himself half with Aron, half with me. I give him a wry look, which he acknowledges with one lifted eyebrow that says, *You know it has to be this way.* At least he's not coddling me.

Clitus begins, "I'm sure you understand that we need to know as much as possible about what the Unnamed is doing and planning. We had a partial report from Bran, based on what Heborian's Drifter—"

"Horik," I correct him.

"Based on what Horik told him, but we need to know anything you can tell us."

My heart speeds up for no reason. "I know."

"The Wardens have had little to report over the past few weeks. Neither the Unnamed nor any of the Seven have been seen in Kelda or beyond. Can you confirm that the Unnamed did not leave the Dry Land?"

It's not even a personal question, but sweat breaks out on my forehead nonetheless. "I cannot speak for every moment of the past few weeks because he wasn't with me every moment."

"What was your impression?"

I shift uncomfortably. This chair is too confining. "It did not seem that he left."

"Why, do you think?"

I retort, "Why, do *you* think?" I rub my face with my hand. "Apologies, Polemarc, I—"

"Warden." His voice is firm, as I've heard it on the training field. "No one here wants to make this harder for you than it needs to be. You understand that?"

I force my hands to unclench. My palms are sweaty, but I don't let myself wipe them dry. "I understand."

Clitus explains, "After Tornelaine, we came to better understand that the Unnamed seeks the destruction of Avydos—"

"You mean Astarti helped you understand that."

Clitus inclines his head in acknowledgement. "What we don't know is how he now hopes to achieve that, the Old Ones forbid it should come to pass. Did he say or do anything that gave you an indication of his current purpose?"

My heart hammers a warning. Images start to flash: Arathos, face gray and slightly decayed, Astarti, smiling cruelly, the Ancorites, with their fingers like iron bars. And, of course, Belos beneath them all, wanting to know what I am.

"Loganos? This is important."

The room comes back into focus. I force my voice to be wooden, unemotional. "Naturally, he did not share his plans with me, but he was very interested in the Ancorites." My voice sharpens on the last word, my detachment lost.

Everyone freezes. This is something we do not discuss. Ever.

Aron slumps in his chair. With one elbow propped on a chair arm, he leans his face into his hand, not looking at me. "And what did he want to know about them?"

"My memory isn't very clear because he was drugging me." All eyes snap to me. "But I think he wanted to understand what they are doing in the tower."

Seconds tick by. No one wants to ask it. Of course, it's Aron who finds the courage. Or, perhaps, the ruthlessness.

"And what *are* they doing?"

"I don't know." I try to keep myself detached. It's just a question. It doesn't mean anything.

Aron whispers, as though to lessen the significance, "You truly have no idea? You were there almost a year."

Immediately, my mind shuts down. I float in that distant, nebulous place I came to inhabit after I fled the tower. I am not here. If I am not here, nothing can touch me. Voices drift to me, some from the present, some from the past. Nothing makes a firm impression.

"Logan?"

"What's wrong with him?"

"*He must be chained.*"

"I don't know what happened there. He's never told me."

"*Dangerous, dangerous, dangerous.*"

"You remember how he was when Clitus brought him back. He wouldn't even speak."

"*He's one of them.*"

"We need to stop. He's getting that look again."

"What did they *do* to him?"

"Which 'they'?"

"Can he even hear us?"

"Bran, for the love of the Old Ones, be *careful.*"

Fingers touch my arm, but I'm still too deep within myself. They squeeze, and Bran says my name once, twice, three times. I try to drag myself out of wherever I am, but I can't. Maybe I will never come back.

But when Bran shakes me, I break free all at once.

I jerk away from him. He recoils, expecting me to strike. My heart hammers in my throat, choking me. I clench the arms of the chair to ground myself. Sunlight, bright from the recent rain, pours through the windows, gleaming over my brothers and Clitus as they sit tensely in their chairs.

A light knock at the door makes everyone jump.

"Tea for the Arcon?" A brief hesitation, then, "Arcon, did you not call for it earlier?"

Aron clears his throat. "Yes, apologies. Please bring it in."

Someone—I don't let myself look at her—sets the tray on Aron's desk and hurries out.

Aron busies himself pouring steaming tea into four cups. Bran hands one to me. I take it automatically, but my hands are shaking so hard the cup rattles in its saucer. Bran takes it away and sets it on the desk.

He says, "I think we should stop."

Clitus studies me. "Warden, do we need to stop?" He uses his training field voice, as though he's beating me bloody with a wooden sword and wants to know whether I'm quitting. It's a voice that once pulled me from the dark, and it does the same now.

"I do not remember my final days with the Ancorites. The memory is…gone." I have never acknowledged this, but it's true. I remember wandering through the spiraling tower alone for days—weeks? months?—as their presence swirled around me, observing. I remember foraging for food along the shore and in the woods. I remember sleeping on a bed of rushes in a dark corner. I remember the wrongness and the fear. I remember the nightmares. I remember them appearing one day, decrepit and hard-eyed. I remember the lashes but not the reason for them. I remember clenching myself tight in some form of resistance.

But I do not remember the final days. I get flashes. The top of the tower, ringed with columns. The wind, the rain. Then it's a blank. The next thing I remember is the fisherman pulling me into his boat, asking my name. I remember opening my mouth and finding no words.

At this moment, I am equally empty of speech. I do not know what to say. I do not know how to explain.

I lurch up from my chair. I shake my head, trying to tell them I'm sorry that I'm useless, that I'm sorry I can't give them what they need.

Bran rises. "We're done. I'm taking him out."

I make it a few steps down the hall before I have to brace against the wall. My head is spinning, my legs are shaking, and if I don't brace on something, I'll fall.

Clitus's voice drifts out of Aron's study. "It's worse than I expected. I haven't seen him like this in years. Whatever the Unnamed did to him, it stirred up things that would have been better left alone."

"Do you think he really doesn't remember what happened?"

Bran tugs at my elbow. "You don't need to hear this."

"Bran, do *not* touch me."

His hand drops.

I push away from the wall.

Bran leads me past the Wardens guarding the front door to the steps of the covered porch, where Astarti is waiting. She tenses as she takes in my face and body language, but she doesn't say anything. I drop beside her on the step. She doesn't ask if I'm all right; she knows I'm not. Perhaps because she's self-conscious in front of Bran, perhaps because she realizes I'm not ready for it, she doesn't touch me.

The rain has brought out the gleam of the white and gray stone buildings. The rain-brightened colors of trees and flowers flow around us. The only hint that this peace and beauty is not absolute lies in the presence of the guards behind us. But the peace of this place doesn't reach into me. It never has.

The silence eats at me, but I don't want to talk about myself, so I ask, "Have you seen Korinna?"

Astarti nods. "I spotted her with Feluvas."

"It's not right, you know. She'd be a great Warden."

"She has an even more valuable gift."

Her words surprise me. "I would think that you, of all people, would understand not wanting to be forced into something."

Color stains her pale cheeks, but she gives me a defiant look. "I do. But I guess in some ways I'm like Heborian: I understand necessity. She saved your life."

"*You* saved my life."

She waves this away and looks out over Avydos.

After a while, I say, "I don't agree with you, you know, about necessity."

She gives me a half-smile. "That's because you're contentious and like to argue."

I bark a surprised laugh. The tension is fading. My hands aren't shaking anymore. How does she do this?

On the step behind me, Bran chuckles.

"Oh, shut up," I tell him, though I don't mean it.

When Feluvas comes out onto the porch, my skin prickles with dread. I know Feluvas well, so I'm unsurprised when she says, "Loganos, if you'll come with me, I'll see if anything can be done for your leg."

"Don't bother."

I know my tone is unduly harsh, but I don't want to get my hopes up. I can tell from Feluvas's tone that she doesn't expect to succeed. This is a formality. She lives for her duty as a Healer, and her duty demands that she try.

Astarti, though, isn't ready to give up. Her fingers clench on my uninjured knee. "Please, Logan."

I want to tell her it's pointless, but her eyes are begging me. I sigh. Leaving Astarti and Bran on the porch, I follow Feluvas.

When I enter the sick room, Korinna is studying the shelves that are loaded with all manner of glass jars filled with powders and dried herbs. Because there are so few Healers, we must be able to treat the ill and injured without earthmagic. Besides, injuries like mine are not unknown. Healing isn't perfect. Korinna slides a jar back into place. At least she looks interested in the Healers' wares.

Feluvas motions me toward the nearest cot. I kick off my boots and drop my pants. As I lower myself to the cot, my knee screams protest.

Feluvas sucks in a breath when she sees the red, angry scar. Korinna stares at it grimly. Feluvas crouches beside me and places her hands on my knee. Warmth spread from her hands, but the pain is still there. She rocks back, frowning.

"How long did you have it before Korinna Healed it?"

I have very little sense of my time in the Dry Land. I don't even know how long I was there. A week? A month?

Korinna's eyes flick to mine, then she answers for me. "It looked a couple of weeks old."

Feluvas's mouth sets in a grim line. "The cause?"

Memory flashes: the earth rumbles beneath me as I jerk against the chains binding me to the dungeon wall. I'm trying to break free. I'm almost there. *He* appears.

I say woodenly, "Sword."

I don't realize I'm rubbing my shackle-scarred wrists until Feluvas's attention falls on them. I stop.

Feluvas looks unsatisfied with my answer, but she knows me better than to push when I don't want to say more. "Do you have other lingering pain?"

My shoulder still aches, but I want her to stop looking at me, so I just shake my head.

"Do you want something to dull it? It won't fix anything, but you will be more comfortable for a while."

I don't want to say yes because it makes me feel weak to ask for help, to even accept it. Feluvas, though, has known me all my life, and she just nods at my silence. She stands and motions to Korinna.

"Come, child, you might as well start to learn."

While Korinna follows Feluvas to the worktable, I tug on my pants and boots. I sit back down and lean against the wall. I must doze because their voices grow fuzzy and the room blurs. I start when Feluvas touches my shoulder. I blink her into focus. She's looking at me with concern.

"You should be resting. You're exhausted. Your body needs time to recover, even with Healing."

I don't answer. I know I'm exhausted, but I don't want to sleep.

A line wedges between Feluvas's brows, the only sign of her frustration. She offers me a steaming drink. Even though I know it's only willow bark or something like that, my heart still speeds up whenever someone holds out a cup to me. Feluvas gives me a questioning look, but I'm not about to explain myself. I take the cup and down the drink, burning my throat.

When Feluvas takes the cup back, I can't stop myself from asking, "Do you think…will my leg get any better?"

"It should grow stronger with time. With strength the pain may lessen, but I doubt it will ever go away completely. I'm sorry, Logan, that's the truth."

I nod, unsurprised, wishing I hadn't asked.

ᘓ ᘐ

When I offer to show Astarti around Avydos, she initially tries to talk me out of it, but she sees how twitchy I am, that I can't stand being around everyone who edges around me like I might burst into flames. Besides, if I'm going to make my leg stronger, I need to use it, and whatever Feluvas gave me has dulled the pain from a stab to an ache.

We pass over the many dozen bridges that span streams and small waterfalls rushing with rainwater. Unlike the cobblestones of Tornelaine, the streets here are paved with smooth white stones, sheened with rain. The gardens are in full spring bloom, weeks ahead of Tornelaine in their growth. Astarti looks around with childlike fascination, and I see the city anew through her eyes.

She sniffs with interest when we pass a confectionary, so I lead her inside.

At her wide-eyed wonder, I ask, "You've never had chocolate?"

She peers through the curved glass cases. "It smells so good in here."

I tell her she can have whatever she wants, but she chooses only two pieces, both dark. When the confectioner hands her a small paper box, she holds it lightly, like it's fragile and valuable. I want to tease her that it's only chocolate, but I won't belittle her new experience.

When I pay for the chocolates with coin I retrieved from my rooms, her eyes follow my hand. She doesn't like me paying for her.

We sit on one of the bridges while she eats the confections. She offers me a bite, but I decline. I bought them for her.

Her eyes close as the chocolate melts on her tongue. She makes an indecent sound, and I laugh. I love watching her.

When both chocolates are gone, she stares into the empty box. She sniffs it.

"You could have had more, you know."

She smiles at me as though I've offered her something much greater than chocolates.

By the late afternoon, when Feluvas's painkiller has worn off, I'm limping so badly that Astarti says firmly, "All right, you're done."

It's a long, painful walk back to the Arcon's House.

The sun hasn't even gone down yet, but I'm so tired that I don't argue when Astarti tells me I ought to go to bed. I don't want to sleep, don't want to dream, but I know I can't hold it off much longer. Astarti follows me to my chamber, which, unfortunately, is in the upper floors. More stairs.

There's food waiting in my room. Despite the appeal of the bed, my stomach grumbles a demand.

When I've eaten, I strip down to my undershorts. I do it without thinking because I'm exhausted, but immediately Astarti's eyes and the rising heat of my body remind me that I'm alone with her. It's not like this is new, but the memory of this morning in the bathing chamber settles over me, and I feel the ghost of her hands. My nerves feel suddenly exposed, humming for the barest touch. In spite of everything, in spite of all the chaos in my head right now, one thing is simple and clear: I want her. I need her.

But she closes her eyes. She turns away.

As she busies herself with the empty dishes, the clatter of pottery breaks the moment into a thousand scattered pieces. Only when I've climbed into bed and pulled up the linen sheet does she come to my side.

"Do you need anything?"

"No," I say, more shortly than intended.

"Logan." She sounds pained.

"What?"

"We're in Avydos."

I'm not sure what her point is.

"Aren't you…worried?"

"About what?"

She rolls her eyes. "The *law*."

She's talking about me being Stricken for being with her. Something cold washes around my heart at the thought, but other, more confused feelings tumble in behind because I can't think about being Stricken without thinking about the question of what I am. If I am not an Earthmaker, they may cast me out anyway. All day, I've held my mother's story at a distance. It's too much, too big, and I can't assimilate it right now. But it comes sweeping back to me like an ocean tide. In its wake come *his* questions, and all the memories he stirred with them.

I can't even finish one feeling before I'm leaping to another. It's too much. My lungs won't expand all the way. I can't breathe. I throw the sheets aside and sit up.

"Hey," Astarti says. "Hey now." She climbs into the bed, kneeling beside me. She pulls my head to her neck. Her pulse throbs against my temple.

"Just breathe."

She takes slow, deep breaths, and eventually my own breathing falls into time with hers. Slowly, everything recedes. My fists unclench.

She lays me down, like I'm a child, but I don't mind. I marvel at her tenderness. Where did that come from? She certainly didn't learn that from Belos.

I stiffen at the name in my mind, but Astarti smoothes the new worry from my face. I'm afraid she'll leave, am tensed for it, but several minutes pass and she shows no signs of getting up. I start to unwind.

But just as my thoughts unravel, my heart thumps hard for no reason, and I'm restless again. I continue through this cycle again and again, but Astarti stays through it all. Finally, exhaustion closes over me.

CHAPTER 21

The windows have gone dark before I'm sure Logan is fully asleep. I slide from the bed and pad across the room. The door opens on silent hinges. I close it as quietly as possible behind me and lean against it. I don't know how much space to give him, don't know how to help him. To make matters worse, even though I should ask for nothing from him, especially right now, I *do* want something. I want more. I want him.

We dance closer to a precipice every day, and I *want* to fall over. It makes me feel rotten and greedy and selfish. When I foolishly broached the subject of his being Stricken, he couldn't even breathe. It must have terrified him. Will I make myself like Belos, taking what I want with no care for those harmed by it?

Disgusted with myself, I push away from the door. I need to move, to walk some of this tension out of myself.

I'm walking down the entrance hall, thinking I'll wander the city, perhaps even make my way to the rocky arms of the horseshoe bay, when Korinna calls my name. I wheel around to find her jogging toward me. Braziers cast halos of light, flashing over her pretty face. An Earthmaker woman I don't know walks behind.

Korinna flows to a graceful stop. She gestures to the woman. "I thought you might want to meet—well, this is my mother. Kassandra."

My heart lurches. Korinna's mother. Sibyl's sister. My aunt.

Kassandra halts beside Korinna. She's beautiful, of course, smooth and elegant, clothed in the flowing gowns of an Earthmaker woman. But there's a fierceness in her eyes that I've seen in her daughter.

Kassandra dips her chin. "Niece. It's been many long years since I saw you, though you would not remember."

My eyes widen. I was born well after Sibyl was Stricken.

Kassandra nods at my understanding. She whispers, "Sibyl always said, 'Obey your heart before the law.' Yes, I came to see her. And you. Come. Prima Gaiana has given us the use of her balcony."

We arrive to find glass-faced lanterns making pools of gentle light around the balcony's elegant furnishings and potted plants. Moonlight pours through the railing, mixing coolly with the warm lantern light. In the distance, the calm waters of the bay gleam under the moon, lovely even in their coldness.

Kassandra takes a seat in one of the deep chairs and settles herself to pour tea from the steaming pot that sits on a nearby table. I take the cup she hands me and sit on one of the stools. Korinna sits beside me with her own cup. Earthmakers are so funny sometimes. It's like they think tea will take the tension out of a conversation. As I lift my cup to my lips, warmed by the bittersweet drink and using it as an excuse not to stare at Kassandra, I laugh silently at myself. Maybe they're right.

Korinna says, "My mother lives in a smaller town on the eastern end of the island. I went to see her this afternoon. I told her you were here."

I say, trying to deflect attention, "You must be very proud of Korinna."

Kassandra inclines her head. "I always told her she would be a Healer."

Korinna protests, "But you know—"

"I know, child. I should never have let your dreams of becoming a Warden grow so big. But we have years to speak of this." Kassandra's eyes shift to me. "I did not know, Astarti, what had become of you. I thought you dead. Had I known, I would have—well, I don't know what I would have done, or what I could have done, but I wanted to tell you that I'm sorry."

I lower my eyes to my cup. "It's no fault of yours."

"I wish I could believe that. But I should have spoken more loudly when she was Stricken. We all should have, those of us who believed her."

Korinna says, "Mother, *I* will—"

"Oh, Korinna." Kassandra's eyes close. She believes she will lose her daughter, as she lost her sister, and she may be right. Korinna will not be silent. When Kassandra opens her eyes again, they are filled with equal parts fear and pride.

My heart breaks a little. Courage always comes with such a price. I spent too many years obeying Belos to judge Kassandra for her small cowardice, for clinging to safety. It is hard, so hard, to do the right thing, especially when you are not even sure what *is* right. Is it right for me to stay with Logan, tempting myself, tempting him, risking his being Stricken? Gaiana's words come back to me: *Please take care of him.* Didn't she realize what that could mean?

I push these questions aside. I have no answers to them now, and I have other, more pressing questions. One, in particular, has eaten at me all day, ever since Gaiana told her story. But it's not a question for Kassandra. It's one I will need to ask Heborian, and I shiver at the immensity of it. I've fought all day to repress my anxiety, my impatience to get away from Avydos and back to Tornelaine, but it seizes me now, and I nearly rise from my stool.

"What is it, Astarti?"

I start at Korinna's voice. "Sorry. I was just thinking of something I need to ask Heborian."

Kassandra's eyes narrow at his name. "I wish Sibyl had never met him. But it was inevitable, I suppose, given her interest in the Drift and in Rune."

That piques my curiosity. "What was her interest in Rune?"

Kassandra's eyes film with memory. "When I visited her, she told me she believed that the Runish tales held some key to Earthmaker history. I do not know what she meant, nor did I care for the idea."

My heart pounds with anticipation. This slides so close to the question that has tormented me. Heborian once told me that the Lost Gods of the Runians and the Old Ones of the Earthmakers were one and the same. Could it be true? And if it is, could the half-remembered tale swimming in my mind hold the key to Logan's parentage? A cool breeze rises from the ocean, stirring my hair. I shiver.

Kassandra rises from her seat. "You have much on your mind, Astarti. I will leave you to your thoughts. I hope you do not mind that I have intruded."

"I'm sorry," I say, setting my cold tea on the ground and rising beside her. "I don't mean to be rude. I'm very glad to have met you."

Kassandra clasps my hands. "We'll meet again, I'm sure."

When she and Korinna are gone, I crouch on my stool, raking through my memory for details of a Runish story about a terrible binding. The wind picks up, as agitated as I am.

Chapter 22

LOGAN

Footsteps sound on the dungeon stairs. I freeze, not wanting my chains to scrape and draw attention. Stupid, of course, because I'm in the very place he left me, but instinct makes me stay quiet.

He *steps into the cell. A whip, glowing blue with Drift-energy, curls around his arm like a snake. I am frozen, unable to speak or move.*

He throws out his arm, and the whip snaps toward me. I cry out at the burst of pain as the lash strikes. It burrows into my chest, forming a glowing thread between me and him. Fear and pain flood me, then fury. At first my rage is clean, but then it shifts to something ugly: a need to hurt back. I *want to be the one doing the punishing.* I *want to be in control.*

Suddenly, I am.

I growl with my power, staring down the length of the whip to the man chained to my dungeon wall. I am stronger. I have power over him, over all of them. I will *be respected! They will see. They will learn what I am!*

I recoil, horrified, ripping myself away from these thoughts.

Now I am huddling against the wall, shaking, wheezing. I claw at my chest, but the whip is gone.

I curl up tight on my thin pallet, knees to my chest. Wind howls around the tower, gusting through the high, thin windows. They're here somewhere, floating like ghosts, the old men who whisper in the dark. A shape wavers near me.

His voice scrapes like dry leaves blown across stone. "Are you one of them?"

Skeletal fingers touch my head. I scream.

ꕥ ꕥ

I jerk awake in a tangle of sheets. I am rigid with terror. Wind has thrown the wooden shutters open, and they bang against the wall, startling me into movement. I scramble up on the bed. Slowly, I remember where I am. In my chamber. In Avydos. I make myself breathe slowly until my heart stops hammering. The wind fades.

I push myself from the sweat-soaked bed and stumble to the window. I rest my shaking hands on the ledge and look out to the moonlight-gilded Wood. Everything looks the same. He is not here. They are not here.

I sink to the floor, shuddering, my sweat-sheened skin pebbling with cold. I curl up on my side on the cool floor.

ꕥ ꕥ

I wake to sunlight warming my hand where it sticks out from under a blanket. I blink in confusion and sit up stiffly, shrugging off the blanket. I jerk in surprise to find Astarti sitting in a chair nearby, watching me.

I look down at the blanket then across the room to the bed, where the covers have been straightened. I feel hot shame creep up my neck. When I try to get to my feet, I'm so stiff from the cramped position that I have to grip the windowsill with one hand and haul myself up. Astarti stands, ready to help, but I don't meet her eyes.

I hobble to the washbasin and pour water. My trembling hand makes the stream jerk and splash, and half the water streams onto the table instead of into the basin. I wash my hands and face and run wet fingers through my hair.

When Astarti's arms snake around me from behind, I stiffen, still embarrassed that she found me curled up on the floor. She draws away, and when I turn to seek her touch again, her cheeks are red with embarrassment of her own.

"Astarti—"

"I'm sorry, Logan, I wasn't thinking."

"Good. Sometimes I wish you would stop thinking so much."

Her eyebrows twitch. She doesn't understand my meaning. But she doesn't ask; she backs away. My thoughts are too scattered to explain.

"Do you want food or tea or—"

Frustration makes me sharp. "I just want to get away from here."

"This room? Or Avydos in general?"

"All of it," I say, not quite sure what I mean.

"What would you say to returning to Tornelaine? I have some questions for Heborian."

That takes me aback. "About what?"

Her eyes dart away, and she busies herself picking up the blanket and folding it. She says, as she carries the blanket to the bed, "Your mother's…story…reminded me of a Runish tale." She shakes her head. "I can't remember it well enough. I need the details."

My brow furrows. "I don't understand."

"I don't either. It might be nothing. I'm sure it's nothing." She says it too firmly, as though to convince herself. "Still, I want to ask him."

My heart speeds up in warning. "You think it has something to do with me?"

"I don't know. Maybe. If you want, I can speak with him on my own, then—"

"No. Just get me out of here."

She smiles wryly. "I think you'll have to get me out, remember?"

I feel my face drain at the thought of entering the Current again. What did it see in me that it hated so much?

"Logan?"

I shake my head, unable to articulate my fears. I grab my spare sword from its rack and throw it on the bed then turn to the wardrobe to rummage for clothes.

I must have slept long under the window because it's well into the morning when Astarti and I sweep through the long entrance hall. The only Wardens in sight are those standing guard at the front doors, which means the others, and Clitus, are engaged in their morning exercises. I shouldn't leave without telling Aron or Bran or my mother where we're going, but I have no patience for that right now. My mother has not, to my knowledge, emerged from the cave. For all I know, she could be deep in the ocean. She has never dealt well with farewells, and she knows me well enough to have realized that one was coming. It's a relief, in a way, not to see her. As for Aron and Bran, they would have questions, and I have no answers.

I ask the guards to inform my brothers that Astarti and I are returning to Tornelaine. No emotion flickers in their eyes. The only indication that they find this spontaneous departure unusual is in a slight stiffening of their backs, but I don't care what anyone thinks.

When we reach the grove of trees beyond the courtyard, the hurry that has been driving me to ignore my stiff knee vanishes. I hover by a smooth-skinned beech tree. I take three deep, even breaths but have to repeat the exercise before I'm calm enough to take Astarti's hand and pull her into the sweeping tide of the Current.

The Wood shivers with agitation. Golden branches snake and writhe. Something inside me twists and tightens, hiding. I flash back to my dream, to the desperate anger and the need to hurt. Suddenly, I am furious. I want to rip the branches from their trunks, blast them to pieces. If they touch me, I swear I will destroy them. They shiver and withdraw, and I am almost disappointed.

CHAPTER 23

LOGAN

When I pull Astarti from the Current, my knee buckles and I'm shaking too hard to prevent my fall. I feel exhausted as the anger drains away. Where did that even come from? What is wrong with me?

I close my eyes to shut everything out: my anger, the Wood's distrust, my dreams, the panic that my mother's story has caused to spike through me when I'm not guarding against it. It doesn't help. Everything crowds in my mind, making my heart thump anxiously. A voice whispers from deep inside me, *What are you?*

Astarti, in that way of hers, waits patiently for me to pull myself together. I hate that I'm all over the place. One minute I'm fine, the next I'm a mess.

I use a nearby tree branch to pull myself up.

Astarti says, "Are you sure you're ready for this?"

"I'd rather be here than in Avydos."

"He's going to ask you questions," she warns.

"I know."

When we get to the castle and are taken to Heborian's study, after being disarmed, he looks surprised to see us. He dismisses the men with whom he's been conferring. Most of them have Runish tattoos, like Heborian, like Horik. Horik gives us a questioning look as he leaves.

When the door closes, Heborian says, "I didn't expect you two back so soon. What happened?"

My temper explodes inside me, shocking me with its force and suddenness. I thought I could be calm and rational in a conversation with Heborian, but I know what a mistake I've made. This is the man who gave Astarti to that monster when she was a child. No, not a child. An *infant.* My hands close into fists.

Astarti says, "I have some questions for you."

Heborian, eyes still on me, comments, "I gathered."

Astarti touches my elbow and says, almost warningly, "Logan, sit down."

I release a shaky breath and follow Astarti to the chairs by the hearth. I lower myself into a chair with my hands, not trusting my knee to endure the strain.

Heborian folds himself into his own chair, wholly at ease. "As soon as the Arcon arrived yesterday morning, I knew you two would slip out. But I'm glad you're back because I have questions of my own."

"Later," Astarti says firmly.

"I must know how he broke Belos's Shackle."

At his words, memory flashes: Astarti screaming, the Shackle's cuff on her wrist, the bone chain connecting her to him. Or was it to me? That slick oiliness inside me. I feel it spread within me, violating my body and mind. I stop breathing.

No.

I'm in Tornelaine.

I am no longer Leashed.

But—

As panic throbs in my chest again, denying reality, I shut my mind down, wrenching away from memory.

"Logan?" I hear Astarti's voice only distantly, then Heborian asking, "What's wrong with him?"

Astarti shakes me gently.

Blood roars in my ears, and everything comes crashing into me as the world reasserts itself. My heartbeat reverberates through my body. I plant my elbows on my knees and lower my head into my hands. I *have* to calm down. Nothing is happening. Nothing is wrong. Why do I keep overreacting?

I count my heartbeats.

"Here," rumbles Heborian's deep voice.

I look up to see him holding out a glass filled with amber liquid. When I smell the vapor of strong spirits, I take the glass, throw back my head, and down the whole thing in four burning gulps.

Heborian's eyebrows lift in surprise. I lift my own wryly. Yes, I've done this before.

The alcohol starts burning its way into my stomach as he returns to his chair.

Astarti looks at me with concern, but I can't meet her eyes. She leans near and puts her hand on the glass. Pressure cracks are forming where I'm gripping it too hard. I let go and she sets it on the floor under her chair.

She says, "I once heard a story of the Lost Gods. Something about a binding."

Heborian's dark eyebrows draw together. "And where did a girl raised so far from Rune hear such a story?"

"I've been many places and encountered many people. But it hardly matters. Tell me the story."

She and Heborian lock eyes in a silent battle of wills.

Heborian shrugs, giving in. "There are many versions of the story. In one, the King of the Gods is a huge wolf, bound in the forest with a magical ribbon made of Drift-energy. It is said that when he breaks free, he will destroy the world."

Astarti says, "Isn't there a story about…the ocean?"

My eyes rip to her, but she's focused on Heborian.

"Why the sudden interest?" he asks.

She growls, "Is it a secret or something? Just tell me."

"You're so pushy."

"And you're so stubborn."

He grins, delighted, and I feel my head about to explode. What right does he think he has to banter with her as though they are friends? His eyes twitch to me, and his grin slowly fades.

"Fine," he says. "There's a story that the gods fought with their children. Essentially, the gods were defeated, and their children cast them out into the ocean. It's said a great chain was laid over them, a chain so heavy even the gods could not lift it. This chain is said to encircle the entire world."

The ocean roars in my ears.

No.

Impossible.

But a voice whispers inside me with a satisfied, *Ah.*

I splutter, "Astarti, you can't mean—"

She cuts me off with a sharp look, but it's too late. Heborian's dark eyes have narrowed on me, the stare intensified by the tattoo hooking his right eye. He looks to Astarti, then back to me. His eyebrows lift. What does he think he knows?

Astarti says, "A woman I met in Avydos told me Sibyl believed that Runish tales have some connection to the Earthmakers. You yourself once told me the Old Ones and Lost Gods are the same."

I dart a surprised look at her.

Heborian confirms, "That was her theory. I believe she was correct. There are too many similarities: the Earthmakers and Runians both claim the gods shaped the world. Both recall an ancient conflict. And in both cases, the gods have vanished."

Panic claws its way through my chest, spiking through the haze of alcohol. No. Ridiculous.

And yet.

And *yet.*

One part of me eases with satisfaction; another screams denial.

Heborian says, "You still haven't told me why you're interested."

Astarti says smoothly, "We're investigating some of Sibyl's theories. We have to start somewhere."

There may be some truth in what she's saying, though there's no "we" here, since I knew nothing of this. Regardless, it's essentially a lie. I know why she's asking these questions, even if I can't quite swallow it. And even though I know she's lying to protect me, it's still unnerving to see her skills in deception and misdirection.

Heborian says, "Did I tell you that Sibyl went to Rune, to speak with my mother about these very stories?"

She answers with a surprised, "No."

"My mother, Sunhild, is a bard of sorts, unusual for a woman, but then, Sunhild is nothing if not unusual. In Rune, bards are the keepers of both history and legend. Runians don't make a very clear distinction between the two. Sibyl never told me exactly what she learned. While in Rune, she realized that she was pregnant, and when she returned here, everything but that had faded from her thoughts. She was more interested in her child."

Anger snaps through me with shocking intensity. Everything that overwhelms me, every emotion and idea that I can't quite assimilate, I allow to pour into this one thing. My hands clench on the arms of the chair, and I'm pushing to my feet when Astarti's arm shoots out to hold me back. I freeze, not wanting to knock her aside, not able to make myself sit back.

Heborian takes a deep, thoughtful breath as he studies me. "Whatever's going on in your head, son, you need to find a way to deal with it."

I snarl, "Oh, I can think of a few ways."

"Do you want to fight me, or do you want to continue this conversation? I can handle either."

"Logan," Astarti hisses.

"Why are you defending him?" I snap at her. "After what he did to you?"

"I'm not defending him. But we're not here to fight."

I force myself to lean back in the chair, but I can't make my hands unclench.

Astarti says, "So you don't know anything more about what Sibyl learned in Rune?"

"Like I said, she got caught up in her plans of motherhood."

My pulse throbs in my neck. "Only she didn't realize you'd already sold her baby."

Heborian is amazingly unfazed. "No, she did not."

I'm out of my chair too fast for Astarti to stop me. Heborian meets me on his feet.

Ignoring Astarti's shout, I growl into Heborian's face, "Do you have any idea what you sold her into?"

I have enough control not to throw the first punch, but I'm waiting for him to grab me, to push me, to look at me wrong. Any excuse.

Heborian only studies my face. "You are wound *way* too tight."

Astarti's fingers close on my forearm. Heborian waits for my next move. Slowly, an inch at a time, I give in to Astarti. I back away. I lower myself again into my chair, but my eyes never leave Heborian's tattooed face.

Astarti clears her throat. "It sounds like we need to take a trip to Rune to speak with Sunhild ourselves."

Heborian, still pinning me with his dark, unemotional eyes, asks, "Can you navigate the Current that precisely? Or will you be traveling the Drift?"

Something cold spills through my gut. "I won't use either."

"What's the problem?"

I can't say it, can't admit to the fury and confusion that surges through me when I'm in either the Drift or the Current. I'm holding myself together with strings. I know instinctively that the smallest thing could break them, and I would come apart. But I can't say this.

Astarti sighs unhappily. "We'll need a ship."

Heborian's eyes are still trained on me, still looking for answers, when he says, "Impractical, but if you insist. What I insist on is that Horik accompany you. You don't know Rune; he does. I can arrange your passage, and you can leave with the tide tomorrow morning."

My skin prickles at the thought of waiting. "What about today?"

"You've missed the tide. If you want a ship, you'll have to wait until tomorrow."

Astarti asks warily, "Why are you helping us?"

Heborian shrugs. "I, too, want to know more of Sibyl's theories and what she learned from my mother."

Astarti's eyes narrow with suspicion. "You had nearly twenty years to ask your mother those questions. Why do you care now?"

Heborian's eyes sharpen on me. "Various reasons."

ഉ ഗ

There are many details to be worked out for our journey to Rune, and I find myself pacing Heborian's study as he and Astarti pore over maps and discuss routes and supplies.

Astarti straightens from the map-strewn table. She closes her eyes for patience. "Logan, you are driving me crazy."

Heborian grunts agreement.

This is my opportunity, so I say as casually as I can manage, "Maybe I'll get some food. I'm hungry."

Arms crossed, Heborian studies me. "I think that's a great idea."

Astarti offers, "I'll come with you."

"No," I say quickly. I don't want her to see what I'm about to do. "I'm fine."

Her dark eyebrows snap together. "You sure?"

I say only, "I'll see you later," and turn away before she can question me further. I feel Heborian's eyes on my back all the way to the door.

Once I get away from the castle, I head straight for the docks, where the drinks are cheap and the crowds rough. I step into a rundown tavern. It's not even midday, so only a few quiet patrons sit at the bar. I move on.

When I find the next tavern much the same, I go to the bar with a grunt of frustration. The sort of crowd I'm looking for won't be out until dark.

I down several tasteless beers.

When I push my mug to the barkeep for the fourth time, he says, "Sure you don't want some food with this?"

The truth, regardless of what I told Astarti, is that I could not possibly eat right now. I know I'll pay for my empty stomach later, but it's not later yet.

I look at the barkeep straight for the first time. His eyes widen when he sees mine, which are no doubt a riot of color.

The barkeep turns to hold my mug under the keg's tap. When he pushes the full mug back across the bar, he says, not looking at me, "Last one."

By midafternoon, I've been in two more taverns. Despite the alcohol coursing through me, I can walk without staggering. Sure, I'm a little hunched, concentrating a little too hard, but I don't get any funny looks; no one avoids me. I doubt anyone even realizes how drunk I am. Practice will do that.

This is just one thing Astarti doesn't know about me, and it's something I don't want her to know. I don't do this very often, but sometimes, when I can't take the pressure in my head anymore, I have to.

And, by the Old Ones, is there pressure in my head right now.

Because it's still too early and my tolerance is a little lower than expected, I slide into a quiet alley between stone buildings. I sink to the ground and let myself pass out.

ꕥ ꕥ

Dioklesus solidifies and drifts toward me. His eyes, vivid green, burn with madness. He holds his skeletal, claw-like hands in front of him, one curled over the other. He is bald, ancient, shrunken like something that should be dead. His loose robes hang still and lifeless from his shoulders.

"It's time," he says. "You must be bound."

I shrink away from him.

He latches onto me with skeletal hands.

ꕥ ꕥ

I jerk awake, shoving away, and fall to my shoulder in the alley. My breath rasps around the scream I won't let out. Dusk has fallen, and I shiver with cold as I push myself up. I climb unsteadily to my feet, still half drunk. I lean against the wall until my heart stops pounding, then I make my way out of the alley.

I wander a few streets, listening for loud voices. I follow my ears to a poorly lit, smoky tavern. The bar is crowded, so I elbow my way into a space. This earns me a few dirty looks. Good. I buy three beers and two shots of spirits before a sly-faced little man, recognizing a drunken fool with money, asks me to join the dice game.

I have enough control not to stagger, but I hear the start of a slur in my voice when I say loudly, "You fellows don't cheat, do you?"

Several heads whip up from the dice game in the corner. One barrel-chested man gets to his feet and stares at me. My nerves tingle with anticipation.

"You'd better watch your mouth," the sly-faced man warns me.

I follow him to the corner, where I roughly brush one of the men as I crouch down. I pretend I'm even drunker than I am and give him a stupid, sorry-I'm-drunk smile. He grumbles something under his breath.

Luck is against me for the first throw. Two dots turn up, and the men chuckle with satisfaction, but luck rides my shoulder on my next few rounds. The men angrily shove their coins at me.

As the man next to me grudgingly hands me the dice again, the sly-faced man whispers in my ear, "You might do better to quit now."

"But I'm winning."

"That's exactly the problem."

I throw the dice, which tumble against the wall. The men shout angrily as two fives turn up.

I hear, "cheater," "impossible," "switched the dice," and a few colorful descriptions of my parentage. A hysterical laugh builds inside me.

As several of the men start shoving me outside, my nerves hum through the haze of alcohol. I don't try to collect my winnings; they're not what I came here for.

The barkeep shouts, "Don't break my windows!"

Everyone in the tavern watches us leave, but no one tries to help. I came to the right place.

The barrel-chested man shoves me down the steps. I fall into the street, and he lands a few kicks in my ribs. The men show signs of leaving matters at that, so I stagger to my feet and growl, "Cowards."

I let them drag me into the alley. The first punch crashes into my jaw with the force of a hammer. I duck the next one, and the man cries out when his fist slams into the wall instead of my face. Someone lands a kick in my gut.

When one of them, getting creative, whips me across the back with a belt, rage leaps through me so fast that my mind lags several seconds behind my body. I'm punching, kicking, and scrambling without thought. I am an animal.

The men pick up their pace, the blows coming harder and faster, more desperately. I throw one man into another, hit a third so hard he crumples. The barrel-chested man slams me against the wall, but I punch him with my right, my left, then make an undercut to his jaw. He falls.

I'm breathing hard, making a strange, wheezing sound. I clench my fists and wait for them to come again. They shout to each other as they scramble up. I want more, but they've had enough, so I make myself let them go. I stagger out of the alley.

I force myself to keep walking until I stop making the wheezing sound, but anger still roars through my veins. I'm not even close to done.

I don't have to go far to find another dice game. I'm not as lucky this time, but when one of the men grabs at a serving girl, tearing her blouse, I latch onto the excuse to start something. Five minutes later, I'm staggering out of another alley, still on fire.

It takes several more taverns for me to be drunk enough, tired enough, and in enough pain to be in any danger. That's when I find my savior. He's huge, he's mean, and he doesn't need much of an excuse to drag me outside.

I land a few good punches, but his fist makes my head snap back. I'm slower now, so the kick I aim at his knee only gives him the chance to get me off balance. He punches me several times in the kidneys, and I go down. The pain is enough to make my body start sending warning signals, but my friend here isn't finished with me. He picks me up by my shirt and drives his fist into my eye. Lights explode in the dark. My head lolls, and he shoves me down, steps over me, and lumbers back to the tavern.

I'm still lying on my back, trying to drag my thoughts into enough order to get up, when a deep voice rumbles from the shadows. "Had enough yet?"

I push myself to one elbow as Horik steps into the sliver of moonlight that falls between buildings.

"How did you find me?" I slur.

"I'm a Drifter, Logan." He crouches beside me. "You know, there are other, less painful ways to work things out of your system. If you would've just asked, I'd have taken you somewhere nice, where they would have treated you really good."

He's talking about whoring, but I would never approach a woman when I have so little control over myself. At least my way, no one gets hurt but those who look for it. Besides, there's only one woman I want. "This way works things out just fine."

Horik draws a heavy breath through his nose. "It doesn't look to me like you're working anything out. It looks like you're just taking more in."

The haze of alcohol, pain, and exhaustion finally sucks me back down, and the little concentration I had for arguing vanishes. I've got nothing left. But then, that was the point.

He rises and holds out a hand. I try to lift my right arm, but the shoulder isn't working. He grabs me under the left elbow and lifts. I cry out as a dozen points of pain flare into my awareness, especially in my lower back.

Horik mutters, "You really messed yourself up, asking for it again and again. If I hadn't watched it myself, I wouldn't have believed it."

That pierces the haze. "How long have you been following me?"

He says darkly, "Long enough."

I grunt and turn away, limping out of the alley. When I reach the street, I stop dead and Horik runs into me.

I spin and have to catch myself on the corner of the building. "Astarti's not—she didn't see—"

"No. She didn't see this. It wasn't easy to get her to stay behind, but I didn't want her to see you like this, and I didn't expect you wanted to be seen."

"How did you even know?"

"Heborian had a feeling. And his feelings are usually correct."

"You won't tell her about this, will you?"

"If she asks me, I won't lie to her. But she's a smart girl, Logan. Don't you think she'll figure it out? You're a bloody mess."

I grunt, queasy at the thought of Astarti seeing me like this. I wasn't thinking that far ahead.

It's a long walk back to the castle and not only is my knee killing me, the sharp pain in my kidneys forces me to stop from time to time. When Horik suggests using the Drift, I stop dead and glare at him. For one second, I'm sober. He doesn't mention it again. By the time we reach the bridge to the castle gates, my mind is tuning in and out, and I don't remember the last few streets.

"We're almost there," Horik says.

When we've crossed the cobblestone courtyard and are climbing the steps to the huge, guarded doors, I halt.

Horik looks back. "What?"

"I don't want her to see me drunk."

"A little late for that, isn't it?"

"I'll just stay…" I sway as I turn to search for inspiration.

Horik exhales noisily, and I give him a hopeful look. He scrubs a hand through his close-cropped hair. "She's going to be so pissed at me."

I appeal to his feelings for Astarti, trying to ignore the bite of jealousy. I let my slur thicken, "You don't want her to see this, do you? After all the trouble you've gone to."

He makes a sound that's a cross between a sigh and a growl. "You can sleep it off in my room."

Horik's room, unfortunately, is several floors up, and by the time we reach his door, he's half dragging me. He deposits me in a chair, and I wince at the stab in my kidneys.

With several lanterns burning, the room is well lit, and he stares at me. "Gods," he mutters. "What a mess."

I'm content to pass out in the chair, but Horik fumbles behind me, grabs the hem of my shirt, and pulls it over my head.

"Hey!"

He throws the shirt down. "I have to see if I need to call the physician, otherwise I'd never hear the end of it from Astarti. It's a *long* way to Rune on a ship with an angry woman."

If I had more focus and energy, I would argue with him, but all I can do is wince when he prods my bruised ribs.

"You weren't fooling around, were you? You could've gotten yourself killed."

"I'm sure you wouldn't have let that happen."

"You didn't even know I was there."

I grunt noncommittally.

He pokes me in the belly, either checking for internal bleeding or just being an ass.

"I'm *fine*."

He ignores me. He feels my bruised jaw and cheekbone to see if anything's broken. He's not gentle.

Dropping his hands, he pronounces, "You got lucky. There are no Healers here, you know."

He goes to the washstand and dips a cloth, which he tosses to me. My reflexes are too slow, so it smacks me wetly in the chest.

"Clean up your face," he orders. "It looks terrible."

I fumble for the cloth and scrub it across my face, surprised when I pull it away to find it streaked with red. Horik shakes his head.

I lean my head back and close my eyes. Immediately, darkness starts to descend.

"Oh no, you don't. Get up."

He drags at me, and I sort of help. I expect him to lead me to the door, throwing me out after all, so I'm surprised when he lets go and I fall onto a mattress. Horik tugs off my boots and shoves me the rest of the way into the bed. I'm on the edge of consciousness and just aware enough to know that my exposed back is to him. A blunt finger touches one of my worst, oldest scars.

He mutters, "Belos wasn't the first one that messed you up."

I'm still trying to pull away when my mind unravels and I pass out.

Chapter 24

LOGAN

Voices intrude into my awareness. I try to ignore them because I want to slip back into the blissful nothingness of dreamless sleep, but the contrast of low male grumble and higher, female anger pierces deep. My mind is too fuzzy to react, but Horik and Astarti's voices start to come through clearly.

"Horik, let me in right now."

"Just let me have five minutes to get him up."

"Why? Why can't I see him now? What's wrong with him?"

"Astarti, *please*."

There's a brief, half-hearted scuffle, then Astarti's boots slap across the floor. She stops near the bed. "*Gods*. What *happened* to him?"

Horik says, "It's not as bad as it looks. Nothing's broken."

"Who did this?"

Horik is silent.

"*Who did this?*"

"Anyone he asked."

Silence.

"*Gods.* I can't *believe* you didn't come get me last night, Horik. I'm *so angry* with you."

Light fingers touch my face, and my eyes open without my consent. In the light of a single lantern, Astarti is frowning, her dark eyebrows pinching together.

For all her sharpness with Horik, she speaks gently to me. "What have you done to yourself?"

My mind is too heavy with exhaustion, pain, and the lingering effects of alcohol to formulate a good answer. I push awkwardly into a sitting position and slide from the bed. Horik catches my elbow as I start to fall.

He pleads with Astarti, "Let him get himself together."

She sighs irritably. "I think we should delay until tomorrow. He's drunk. I can smell it from here."

"No," I protest, pulling away from Horik. "I'm fine. I'm ready."

Horik laughs humorlessly.

Astarti says skeptically, "We need to be down at the docks by sunrise to catch the tide."

"He'll make it." Horik claps me on the shoulder, and my bad knee gives out. He adds, "I can carry him."

ꕥ

Fortunately, after a few glasses of water, I'm sober enough to walk on my own, even if slowly. It's still dark when we cross the bridge. No wonder I feel like shit. I've only been in bed a few hours. Well, I suppose there are some other small details contributing to my general misery, not that I'm blaming anyone but myself. The worst is my lower back from the blows to my kidneys. I pissed blood into the chamber pot this morning.

When Horik said before we left his room, "Maybe we *should* call the physician," I knew he'd looked, which annoyed me. Some things are private, and the color of a man's urine is one of those things. If he tells Astarti, I'll kill him.

My mind is fuzzy enough that I can ignore Astarti's angry silence all the way to the docks. She's not angry enough to let me fall in the water, though, because she grabs my arm when I sway on the boarding platform. She gives me a dirty look as she does it, of course, but still. I make it into the ship without a major incident and collapse onto a pile of ropes, leaning my forehead against the gunwale.

After a few shouts from the captain to the crew, the ship swings out into the harbor, and I realize the worst consequence of my actions last night. The motion rolls ponderously through my stomach. We're not even out of the harbor before I'm leaning over the side of the ship and puking my guts out.

Astarti sits beside me, which makes me miserable. I'm so embarrassed to have her see me like this. Horik tries to get her to leave me alone, but when he goes silent and retreats, I can imagine the look she must have given him. I curl up on the rope, moaning.

I must pass out again because I wake to the sun in my face. I throw an arm over my eyes. *Way* too bright.

"Here."

Astarti nudges me, and I peer around my arm to squint at her hand. Bread.

She wiggles it in irritation. "You need something in your stomach."

I groan at the mention of my stomach. I claw my way up the side of the ship and hang my head over. I wait but nothing happens. My stomach, apparently, is now content to quietly torment me with nausea. I slide back down. When Astarti thrusts the bread at me again, I take it. It sticks drily in my throat, and the next thing Astarti pushes at me is a wooden tankard of water.

I say, staring at the salt-stained stretch of deck beyond my rope pile, "You're really angry with me."

She says crisply, "I'm not angry that you got drunk."

"But you're angry about something else."

When she doesn't answer, I let my head roll in her direction. My eyes travel slowly from the wooden barrel she's sitting on to the curve of her buttocks, which even in my appalling state makes my groin tighten, to the angry straightness of her back and her wind-whipped dark braid. Her jaw is tight, and she's pointedly not looking at me. Well, good. I get to study her. Her skin is so fair it's like the translucent porcelain that comes from the east. Her eyes are as pale as winter morning. Gorgeous.

When I tell her this, she mutters, though with less bite, "I think you're still drunk."

I spend the rest of the morning on the pile of rope, drifting in and out. Sometime around midday, I have to relieve myself. That's not something you do over the side of a ship with the wind blowing, so I make my miserable, unsteady way below deck. Fortunately, Astarti is nowhere to be seen and Horik is talking to the captain at the helm, so only the crew witnesses the spectacle of me clutching my kidneys as I hobble to the stairs. Some of them eye me warily, but they're busy with their duties, so no one says anything or makes any jokes, at least not that I can hear.

Judging by the size and big-bellied structure of the ship, this is a merchant vessel, but when I drag myself down the stairs, I find there are a few private cabins.

When I emerge from the privy, Astarti opens one of the cabin doors. She takes in my undoubtedly horrible appearance and sighs.

"Please tell me you're not passing blood."

That's it, Horik must die.

She reads my face. "I thought so. And, no, Horik didn't tell me, if that's what you're thinking, though I have some words for him on that account. I can tell by the way you're standing."

Knowing I'm asking for a fight, I snap, "What do you want me to say? It was stupid; I know that. I'm sorry, all right?"

She leans against the doorframe and shakes her head in that way women do sometimes. She wasn't even raised by women—they must come out of the womb like this.

"What?" I growl, all the sharper because I know I'm in the wrong.

Her eyes flash. "Stop trying to pick a fight with me. Come in here and change your shirt. That one's filthy. It's about to crawl off your body."

Though I remember bringing clothes from Avydos, I didn't carry any on board. Or my sword, which I wisely left behind yesterday before my trip to the taverns, but which I wish I had now. Not *right* now, of course, but in general.

She represses an eye roll. "I packed for you."

Feeling like more of an ass than I've ever felt before, I follow her into the cabin.

Astarti's bluish Drift-light reveals a cramped space with a bunk bolted to the wall and a narrow stretch of floor. Bags are stacked in the corner, and my sword is pressed to the wall behind them. All of this makes me feel even more miserable and embarrassed. The depression that I knew was coming starts to set in. It's always like this. I feel better at first, for those brief euphoric moments, during every release of my fist and every mind-clearing blow I take, then I hate myself. I know how appalling, how stupid, how lowly and pathetic my actions were. Oh, believe me, I know.

Astarti tosses a clean shirt and a pot of white paste on the bed. Taking the not-so-subtle hint, I twist off the lid and scoop out some paste with the brush Astarti thrusts at me like a dagger. I scrub through my mouth. Belatedly, I look around for a bowl for spitting.

"Just use your shirt," she says. When she sees me hesitate to expose my torso, she adds, "I can already imagine how bad it is."

When I still hesitate, she actually snaps her fingers.

I pull off my blood-stained shirt, but I don't look at her. I spit the paste into the cloth and wad it up. Astarti practically rips the shirt from my hands. I don't like her touching it because it's too dirty, but I don't have to worry long because she chucks it into the corner like it has misbehaved. If she were directing this at someone else, I might be enjoying it. She's adorable when she's angry—that is, so long as she doesn't have her spear in hand.

Before I can reach for the clean shirt, she stops my hand. Her fingers trace my right arm up to the shoulder. It's sore and bruised from having gotten out of joint again, though it's back in place now. Her fingers trail over my chest to my purple and blue ribs. Despite the pain and my foggy head, her light touch teases me. My body's automatic response is all at odds with the way I can't quite look at her.

She says softly, fingers hovering near my bruises, "Don't do this again. Ever."

I close my eyes. I don't think I can make that promise.

"Logan."

Her pale eyes are too bright, like she's on the verge of tears. My heart constricts to see it; she never cries.

She says, "I should have prepared you for what I was going to ask Heborian. I wasn't sure if I was right—well, I'm still not sure—and I didn't want to scare you. That was stupid of me because then you just ended up with it sprung on you. I'm sorry for that. And then I didn't know what to say to you and didn't know what you needed from me. But it's no excuse. I could see you were upset, and I shouldn't have let you go."

I let my thoughts go fuzzy. I don't like where this is going. I want to tell her it's not her fault, because it's not, but I can't discuss this. That voice whispers, *Because you know.*

"Do you want to talk about it? Logan?"

"*No.*"

She chews her bottom lip, unsure what to do. "I'll get you some food, then you should rest." She's gone before I can gather my thoughts enough to protest.

When she returns a few minutes later, I'm standing in exactly the same spot, staring at nothing, trying to drive that whispering voice into the dark. *Yes, yes, yes.*

Lips compressed with either annoyance or worry, she hands me bread wrapped around a wedge of cheese. I stare at it with no appetite. For a second, I think I'll be sick again, but I know I need the food. My throat is horribly dry, and the bread goes down hard. Astarti digs through the stacked bags and hands me a water skin. I suck down over half of it.

As Astarti turns down the sheets, I strip off my belt and let it slither to the floor. The cabin is cramped, and Astarti brushes my hip as she straightens. Heat spikes through my body, and I suck in a breath. When her eyes slowly travel my torso to my face and her breathing quickens, relief shudders through me. She wants me, too. I've been afraid that seeing me so weak and pathetic, seeing the evil I did when *he* had me, would lessen me in her eyes.

When I cup her cheek, brushing my thumb over one dark eyebrow, her eyes close with pleasure. I *know* this is not the time. I'm filthy, hungover, still looking like an idiot after what I did last night. And yet, I find myself leaning down.

Her soft lips part when I kiss her. Desire lashes through me, and I press myself against her. Her breasts rise and fall with her quickened breathing, and my mind threatens to splinter, to abandon me to my body. By the Old Ones, I have so little control.

I make myself pull away. I feel certain she's never been with a man before, and I won't let her first time be with someone who stinks like every alley in Tornelaine, someone hungover and with too little control to make this a good experience for her.

Unable to let her go entirely, I brush my fingers across her smooth, blushed cheek and behind her ear to her neck. I don't realize my fingers are on her Griever's Mark until she stiffens. I know it's a tattoo the Runians bleed into those about to die, such as the babies they sometimes cast off in hard winters, and I know who gave it to her. I suppose Heborian meant it to be a sign of protection, but for Astarti it's only ever been a mark of shame and rejection.

I lift her braid slightly. She shifts uncomfortably when the Mark is exposed. I press my lips to it. She starts to tremble. I worry that she'll pull away, that she'll misunderstand me, but then she throws her arms around my neck and hugs me tight. I slip mine around her waist. I squeeze my eyes shut and hold on for all I'm worth.

Chapter 25

Standing to the westward side of the bow, I watch the sun sink toward the horizon. I keep a hand over my Mark, not wanting to let go of the warm, tingly feeling of Logan's kiss. No one has ever touched my Mark like that, and, for some stupid reason, it makes my eyes prickle.

As I stare at the blinding disc of the sun, dragging wind-blown hair out of my eyes, I torment myself by remembering all my errors over the past two days. How could I have been so stupid as to let Logan get that Runish story sprung on him? He's been on edge since we got him out of the Dry Land, and little wonder. I still don't know any details of what happened to him there—he hasn't offered to speak of it, and I haven't pushed him—but I know he's hurt, way deep down where no one can see.

Because he handled the conversation with his mother surprisingly well, I pushed him into another, even though I should have known he wasn't ready. When I found him on the floor of his room in Avydos, curled up under the window, far from the twisted, sweat-soaked bed, I knew. When I saw his energy form in the Current, where at the region of his heart his golden energy coiled tight, constricting and restless, I knew. Oh yes, the warning signs were there. *I* was the one who wanted to talk to Heborian, to chase down a half-remembered story, and I dragged Logan with me. The result? Something he's likely been trying *not* to think about got thrown in his face. Frankly, that conversation with Heborian would have been enough to shake anyone's foundations. Stupid, stupid, stupid. Logan's mind must be in a thousand pieces.

And yet, I'm still mulling over the question that our conversation implied. Could his father really be one of the Lost Gods, one of the Old Ones? I shiver, chilled to the bone by the immensity of this idea and all the other questions that rise in its wake. Who are the children referred to in Heborian's story? Why did they bind the gods? *What* is really binding them? And most importantly, why is Belos so interested?

Wait, I caution myself. *Get more information before drawing any conclusions.*

One thing that haunts me from the conversation with Heborian is that Logan did not seem more surprised. He didn't handle it well, as evidenced by the battered state of his body, but he didn't seem to reject the idea.

I scrape back my hair at the thought of his physical condition. Of all the stupid things to do. Yesterday when Logan left Heborian's study, I figured he needed to work through things on his own, as I would want to do, so I gave him what I would have wanted: space. Besides, he had made it clear that he didn't want my company. Later, when Horik convinced me to stay behind while he went to find Logan, I expected that Logan might be drunk and decided to continue respecting his privacy. I didn't, however, expect him to be getting himself beaten half to death all over again.

The wind, annoyingly gusty, makes my jacket flap, and I wrench it to stillness. I frown at the wind, but it just blows hair in my face. It seems like the wind should be calming down at this time of day, not whipping back and forth in fits and starts.

Long-strided, rolling footsteps announce Horik's approach. He leans down beside me and plants his elbows on the rail. The sun has just disappeared, and Horik stares out over waves painted pink and orange by the afterglow.

I shake hair out of my eyes. "Why would he do that, Horik? What he did last night." Maybe another man can understand it.

Horik breathes out heavily, considering. "He thinks it's a safe way to release his frustration."

"Safe!"

"Safe for others. I mean, relatively, of course. As far as I saw, he never threw the first punch and never fought anyone who couldn't handle him, never even gave himself fair odds. At least it was just fists. He didn't have a weapon and never touched his earthmagic. You saw him in the Dry Land, Astarti. He's right to think himself dangerous. How did he break that Shackle? How did he tear down Belos's whole fortress?" Horik shakes his head. "He has too much power and not enough control, and he knows it."

"It's not his fault," I protest.

"It doesn't matter. It's still the truth."

Distrust creeps over me. "That's why you're here, isn't it? It's why Heborian sent you. He doesn't trust Logan."

The wind gusts again, making me shiver.

"Heborian doesn't trust anyone."

"You didn't answer my question."

"Heborian also never does anything for just one reason. He'd call that downright wasteful."

"So I'm right?"

"That might be *one* reason."

I clench the rail in frustration and rock on the balls of my feet. I hate being on a ship, my boundaries set by wooden planks and water. In some ways the ocean is as desolate, as prisonlike, as the Dry Land.

"Horik, you saw what Belos had done to Logan, how he'd taken his mind. You have no idea what that's like, to have another take control of you. It is the worst violation."

Horik's face turns toward me, but the little remaining light is at his back, leaving his expression in shadow. He says softly, "It makes him no less dangerous."

"That's what Heborian would say. What do you say?"

"Are you assuming I only repeat what he says?"

"What do you say, Horik?" I don't know why, but his opinion seems to matter to me.

Horik blows out his cheeks. "He's like a Runish berserker. The old stories tell of berserkers who would turn into animals when their fury was upon them. Point them in the right direction and step back! One berserker could change the course of a battle. Logan is like that. When he really loses it, watch out. I still say he's dangerous, but it's an incredible power to witness."

I rest my chin in my hand, scowling into the wind. That wasn't what I wanted to hear.

"Oh, don't be that way. I'm trying to tell you that I like him." His voice turns playful when he adds, "But then, I like everyone. I'm friendly like that."

I try to play along. "You don't look friendly."

"Well, I do have my reputation to think about."

I go silent, unable to keep up the levity.

Horik sighs. "Whatever Logan is, it isn't his fault. What happened to him isn't his fault. What he did under Belos's control isn't his fault. The fact that you grew up serving Belos isn't *your* fault. But as you know, there are still consequences of those things."

I pinch the bridge of my nose, overwhelmed by the truth of Horik's words.

He straightens. "Come on. No brooding. I'll teach you to play dice."

"I don't have any money."

"I'll lend you some." He grins. "You can owe me."

My resistance is half-hearted, and when Horik tugs the sleeve of my jacket, I follow him, hoping I can stop thinking about all this for a little while.

Chapter 26

LOGAN

Moonlight paints the smooth, curving face of the tower. There are no doors or windows, no seams. I begin to walk around the base, stumbling over the jumble of loose rock. I can't go all the way around because the tide is high, licking the base of the tower on the seaward side. The tower casts a long shadow across the moonlit waves.

I crane my neck, straining to see the top. I know they're in there.

I grope clumsily for the Drift, but it's distant, deadened. I growl in frustration.

ꟸ ꟸ

Rage writhes within me. I strike him again, shouting, "Tell me! What are they doing?"

His head lolls to the side. He tries to squint me into focus with one eye. The other is swollen shut.

I grab his hair and rear back, my fist tight and angry, glowing with Drift-energy. His jaw sets stubbornly, and that eye swirls blue and green. Furious, I swing.

* * *

My fist slams into smooth, hard wood. Rage boils so hot inside me that I don't feel any pain. I scramble up, my chest heaving. Something tangles around my feet. I grab and rend it, exulting in the sound of ripping cloth. I try to stand, and my head strikes a low ceiling. I grope frantically and find myself in a small room. I am desperate for light. The faintest blue light blooms, revealing a cramped cabin. Bags are stacked in a corner. My sword is pressed to the wall behind them.

My sword, its pommel gleaming in the faint bluish light.

Drift-light.

I gasp, and the light vanishes.

I huddle on the bed, in the dark, trembling, my stomach rolling with the wind-tossed ship. I squeeze my eyes shut, trying to drive the image of the light from my mind, trying to drive my dreams into the deepest, darkest corner of myself.

The ship rocks to steadiness.

Chapter 27

When I emerge from my cabin in the morning, I find that Logan's is empty. I frown at his torn sheets and a fist-sized dent in the wall over the bed.

Last night, after playing dice with Horik for far too long and getting myself in grotesque "debt," I checked on Logan and found him sleeping crouched at the foot of the bed. Horik helped me get him straightened out. Because Logan didn't wake when we moved him, I knew he was exhausted, so I left him alone, never using any light. During the night I never heard any sounds from his chamber, so the damage must have been done before Horik and I moved him.

I find Logan in the open space of the bow, working forms with his sword. There's strain and rigidity in his movements as he forces his body to obey despite his obvious pain. My jaw clenches. He needs to let himself rest and recover. His hand is too tight on his sword, blanching his knuckles around the purple of new bruising.

I am frozen, uncertain whether to say something or just leave him alone.

He sees me and drops his form. I make my uncertain way up the steps into the bow. His mouth tightens when he gets a good look at my face. He looks away, embarrassed, clearly assuming I saw the damage.

I have no idea what to say or do. I'm way out of my depth with all this.

Awkwardly, I ask, "Have you eaten?"

His shoulders slump with relief that I haven't said anything more serious. "Not yet."

"I'll get something."

When I return with two trenchers of boiled oats, we sit on the deck, leaning against the railing. We eat our lumpy, tasteless portions in silence.

Horik joins us in the bow. He stretches until his back cracks. "Horrible bunks," he mutters. "I had to sleep with my knees bent."

The day is long and tedious. I try to be helpful, but I just get in the way of the crew, so I spend most of my time sitting on a barrel, bouncing my knee. I do some forms practice of my own, ignoring the wide eyes of the crew as I shape my Drift-spear. I find it amusing that they are more worried about me than about Logan.

By evening, I can't take it anymore. I find Logan, little more than a shape in the dimness, on the steps leading to the bow. I drop beside him. Of course, my courage abandons me at the last moment, and I can't think of anything to say.

I hear his deep exhalation. He says softly, "I'm not trying to be difficult."

"I know. I'm not trying to be pushy."

"I know."

I shiver pleasantly when his hand slides along my forearm. His fingers twine with mine. I squeeze. He squeezes back.

When he rests his chin on my shoulder, I wince. He draws away immediately.

"What is it?"

"It's nothing," I assure him. "Still healing, but it's nothing." I plucked out the stitches from my shoulder and thigh some days ago, but the flesh is still tender.

"Did I do it?" His tone is dark, fearing the worst.

"Of course not. I don't even remember who did it. It was a battle."

"Then how do you know it wasn't me?"

I say firmly, "Stop it."

"I don't like seeing you hurt."

I give him an incredulous look, which I know he can't see in the dark, so I do my best to make him hear it. "Do you *want* me to throw you overboard? Because you just tempted me like you would not believe."

"What do you mean?"

"What do I mean? Let me poke you in your bruised ribs and see if you can figure it out."

"Oh."

"Yeah, 'oh.'"

We both fall silent for a time. At first, the silence is uncomfortable, because I'm annoyed with him and he knows it, but it eases. I lean against him. He's warm, solid, strong.

"Do you think—" He cuts himself off. The tension in his body tells me he's talking about something big, maybe even Heborian's story.

I nudge him gently, hoping he'll go on.

I feel him shake his head.

After a time, he asks, "Have you ever been to Rune?"

I try not to be frustrated that he's changing the subject, but I can only offer a short, "No."

"Hmm."

"What?"

"Where did you hear that story? You didn't want to answer Heborian when he asked."

I stiffen. With everything Logan must have been thinking about at the time, I am stunned he picked up on that. And appalled. My heart knocks against my ribs.

"What is it?"

I pull away from him.

"Astarti?"

With someone else, I would not be so unsettled. A lie would rise smoothly to my lips; I would barely even have to think about it. But with Logan I always seem to have my guard down, and I don't want to lie, not to him.

Yet I cannot tell him the truth. I could not bear to watch myself fall so far in his eyes.

He stands. "You haven't pushed me, Astarti. I'm not going to push you."

I close my eyes. We both have so many secrets.

"Do you want me to leave you alone?"

I don't want him to leave me, but I can't look at him right now, even in the dark.

He's gone before I can bring myself to speak.

᪥ ᪥

The wind has been gusting sporadically all night, whipping my braid into a dreadful tangle, but it's quiet for the moment. I'm dozing on the gunwale, leaning into the ropes.

"Careful," Horik advises, stopping beside me. "You fall asleep like that you're liable to take a swim."

"Then let me hold onto your sleeve so I can take you with me."

He snorts. "I'm three times your weight."

"I doubt that."

"Close enough."

The wind gusts suddenly, making the ship rock and the waxed canvas sail slap. The captain, bustling onto the deck from his chamber, shouts for the crew to start taking the sail in before it rips. I wrap my arms around myself for warmth, tugging my jacket tight.

The wind switches directions and whips my braid into my face. Eyes watering from the sting, I toss the braid behind me.

Horik mutters, "What is with this wind? It's not even coming from the right direction for this time of night."

"Oh?"

He comments wryly, "A mariner you are not."

I'll have to take Horik's word for it, but the wind does seem wrong somehow, as it did last night, though now it's even worse. Angry. Fitful.

A sudden gust rips across us. Water sprays. Barrels roll and clatter. The deck tips, making my stomach soar into my throat as I latch onto the ropes for balance.

A chill spreads through me.

Oh no.

This isn't just wind.

It's—

I launch myself from the gunwale and charge across the rocking deck, ducking around crew members as they scramble to adjust ropes and secure loose gear. Shaping a Drift-light, I thud down the dark steps to the cabins, getting thrown into one wall then the other.

Horik is hard on my heels when I wrench open Logan's door. My bluish Drift-light reveals Logan's thrashing, nightmare-ridden form. He's making low, inarticulate sounds. Remembering what happened last time I startled him from a nightmare, I hesitate.

The tipping ship throws Horik into my back, and I stumble into the cabin. The hand I thrust out to catch myself lands on Logan's ribs.

He explodes awake, snarling, leaping from the bed to drive me and Horik through the doorway. Horik slams into the passageway wall. I am briefly pinned between the two men, but I slip free and skitter down the hall.

"Logan!"

His head whips toward me. By some trick of shadow and Drift-light, his eyes look black. My blood runs cold.

Horik grabs Logan's arms and pins them behind his back. He tries to wrestle Logan down, but Logan slams the back of his head into Horik's face. Horik reels, and Logan tears from his grip.

Logan stalks toward me.

Behind him, I see a brief glow of Drift-work as Horik shapes his axe.

"No!"

I lunge to shove Logan out of the way, but Horik's swing cannot be stopped. In the last moment I realize Horik is swinging the handle, not the blade. He cracks Logan in the head, and Logan crumples against the wall.

The wind dies, and the ship rolls on the quieting waves.

ꕥ

With my Drift-light hovering over the bunk, I peer behind the cool damp cloth I've been pressing to the bruise at Logan's temple. He's been unconscious for over ten minutes.

"Did you have to hit him so hard? You could've killed him."

Horik shifts guiltily in the cabin doorway. "Is he all right?"

"Do I look like a physician?"

"Astarti, he was out of control. I thought he was going to hurt you."

"He was having a nightmare."

Horik grunts.

"He's been out too long," I worry.

"I'll see if anyone has smelling salts."

Horik's feet beat a quick rhythm up the steps to the deck.

My fingers curl on Logan's chest, feeling the rhythm of his heart, a steadiness that belies all the turmoil inside him.

An image of his eyes, unnaturally black, surfaces in my mind. I will it to recede. That was nothing more than a trick of the light, a vision of my own fears.

When Horik returns with a jar of salts, I waft it under Logan's nose. He twitches awake. His eyes open to reveal blue irises threaded with brown and green. Relief makes me dizzy.

He groans and rubs his face with both hands but flinches when his fingers brush the new bruise from Horik's axe handle. "What happened?"

I look over my shoulder at Horik.

Logan's eyes follow mine. "Horik? What happened to your nose?"

Worry crawls over my skin. "You don't remember?"

"Remember what?"

"You had a nightmare." I try to say it neutrally, but he stares at me.

He asks warily, "Did I do something?"

"You really don't remember?"

He pushes himself into a sitting position. He looks from me to Horik and back to me, trying to gauge us.

"Do you remember what you were dreaming?" I'm amazed by the calmness of my own voice; my heart is hammering.

Logan's eyes drop to his lap. His breathing grows shallow. He shakes his head in denial, though I don't know what he's denying.

"Logan?"

His head snaps up. "Did I attack you?"

I say carefully, "Everyone is fine."

"Everyone is—?" Logan throws the sheets off the end of the bunk and edges around me.

"Logan—"

He brushes past my hand then growls at Horik, who moves out of the doorway.

I follow Logan as he limps along the passageway and up the narrow steps. He stops, and I peer around him to see silhouettes of the crewmembers busily straightening out a mess of broken barrels and tangled rope.

Logan staggers back, nearly knocking me down the steps. He slides down the wall.

"I could have killed us all."

My Drift-light hovers over my shoulder, painting his haunted face with bluish light.

"Logan, it's not—"

"Don't you dare say it's not my fault!"

He's sucking hard for air, like his lungs won't expand. He claws at his chest. I try to reach for him, but he jerks to his feet. He bolts up the last few steps and onto the deck.

A sharp wind cuts across the deck, making the ship rock, then it's gone—and Logan with it.

Chapter 28

I scan the dark, empty water, alert for any trace of wind. The night is growing cold, and I keep my hands tucked under my arms. I consider going to the cabin for more clothes, but what if Logan returns while I'm gone? My heart starts pounding when I think, *What if he doesn't return at all?*

Horik is still talking with the captain, who was quick to lay the blame at the feet of the Drifters on board, which means that he, like most people, doesn't know anything about the Drift at all. I should be giving Horik a hand with the man. After all, lying and smoothing things over is my specialty, not his. But I don't think I could manage it right now.

It scares me that Logan was right: he could have killed everyone. For one second, I feel a glimmer of understanding of why his father—well, Arathos, that is—sent him away. I cut myself off.

No.

Absolutely not.

Where Logan has needed help, he's found only abuse. Why did any of them ever think that would solve this?

But, then, what will?

I'm spared my own chilling failure to answer that question when Horik joins me at the railing.

"Well?" I prompt.

Horik's swollen nose makes his voice funny. "I was as vague as possible, swore nothing more would happen, and promised that Heborian would triple his fee when he gets back to Tornelaine."

"So we're all right with him?"

Horik tilts his hand in a so-so gesture. "I'd steer clear if I were you."

"I'll be happy to," I mutter.

"Astarti…"

"There's nothing you can say that I haven't already thought of. I know, Horik. It was bad."

"Astarti, he could have—"

"I *know*."

Horik waits with me for a while, but when his yawns start to grate on my nerves, I tell him to go to bed.

"What about you?"

"I couldn't possibly sleep."

I'm watching the sun bleed its light across the eastern horizon when the waves chop and a sudden wind whips around me. I spin so fast I lose my balance. Before I can either fall or catch myself, Logan wraps his arms around me. My back is pressed to his muscled chest and stomach. Though he's still recovering from his imprisonment and his stupid fights, his body is strong and sure. I don't want him to let go. I don't want to turn around and look at him and start facing what's happened.

And yet, despite the way he clings to me, there's an undercurrent I don't like. Something too fierce, too final.

When he steps away, I rock unsteadily. His jaw is set, his eyes a flat blue that doesn't look right on him. The bruises from the other night are showing yellow at the edges, but the one across his temple is dark and awful. His head is tilted slightly to the side, his left eye squinting. He must have a crushing headache.

He says firmly, "I want you to go back to Tornelaine."

My heart lurches. "No."

His chest gives one heave, then he's under control again. "You have to."

"No, I don't. Besides, you don't know how to find Sunhild."

"So tell me."

"No. You're stuck with me."

Emotion breaks momentarily over his face then vanishes. "What if—"

"There are too many 'what if's' to even begin. We'll deal with it."

His eyes swirl with green, showing how thin that skin of calm really is. "Please go back. If I hurt you…"

I reach for his hand, but he closes his fist.

"No one was hurt. Horik or I will watch over you when you sleep. It won't happen again."

"No," he says stiffly, "it won't happen again." His meaning seems different from mine, and I don't like it. I don't know what he's saying.

When he retreats across the bow and disappears below deck, I sink against the railing, both relieved and unhappy.

൬ ൫

In the afternoon, with nothing else to do, I once again make use of the empty space in the bow for some forms practice with my spear. Horik joins me, but it's too small an area for sparring, so we have to take turns using the space for forms.

When Logan emerges onto the deck, walking to the side to look out, his slow, careful movements speak of lingering pain in his shoulder, knee, and lower back. His head is still tilted oddly from his headache. I wish there were a physician on board to look at him. I wish I knew something of Healing.

I also wish he would join me and Horik, but he doesn't even look at us. Horik clamps a hand on my shoulder in sympathy.

In the early evening, we make port in the northwestern Keldan city of Avarre. While the captain haggles with a merchant and the crew unloads crates of wine, I change into a fresh shirt, thrilled to get off the ship for a while. Horik has suggested we seek out what he termed "real food." He even talked Logan into it, and I find myself hunting through my bag for the one pretty shirt I brought, just in case. The silk slides over my skin like water. Silk. Am I growing so used to fine things already? I have no mirror, so I scrub my face with a damp towel, hoping I've gotten it clean.

Horik and Logan are waiting on the dock. The way Horik's eyebrows jump tells me he's noticed that I've dressed for the occasion, and it also tells me that I usually don't dress very well, considering that all I've done is put on a nice shirt. But what matters to me is that some of the deadness leaves Logan's eyes, and he walks close to me as we wander along the dock road.

I gravitate toward a well-lit tavern where laughter and music sound from within. The only empty table is in the corner, and when Horik plants an elbow and it tips, we see why it's empty. When the serving girl brings our beers, we hold them off the table. Dinner should be interesting.

Logan stares into his beer with a slightly ill expression. I can't help it; I laugh. The corner of his mouth lifts.

Horik ends up drinking Logan's beer, and the serving girl brings Logan some water. When our food arrives, we hold the plates in our laps. It's kind of like being on the ship, but the food is undeniably better.

After Horik clears a second plate of lamb, potatoes, and spring onions, I comment, "It *is* nice to eat something green and fresh. And *real*."

Horik looks at me with a stunned expression. "Real food means meat. I thought everyone knew that."

The fiddler and flutist across the room play energetically, their cheeks red and shoulders bouncing. Some of the patrons clap in time to the music. When a voluptuous woman in layers of brightly colored skirts joins the musicians for a few ribald songs, I find myself laughing along with the others. The lines that make the men roar make my ears grow hot, which means they're likely bright red. Horik chuckles at my discomfort. When I glance at Logan, I see him leaning back in his chair, watching me in a way that says he's not seeing or hearing anything else. He is completely focused. On me. If someone else were looking at me like that, I would be uncomfortable. With Logan, it spreads warmth through my body.

As the band leaps into another song, a few people push back the tables and start dancing. Horik gets up and puts out his big hand for me.

I recoil.

"Come on," he says, flexing thick fingers.

"I've never danced before."

"You dance with me all the time in the training yard."

"This is *way* different."

"Get up, you coward."

I look to Logan for support, but he says, "Go on, Astarti. Enjoy yourself." For the first time all day, his face is relaxed, like he's forgotten to hate himself for a moment.

Horik flexes his fingers again.

Blushing and feeling ridiculous, I put my hand in Horik's. He pulls me from my chair. With his size, his fierce Runish tattoos, and his bruised and swollen nose, he manages to command some space for us.

Like the other dancers, Horik claps in time with the music and starts to move his feet. He stares pointedly at mine, so I try to mimic him. He tries not to laugh at me, but I can't help laughing at myself.

Still tapping to the beat, Horik takes my hand and spins me. When he grabs me by my hips and lifts, I give a surprised squeal. Laughter breaks out around me.

Horik quickly gives up on serious dancing, and we hop and spin comically around the other dancers. I accidentally nail Horik in the gut with a poorly timed elbow and mash his toes several times. The singer breaks off once or twice as we distract her, but no one seems to mind.

By the end of the song, Horik is laughing so hard he can barely stand up straight.

"It wasn't *that* bad!" I protest.

The good-natured laughter around me suggests otherwise. I bury my face in my hands, more to hide my grin than my embarrassment.

When the musicians begin another, slower song, Horik puts a hand on my hip. Someone else's hand—with familiar, bruised knuckles—closes on Horik's bicep.

Horik backs away with an exaggerated bow.

I eye Logan skeptically. "You sure about this? Horik seems to have proven that I am a terrible and highly dangerous dance partner."

"He did that on purpose."

"What, reveal that I'm a dangerous dance partner?"

Gold swirls through Logan's eyes. His voice is rough. "No, not that."

He pulls me to him. His hands rest on my hips. My arms snake around him. At first, I hold him lightly, conscious of his injuries, but after a few verses, I'm pressed along the length of his body, and his arms have closed around me. My cheek lies against his muscled chest, his rests on top of my head. I sigh with utter contentment. Nothing has ever felt so right.

Far too soon, the last hum of the fiddle dies away. Logan grips me more tightly. I don't want to let go either.

On our return to the ship, Logan's hand touches my back. The touch is yearning, almost possessive, before he snatches his hand away. And yet his fingers return as though he cannot stop himself.

When we reach the ship, Horik wanders over to join the dice game underway near the mast. He doesn't look at us; he knows. When I head down the steps to the cabins, driven by instinct, with excitement fluttering in my belly, Logan hesitates.

I hear his ragged breathing. Panic? I touch his stomach to see if he's all right, and my fingers, with a mind of their own, trace one notched muscle, then another. He groans. No, not panic.

Part of me wants to grab his hand and tug him along, but I'm too shy. I know that I want him, in every way, but I don't know how to ask.

And, of course, there's still the matter of Earthmaker law.

I wish I could force myself to not think about that, but I don't want Logan to do something he'll regret. I couldn't bear if he resented me for this.

His breathing roughens. His hand finds mine. He starts down the steps.

I fumble with the door latch in the dim light of the passageway lantern. My heart thunders as I step into the dark room. My hands instinctively seek his body, skimming the hard cut of muscle at his hip. He lets out a low groan that has me pulling him against me. He pins me to the wall, his lips finding mine in the dark.

Finally, I am falling over that precipice. I am soaring toward freedom, toward completion. The barrier between us is crashing, and I will know him, in every way. My hands slip under his shirt to explore his muscled back. His lips graze a dizzying path up my neck and along my jaw.

Then, with no warning, he tenses.

His forehead thumps into the wall above my shoulder, and I feel his jaw clench where it brushes my ear.

He's trembling against me, his ragged breathing and obvious arousal telling me he wants this. At least, his body does. But his mind?

I say miserably into his neck, shame already setting in, "I know we can't do this. I don't want you to be…." I can't bring myself to use that shattering word, though it rattles inside me. *Stricken.*

He rears back. "You think that's what's stopping me?"

A horrible possibility occurs to me. "Well, I thought. Or maybe you don't really…" *want me*? Have I misread him?

"Oh, Astarti," he groans, "why don't you understand?" He lays his hands on my face and gently kisses my lips, my chin, the hollow of my throat.

I feel a melting sensation low in my belly, and I have to close my fists to keep my hands off him.

"Then what *is* it?" I can't keep the snap out of my voice.

He takes a shuddering breath. "I want you, Astarti, like I've never wanted anything in my life. It"—he shakes his head, searching for words—"*floods* my mind. It seizes me to where sometimes I can't even *think*." He falls silent a moment before forcing the last bit out. "But I want better for you."

Annoyance surges through me. "But I don't want anything else!"

"But you don't *know* anything else. You have to understand that you're very young, younger than I am, and, for all your experiences, you've never had a chance to live, to *decide*. There are more possibilities before you than you realize. I will crush them, I will *destroy* them. And I can't do this just once. There would be no going back, not for me. And what if I—oh, Astarti, what if I ever hurt you? I mean, *really* hurt you."

"*Stop it.* Just stop it. I'm not afraid of you. I trust you, and I wish you would trust yourself a little."

He barks a disbelieving laugh. "I killed two people when I was five years old because I couldn't control myself. Just last night I could have taken down this ship and killed twenty men without even knowing I was doing it. My earthmagic is boiling up, slipping through the cracks. It's like I'm ten years old again! And I can't—I'm *feeling* too much, and it's all in conflict." He ends harshly, "I don't know what to do."

My heart constricts. I don't know what to do either. By default, I slip my arms around him. I do not touch other people, but I find myself constantly touching him. Because he needs it. Because I need it. He's trembling with suppressed emotion. I wish he would just let it out, but he doesn't.

And yet, inch by inch, he unwinds. When his limbs have loosened, I nudge him toward the bunk. He sits, his back against the wall, his knees up. I settle myself between his legs and lean against him. He lets out a deep sigh and presses his face to the side of my head. His arms tighten around me.

I have never been held like this. The sensation is new and fragile, and I'm terrified of breaking it. But I do, with my own restlessness.

The need to confess has burned in me for days, and Logan's honesty has made it knock against the back of my throat, desperate to be let out. I try to think of a preface, but it comes bursting out of me. "I Took a soul once."

Logan draws back, stunned.

"You asked me where I heard that Runish story of the binding. Well, I never 'heard' it. When you Take someone's energy—their soul, if you want to call it that—you absorb it into yourself. Our emotions and memories are part of us, woven into our very essence, and when you Take someone's energy, you Take those things, too. Nothing is clear. Things come in fragments, bits of images, a few words. The man whose soul I Took was a Runian, and that is how I came by a fragment of that story."

Logan's heart pounds against my back.

Even though his horror is justified, I find myself snapping, "What? Did you think I served Belos for seventeen years with clean hands?"

"I think you're not telling me everything."

"I'm telling you what matters. I'm telling you the truth."

"There's more to it."

"And if I did it to save myself, does that excuse it?"

"Astarti—"

"Answer my question." I don't know why I'm doing this to him, but now that I've started, I can't seem to stop myself.

"No, it doesn't excuse it. But I still want to know the circumstances." He nudges me. His heartrate is slowing as the shock wears off.

I close my eyes. "I refused, at first. I refused for quite some time. But then Belos took my mind—"

"But if—"

"Let me finish. I found myself teetering at the edge of the fortress roof, staring down hundreds of feet to the plain below. I had only a mixed recollection of getting there. I lunged away from the edge, into Belos. He asked me if I understood, now, how much power he had over me. Or *could* have, if he chose. He asked me if I understood how much freedom I had been enjoying. He said that I could either Take the man's energy of my own free will, or I could do under his will. That was the only time he took my mind. It was the only time he needed to. I did what he asked. Of my own free will."

In the wedge of light from the hallway lantern, Logan's knuckles blanch as he clenches his fists. "That is not 'free will,' Astarti."

"It doesn't matter. I did it. I chose to save myself."

"Your refusal wouldn't have changed the outcome."

"So I've told myself many times. And, yes, it's true. What I did was practical, and it changed nothing of the outcome. But it changed me, and I still wish I had refused. If Belos had done it, even using my body and power, it would not be my fault, just as what Belos did through you was not your fault." Logan stiffens, but I don't give him a chance to protest. "There's a big part of me that is cold and practical, and whether that comes from Heborian by nature or Belos by conditioning, I don't know. But there is another part of me that speaks of right and wrong, regardless of practicality. I don't always know which one to listen to, and sometimes I think they're liable to tear me apart with their bickering. But I *do* know that the one that speaks most loudly—and longest after the fact—is the one that speaks of simple right and wrong."

Logan is silent. There is, of course, nothing to say.

But words are still bubbling out of me. "Do you know why I hate Belos?"

Logan whispers brokenly, "Yes, Astarti, I do."

"It's not because of what he's done to me."

"I know." His voice cracks with emotion.

"It's because of what I've done to others. Because it is both his fault *and* mine."

Logan's arms tighten around me. His legs are on either side of me. Eventually, I stop trembling. Eventually, I believe he is not going to leave me.

ꕥ ꕥ

At some point, I hear Horik stumble to his cabin. When Logan starts to slump, I scoot away.

"Lie down. You're exhausted."

He snaps awake. "No. I just need to walk around and get some fresh air."

Ah. Now I understand his words this morning. He means not to sleep at all. Idiot.

I assure him, "I'll stay here and watch over you. Besides, we're in the harbor."

"But you're tired, too. I couldn't allow myself to sleep while you have to stay up all night."

"I'll make you a deal. You sleep the first half of the night, then I'll wake you up so I can sleep the second half."

He considers. "Only if we reverse that. You sleep the first half."

"What, so you can let me sleep the whole night and I won't be any the wiser until morning?"

His stillness tells me this, indeed, was his plan.

"Logan, give me a break. I cut my teeth on deception. You're not going to pull one over on me."

He grumbles, "I'll never win with you."

"Now you're catching on."

"So how do I know you won't play the same trick on me?"

"I guess you'll just have to trust me."

"Didn't you just tell me that you cut your teeth on deception?"

"Hah. Now, lie down. I'm done arguing with you."

He doesn't move.

I close my eyes for patience. "You'll fall asleep eventually. You won't be able to help it. Wouldn't it be safer to do it now, here?"

At last, logic prevails, and he lays himself down on the bunk. He's asleep before I even get the sheet over him.

As expected, his sleep is troubled. The first few nightmares pass without me waking him, but when he starts to sweat and mumble, I shape my Drift-light so he won't wake in the dark. I gently shake his shoulder.

He lunges away from me, slamming into the wall.

I shout, "It's me!"

I'm ready to shape a shield of energy, but he keeps moving away, scrambling to the foot of the bed. He's kneeling, hanging his head over the edge like he's going to be sick. His stomach heaves twice, but he holds it down.

When he draws back, his face is pale and ill-looking in the bluish light. He claws at his chest. "He's—still—in here."

"No, Logan, he's not."

"But he *is*."

I slide onto the bunk beside him. He's not ready to be touched, so I fold my hands in my lap. "Why do you say that?"

"I can feel it. And in my dreams, I *am* him."

I don't want to dismiss what he's feeling, but I have to say, "I think that's probably pretty normal after what you've been through. I still dream that I'm…Leashed." Gods, the word still feels filthy in my mouth. "Dreams are where we torment ourselves with all our fears. He took your mind, Logan. It doesn't surprise me that your dreams reflect it."

"It's more than that. I dreamed that I was in the Dry Land, shifting through the rubble of the fortress. I dreamed a conversation with the sly-looking one—"

"Straton."

"And Straton said, 'Where is he now,' and I said—or *he* said, I guess—'On his way to Rune.' Explain that!"

"That's quite easy to explain. Of course you're afraid he knows where you are. It's—"

"No, Astarti, *no.* It's more. I know it. Step into the Drift and see if I'm still Leashed."

"Logan—"

"Please."

To please him, I slide into the Drift. The world simplifies itself as the details fade and everything is rendered in its most basic forms. Two dozen men sleep in the hold. Horik sleeps on the other side of the wall, and beyond the harbor the city glows with thousands of quiet energies.

Logan is crouched on the bed, tensely awaiting my pronouncement. Of course there is no Leash, but his energies churn. I expect the turbulence, the wild lash of power that defines him, but I am troubled to see again what I saw in the Current: the tightening and twisting around his heart. His energies coil and writhe. How badly must Belos have hurt him to cause this?

I slide out of the Drift.

Logan's hands are clenched on his knees. "Well?"

"You're not Leashed. This is all in your mind." Part of me denies that even as I say it. What I saw in his energies runs deeper than the mind, all the way into his very essence.

Into his soul.

Can damage so deep ever heal?

Logan looks doubtful, almost like he doesn't want to believe me.

I want him to sleep again, but I can see that he won't, so when he urges me to lie down, I give in, too exhausted to argue.

And, yes, I too dream of Belos.

Chapter 29

It takes three more days to reach Rune. After leaving Keldan waters, we sail around the marshy coast of Heradyn. Because the coastal waters are less rocky here, we stay in sight of the coast much of the time. The towns grow fewer and farther between as we move north. When I ask Horik about this, he explains that all of Heradyn's major ports are in the south because people have steadily receded from the north, where the Runians have raided for centuries.

"Ah, yes," I tease, "the gallant occupation of the Runians: stealing."

Horik only shrugs, upset by neither my joke nor the truth of it.

Though Horik doesn't say it, I can tell he's excited to be nearing his homeland. He would have been a young man when he went south with Heborian two decades ago, yet the way he dresses with hints of Runish style, his preference for the axe instead of a Keldan sword, all speak of an unwillingness to let go of where he came from.

By the time we reach the island-studded straits between Heradyn and Rune, the air has grown noticeably cooler, and I start to understand why Heborian insisted we bring warm clothes. On the last day of sailing, I even swing a wool cloak around my shoulders as though it's winter instead of spring.

Horik chuckles. "Southerners."

I'm standing in the bow, fidgety with anticipation of getting off this ship, when the dark landmass on the horizon breaks up into jutting fjords. Beside me, Horik grins. Logan, sitting on the railing and hanging onto a rope for support, perks up from his exhausted slump. Though I've convinced him to sleep some each night, with either me or Horik watching over him, he never makes it long. His nightmares are getting worse.

Around midday, we sail between two rocky, rearing fjords and into the calm waters of a long, narrow bay that leads to the port city of Gruneborg. As we pull up to the dock, I scan the city with interest. The buildings are constructed of wood, the roofs thatched with golden reeds.

When the loading platform thuds to the dock, Logan, Horik, and I are the first ones off the ship. Logan has his sword strapped to his back and a leather bag slung over his shoulder. Horik and I carry our own bags, though naturally we appear unarmed.

As we trudge down the dock, people stare at Logan. His blond hair stands out among all the dark heads, and I'm selfishly glad that my own is dark. No one seems to think much of me. Of course, my anonymity lasts only as long as I keep my mouth shut. As soon as I ask Horik where we can find horses, people stare.

Horik mutters, "Keep your voice down. Gruneborg may be more open to foreigners because it's a trading port, but it's still best for you to keep a low profile."

Someone shouts behind us. "Foldsmitha!" I know enough Runish to realize he called Logan an Earthmaker. Though I can't follow the rest of his harsh, guttural words, I can infer from his tone that he's not happy about it.

Horik steps between Logan and the man who shouted. A brief argument in Runish ensues. When Horik shapes his axe, the man's eyes widen and he seems to notice Horik's tattoos for the first time. His tone becomes conciliatory. He backs away, hands raised in the universal I-don't-want-trouble gesture.

I whisper to Horik, "Why do they hate Earthmakers?"

He looks surprised. "Don't you know? The Earthmakers slaughtered hundreds of Drifters. It almost crippled Rune."

My eyebrows jump. "What?"

"Sixty years ago, Astarti, in the war with Belos."

"What?"

Horik scans the street. "This isn't the place for this conversation. Let's just get some horses and go. Unless you think you can change Logan's mind about the Drift?"

"At this point?"

"Right. Follow me."

We make our way along several unpaved streets. Now that I'm closer to the buildings, I see that every lintel, awning, and support beam is carved with Runish symbols and painted in a range of colors: blue, red, yellow, green. In some places, the paint is new and bright; elsewhere it has flaked away to expose bare wood. We pass numerous stock pens where sheep, goats, and pigs fill the air with their noises—and smells.

When we reach a blacksmith's open-sided shop, Horik yells until the burly man pounding out a horseshoe straightens from his anvil. The man's eyes slide to Logan, but Horik recalls his attention with the word "fee." The man shouts into the back of his shop, and a young, dark-haired boy hurries out.

The boy leads us into the adjoining stable, where horses are tied in narrow slots. We pass down a row of round rumps, and Horik has the boy take out one horse after another.

I mutter, "Horik, it's not that far. What, ten, fifteen miles? We could just walk and save the money."

He gives me a horrified look. "We are not arriving at Sunhild's hall on foot."

I shrug, not seeing the point, but Horik only shakes his head and tells the boy to take out another horse.

Eventually, Horik settles on three horses. His is a heavy-bodied gray that he calls disparagingly a "plow horse" but says is the only one big enough for him. Logan gets a tall, lean brown horse with a black mane, and mine is a short, round-bellied speckled thing. "A roan," Horik informs me, appalled, "not speckled."

We lead the horses to the edge of town, where a dirt road leads away into the rocky slopes. My hands are sweaty on the reins, and I eye the saddle with suspicion.

Horik grins deviously. "Let's get you up there."

"I'll help her," Logan says, handing his reins to Horik.

I whisper, "I've never done this before."

Logan grunts in a way that says he's well aware of that.

Logan hooks a hand in my horse's bridle to keep her still. He shows me where to put my hands on the saddle then angles out a stirrup.

When I've made it into the saddle without much trouble, Logan hands me the reins and explains the basic mechanics of riding. It doesn't sound hard.

When Horik and Logan mount their horses and we start down the road, the sudden, unfamiliar motion of the horse makes my stomach flop. I sway and hunch, knowing I look ridiculous.

"We really couldn't have walked?" I shout at Horik's back.

He grins over his shoulder.

"Bastard," I mutter.

"Payback," he says, his grin widening, "for my hair." He runs a hand over the stubble. "My head's cold."

Logan draws his horse alongside mine. "You're doing fine. Just relax. Try to sit up straight."

"What if she takes off?"

Logan eyes my mare's drooping head. "I don't think that's likely."

After a few tense miles, I begin to believe him. In fact, I have to keep shaking the reins to get her to speed up.

"Try squeezing your legs instead."

"But this is what the cart drivers do," I say in confusion.

"Riding is different." When I give him a puzzled look, he insists, "Just trust me on this."

It does seem to work better, but pretty soon my legs are on fire from the unfamiliar exertion.

We leave the main road and take a smaller, narrower one that cuts through steep, rocky hills. Fingers of dirty snow linger in the crevices. To distract myself from the way the saddle is rubbing all the skin off my legs, I ask Logan if he knows what Horik was talking about when he said that the Earthmakers killed so many Drifters.

Green swirls through his eyes. "Earthmakers don't acknowledge it, but, yes, Horik speaks the truth."

"But why? What happened?"

"Belos was Leashing Drifters here, stripping some of power to add to his own, controlling others. You know that's how he first learned to use the Drift, right?" When I nod, Logan goes on, "He came here, found someone willing to teach him. Then he Took his teacher's energy, and that was the first seed of his power. But he wasn't content with that; he was Taking more and more, becoming dangerous. The Earthmakers attacked here, killing the Drifters to keep Belos from Taking them."

"But why didn't the Drifters fight?"

"Oh, they did, but the Earthmakers had surprised them, killed many before they knew what was happening. You have to understand that Rune is not, never has been, well organized. Gruneborg is one of the biggest towns, and you can see it's not a tenth the size of Tornelaine. Mostly, the people live in isolated communities, with a chieftain who rules a few hundred. Heborian tried to unite Rune, but he wasn't very successful. He had to leave Rune, taking with him likeminded people, and start somewhere else. The Runish people are fierce and independent, but they don't work well together." He shrugs. "At least that's what I've been taught about them."

Horik, listening in, comments, "The land itself divides people here. Look at the hard trek we have to reach a chiefdom only twelve miles away."

"Chiefdom?" I say, surprised. "Who is the chieftain?"

"Sunhild, of course."

The sun is near to setting and my hands are stiff with cold by the time we're heading down from the rocky slopes and into greener land. A valley opens before us. Plowed fields and grazing pastures with the first hints of spring grass spread wide from a cluster of perhaps forty buildings. A wall of sharpened pikes encircles the largest structures in the center.

We've barely started down the slope when a woman appears before us, a faint glow of Drift-work fading around her. I shape my spear automatically, and my horse skitters in surprise. Unprepared, I tip precariously in the saddle. I grab at the reins with one hand, yanking them to my chin, but manage to keep my spear steady.

The woman's face is weathered, lined with age and hard living. Faded blue tattoos hook each temple. A thick gray braid hangs down her back. She is dressed in what most consider men's clothing: woolen trousers and a tunic. The deep orange tunic looks to be of fine weave and has a border of red embroidery, but it's thick and shapeless. Her lower legs are wrapped snugly with three-inch wide cloth, as one might wrap a horse's legs. I first saw this curious style in town, but only on the men. The women wore heavy woolen dresses.

Her jewelry speaks of some femininity. A necklace of amber nuggets hangs down her front, and gold bracelets circle her wrists and upper arms over her tunic's long sleeves. In one tattooed hand, she grips a spear faintly glowing with Runish marks. She eyes my spear, looking surprised.

She says something sharp in Runish, probably demanding to know who we are and what we want.

"Hello, Sunhild," Horik greets her in Keldan. "It's been a long time."

Her eyes flash to him, slicing up his body to his face. "Horik Hornirson?"

He inclines his head.

"What are you doing here?" she asks in heavily accented and guttural Keldan.

"I've brought your granddaughter."

Sunhild's eyes latch onto me. They run up the length of my spear and back down, traveling my arm to my shoulder and face. My cheeks warm under her scrutiny. What do I look like to her?

But she seems to dismiss me quickly. Her eyes flick to Logan. "And the Foldsmitha?"

"He is with her, Sunhild." Horik's tone carries an edge of warning.

Her eyes fix on Logan's then widen with surprise.

Logan is as still as stone.

Sunhild announces, "I'll throw another log on the fire," and vanishes back into the Drift.

I stare at Horik. "What does that mean?"

"It's a Runish invitation to dinner."

Chapter 30

Sunhild's house—or hall, as Horik informs me it's called—is a long, rectangular building with wood-planked walls and a roof of thatch banded ornately along the peak. I detect a slight curve to the walls, tapering toward the short ends, and Horik says that in the oldest days Runians lived in overturned boats during the winters, hence a tradition of bowed walls.

The majority of the interior space consists of a huge open room with a massive central hearth. Raised platforms spanning the long walls look to be sleeping space. I'm reminded of Heborian's words: *in Rune, the king lives with his people.*

A dozen tattooed men, dressed similarly to Sunhild, mill about in the hall, speaking Runish too quickly for me to catch more than a word or two. Even without words, however, their glances at me and Logan make it clear they're talking about us. Sunhild's words to them seem to be both sharp and humorous. Horik, leaning over from his stool, quietly explains that these men are her huskarls—retainers—and that they both defend the settlement and represent her in the summer raiding parties organized in Gruneborg.

Sunhild's men apparently do not speak Keldan because when Sunhild turns her attention to us, they quickly lose interest and break away into smaller groups. A few sharpen swords or knives. Others play some kind of board game with colored stones. They all glance at us from time to time.

Sunhild, relaxing in a carved chair on the other side of the crackling fire, nods to my trencher. "You are magr…" She snaps her fingers as she hunts for the Keldan word, then exults when she finds it. "Slender! Like your mothir. Eat, maer, put on muscle."

My eyebrows lift in surprise. I've always considered myself quite a dedicated eater, and this is my second trencher. Then again, Sunhild is a large woman. Not fat, certainly, but tall and strong.

"You also, Foldsmitha," she directs at Logan. "You have had kvilla…uh…" More finger snapping. "Illness? What happened?" She gestures around her own face.

Logan mutters under his breath, "She's very direct, isn't she?"

Sunhild, having heard him, laughs. "Foldsmitha. So shy. Tell me, Horik Hornirson, how fares my sonr? Does he yet find the suthland better than his own? Do you?"

Horik colors slightly at her implications, but he answers steadily. "The Nottmann. Belos," he explains to me under his breath, "makes trouble. We could use your help."

Sunhild waves this away. "Runians do not belong in the suthland, fighting Foldsmitha battles."

"He may come here, as he once did."

Sunhild sniffs loudly at this, either denying the possibility or trying to show that it doesn't worry her.

She jerks her chin at me. "I see some of my sonr in you, but you look more like your mothir. She came here once, do you know this?"

This seems as good a starting point as any. "I know. We've come for the same reason she did. We need to know whatever you can tell us of the Lost Gods."

She scoffs, "You come so far for that?"

"My mother did also. She must have thought it important."

Sunhild's eyes dance, and I begin to suspect that she's toying with me, weighing and judging me. What does she want to see?

I sit back with annoyance. "Perhaps we've come all this way for nothing. Perhaps you're not so knowledgeable as Heborian led me to believe."

A grin spreads across her face, making the lines fanning her eyes deepen. "Ah. There's my blood in you."

I glare at her.

"In Rune," she says, lifting her feet to the hearthstones and crossing her legs at the ankles, "you don't get something for nothing. I want to know about him." She points at Logan. "His…dath…uh, Horik?"

"Energy," Horik supplies.

"Energy! It is not right. What's wrong with him?"

Logan goes very still, though blue and green whip through his eyes.

I shoot Sunhild my most dangerous look. "Leave him alone."

She nods appreciatively. "A Runish woman should be…" She mutters under her breath, looking for the word. "Protecting. Of her man, as he should be protecting of her."

Logan rocks forward on his stool, as though Sunhild is threatening me.

She grins. "That's better."

Logan's eyes burn vivid green. He doesn't like her needling any more than I do.

But Sunhild only resettles herself in her chair and gropes around on the floor for something. "I like you, sonrsdottur, so I will tell you the story I told your mothir. She wanted to know of the world's beginning."

Sunhild lifts a compact six-stringed lute into her lap. She plucks a few strings, which sound with deep tones. The men scattered throughout the hall stop what they're doing and shift in their chairs to listen. Sunhild clears her throat then begins to sing in Runish. Really, it's more like chanting, with a rolling rhythm punctuated by repeated consonant sounds. Though I can't understand much of what she's saying, gooseflesh rises on my arms. The tone is stirring, deep and mysterious, full of both promise and despair.

As the last note fades, she says in Keldan, "That is the world's making."

I rub my arms. "Why is it so dark?"

She smiles approvingly. "Very good ears. Yes, it is dark." She thinks for a moment, perhaps searching for Keldan words. "Creation is destruction, life and death the same. In Rune, we hold this truth dear."

I frown. Creation is destruction? What does that mean? And how can life and death be the same?

Sunhild does not seem inclined to explain. She plucks at the strings of her lute, filling the air with an eerie tone.

She says, "In the beginning, the gods wept for loneliness, and their tears formed the sea." Though her Keldan is starting to flow better, she pauses between each sentence, preparing it. "They plucked the bones from their bodies to build the mountains. They drew hair from their heads to shape the grass and the trees. They blew their breath into the world to make the grass sing and dance. One plucked out his eye and cast it into the sky to burn forever so that they could see their work. Do you understand?"

"They were like the Earthmakers."

She nods with satisfaction. "But they were still lonely. They wanted children, and so they shaped them. Some they shaped from the earth, from water, soil, fire, and air. Others they shaped from within themselves. How to explain? From their own great spirits, their dath. What was that word again, Horik?" She stops strumming the lute.

"Energy."

She strums again, and the eerie notes float around us once more. "Yes, from their energy. Those children of dath honored the gods as the great source of life. But those of the earth thought themselves separate. They cared only for the earth and believed themselves its chieftains. What is another word?" Her eyes light with pride as she finds it. "Its masters. The gods wept. The world was drowning in their tears."

The lute notes drop lower. Sunhild prepares more words.

"Seeing their land all but swallowed, the children of the earth waged war on the gods, and all creation was nearly destroyed. When the children of the earth prevailed, they cast the gods into the ocean and bound them with chains of water and stone."

"What does that mean, 'chains of water and stone'? How did they bind them?"

Sunhild's eyes flick to Logan.

He's leaning down, elbows on his knees, head hanging. When I lay my hand on his back, he flinches.

Sunhild says, "He knows something."

"Logan," I whisper, "are you all right?"

Sunhild plucks a lute string, sending a note drifting through the air. "Ask him what he knows of the Chainmakers."

Logan's body clenches.

Another, higher note. "Are they the ones who did this to him?"

I snap, "Belos did this to him."

Logan stands abruptly, and his stool clatters to the floor. He stalks across the hall. He wrenches open the door and slams it shut behind him.

I am torn between following him, and demanding answers from Sunhild.

Horik voices my own question. "Who are the Chainmakers?"

A low note. "The first children of the earth. I believe the Foldsmitha call them the Ancorites."

Horror melts my face. "Oh, gods."

Horik's eyes jump to me. "What is it?"

I shake my head. I won't divulge Logan's secrets in front of Sunhild.

Sunhild, though, seems already to know. "Your mothir told me of the Ancorites. I had never heard the name, but it wasn't hard to place them from her description." Sunhild hunts for more words. "She said they live on one of the outer islands, isolated from the rest of their people. She said the Foldsmitha knew—or perhaps I should say, *remembered*—nothing of them. She told of a young boy sent to them because he could not control his magic."

I close my eyes.

Horik makes a surprised sound as he puts it together.

I demand, "How did you know Logan was that boy?"

"Your mothir said the boy had strange eyes." She adds something in Runish, phrasing repeated from her earlier song.

Horik translates, "And the gods wept blue and green for the world, and when they looked at the golden eye of the sun, their own eyes caught fire with it."

Horik's eyes roll warily toward me. He doesn't know Gaiana's story, but the parallel is hard to miss.

I push up from my stool. As I stride for the door, I feel Sunhild and Horik's eyes trail me the whole way.

When I step onto the covered stone porch, I'm relieved to find Logan leaning against one of the columns. I was afraid he would have vanished again.

His fists are pressed to the column, his forehead pressed to his fists. Even in the wavering light from the brazier, I can see he's trembling.

When I touch his back, he starts. He didn't even hear my approach.

I can't think of anything to say, so I just wait.

He mutters, "I can't do this, Astarti. I can't, I can't, I can't."

"I know."

"I will *not* go back there."

"No one's asking you to."

"*He* is."

I freeze, chilled by his tone. "What are you talking about?"

He shakes his head as though to clear it, then he presses into his fists again. "I *can't* go back there."

"What did they do to you?" I know some basics, from Bran's story, but a lot is missing.

His eyes squeeze shut. "I think they knew. Not at first, but by the end."

I close my own eyes. "What did they do to you, Logan?"

Fire flares suddenly from the coals of the brazier. Wind whips through the porch, making the brazier teeter and the flames lick at the wooden wall. I rush to steady it before the hall catches fire.

"Logan, stop!"

The wind dies. The flames settle.

He says quietly, as though nothing just happened, "Do you know what bothers me? That no matter how much I try to hate them, I know every day of my life that what they tried to do was right. I should not have run."

I have no idea what he's talking about, but I say firmly, "Whatever they tried to do was *not* right, Logan. Even if all our guessing is correct, even if your father was one of the Lost Gods or the Old Ones, or whatever you want to call them, that doesn't mean there's anything wrong with you."

"But you heard Sunhild. The Lost Gods—the Old Ones—were destroying the world."

"It's a story, Logan. We don't know the facts of what happened then. Besides, they also *made* the world. Do you see how amazing this is?"

"No," he says stiffly. "I don't."

"Can we just go back inside and forget all this for one evening? I want to try the mead. It smelled like honey." I hold my breath, hoping he'll give in.

He turns, putting his back to the column. "Mead is fermented honey. It smelled strong."

"Good," I say. "Come on, it's cold out here." I hold out my hand.

He takes it.

CHAPTER 31

LOGAN

I try to put Astarti at ease by sitting at the hearth with her, but I don't like the way Sunhild keeps watching me with that knowing expression. Even worse is the way Horik's eyes shy away from mine. What happened while I was on the porch?

Astarti tries hard to keep the conversation light, asking about the fermentation process for the mead, asking where the tradition of drinking from a hollowed horn comes from. I manage to pay attention when she's speaking, but when anyone else says anything, my mind drifts again.

While Sunhild was telling her tale, I know I heard his voice inside me, urging me to go to the Ancorites. I *know* it. I mean, why would *I* want that?

I drain my mead horn.

Every time an image threatens to rise through my memory, I dig my fingernails into my sore knee. I try to hide what I'm doing, but Astarti notices. She doesn't try to stop me, but she looks unhappy. Sometimes I wish she would ignore me, would look away from me and toward better things. Other times, I'm terrified she'll do just that.

When Astarti droops tiredly, worn out by her attempts to force the conversation into submission, I suggest we withdraw. I half expect Sunhild to tell us to roll out our blankets here in the common room, but she leads us to a linen curtain that hides the hallway to the private chambers.

Astarti wants to watch over me tonight, but she did it last night. Besides, I can see she's exhausted from the ride here. Horik, though he still won't meet my eyes, insists he doesn't mind. Sunhild listens to our arrangements with embarrassing interest. I hate all this attention. It makes me feel pathetic. But I can't risk hurting anyone, so I'll just have to deal with it.

When Astarti disappears, grumbling, into one of the guest chambers, Horik follows me into the other. A brazier at the foot of the bed offers the only light, but it's enough to reveal a rush-strewn floor, narrow bed, and wooden chair with a lumpy cushion.

I make my way toward the chair. "I'll let you sleep first."

"I promised Astarti I wouldn't fall for that trick."

I sit in the chair. "She doesn't need to know."

"Have *you* ever tried lying to her?"

I grunt. He has a point. It's like she knows you're going to lie before you've even decided to do it. But I don't acknowledge this. "Come on, Horik, you don't really want to babysit me, do you?"

He hooks his thumbs in his belt. He wanders to the brazier, where glowing coals pulse with warmth. Orange light paints the underside of his bearded chin. Finally, he says it.

"Is it true? Are you…you know?"

Even though I expected something like this, my heart gives a nervous thump. I delay the inevitable. "Am I what?"

"Sunhild said the Lost Gods had eyes like yours. I mean, I've heard the story before, but I never took it to be literal. I certainly never thought about it in relation to you."

"It's just a story." I'm not the smooth actor that Astarti is, and I'm sure my stiffness is obvious.

Horik's eyes flick to mine. "I don't believe we came all this way for a story."

I know I owe him some honesty. He and Astarti got me out of the Dry Land. And here he is now. I realize it's more for Astarti than for me, but all the same, he's here.

I take a deep breath. "Even my mother doesn't know for sure, but it's possible that…" I can't finish it.

Horik says wonderingly, "That your father was one. But how? Where?"

I can only make myself speak of this by detaching myself, pretending it's not about me. "I think the story is right, that they were bound in the sea."

"But they're *gods*! How could they be bound?"

"I don't know. It's *your* story."

"But did your mother—"

"She doesn't know. At least, she wasn't specific."

"But these Ancorites—"

Blood roars in my ears, drowning out the rest of Horik's words.

Dioklesus's skeletal hand closes on my wrist. "You must be bound. It is time."

"Logan?"

I jerk when Horik prods me.

He rocks back on his heels, his jaw set. At least he's looking at me now. He sighs, clearly wanting to continue the conversation, but he jerks his chin to motion me out of the chair and into the bed.

I'm tempted to argue, but I just don't have it in me right now. I kick off my boots and lie down on the feather mattress. I'd like to say that I won't sleep tonight, but as soon as I lie down, weariness and the heavy effects of mead drag me into the dark.

ℵ ℵ

I gaze across the vastness of the Drift, the dark canvas pricked with points of light. I wonder: is it coincidence that the Drift looks so much like the star-studded sky?

But then, where is the moon?

And I realize: I *am the moon, huge and powerful, drawing the tides.*

I slide from the Drift into the cold night. Dark fjords rear around me. The narrow bay stretches out like a knife, moonlight glinting on the blade of it.

A son of the Old Ones. Yes, oh yes.

I lift my face to the sky, exultant.

ℵ ℵ

Astarti finds me on the stone steps of Sunhild's porch as night fades in the east. With this valley buried under the horizon, true daylight is still an hour away. Astarti tucks her hands inside her padded leather jacket against the chill. I pull her close to me and rub a hand up and down her arm for warmth. She leans her cheek against my shoulder.

Given her upbringing, I am, as always, amazed by her affection. It seems impossible that someone raised in such a harsh environment could be so tender-hearted. I know very well that such a thing speaks not in the least of weakness but of immense strength. Warmth spreads through my chest. I did not know I could love anyone so much. I press my cheek to her forehead.

She twitches. "You're freezing."

I tug her closer. "I know. I'm stealing your body heat."

She takes my free hand between hers and chafes my stiff fingers. "How long have you been out here?"

"A while."

"Mm-hmm."

The truth, as I'm sure she suspects, is that I've been here for several hours. After I woke from my dream, I could not sleep again, so I gave Horik the bed. His snores, made worse by his still-swollen nose, quickly drove me out of the chamber. There was no chance of me sitting in the common room, not with all the strangers rolled up in their blankets along the walls. So, yes, I've been here a while.

Astarti releases my hand, and I flex my fingers, which sting with returning warmth. She draws my other hand away from her shoulder and works on it.

"Gloves," she mutters, "are made for a reason."

When she's done with that hand, I put my arm around her again. She presses a palm to my thigh, and the heat of her hand tells me she can feel the cold of my leg. She rubs a hand briskly along my thigh. Sometimes I forget her inexperience. She has no idea how arousing that is. My breath hitches in my throat, and I catch her hand. She looks a question at me, but when she sees my eyes, color blooms in her cheeks.

Unable to stop myself, I nuzzle at her neck, driving my body on. She makes a small sound of "oh."

Is it wrong that I want this with her? I have never trusted my mind, never trusted my body, so when everything in me says to kiss her, to touch her, to let my body know hers and let hers know mine, I don't know whether to listen.

Because I'm not sure, I make myself stop. I breathe in the scent of her hair and draw back a fraction.

Her breathing is shallow now, as mine is, but we both slowly relax and mold to each other again. Everything with her feels so right. But should I trust myself? And even if it is right for me, is it right for her? How can I know? How can she know?

I let out a shuddering breath, and she presses hard against me, hugging me to her.

I try to turn my mind to other things. "Are you still sore from riding?"

She groans. "I had no idea what I was getting myself into."

"You did really well, you know. You have excellent balance and you're strong."

"I felt absurd."

She's always so hard on herself. "You didn't look absurd."

I brush a hand over her thick, messy braid. I love her braid because it's just so…her, but I've never seen her hair loose. The tie at the end is already coming undone, so I help it along. The thick ropes slip out of their plaiting and dissolve. I comb through with my fingers. She moans softly, and her head falls back a little.

I work through the tangles until her hair spills free across her back, hanging to her waist. I wish I had daylight to really see it, but the orange glow from the brazier behind us highlights the silky dark flow.

She rolls her neck.

"Is your neck sore?"

"Sometimes the braid is heavy. I should just cut it."

I spread a hand protectively over her hair. "Please don't."

She turns to look at me.

"I mean, it's your hair, but…it's…" I shake my head, at a loss for words at the waste it would be, but it *is* her hair.

She asks uncertainly, "You like it?"

I bury my nose in it. "Oh, yes."

"But it's always such a mess. All the Earthmaker women have such silky, perfect hair."

"Astarti, do not compare yourself to them."

Her eyes drop as though I've just told her that she doesn't hold up in such a comparison. I'm stunned. Doesn't she realize?

I say, almost sharply, "You are the most beautiful woman I've ever known."

"Oh, shut up."

I blink, stunned. She actually doesn't believe me, maybe even thinks I'm teasing her. I wish I had the kind of fine words a woman likes to hear, but all I can say is, "If you think I don't mean that, I will kick your ass down these steps."

She huffs, "I'd like to see you try."

I tilt her chin until she's looking at me. Heat rolls through me.

Her lips part slightly. "I love when your eyes turn gold."

"What?"

"Your eyes. They turn gold when, well, when…you know. You didn't know?"

I've never been told this before. But then, I've never felt like this before. I draw her against me. "I think that's just for you."

Her arm slips under my jacket, around my waist.

My mind stays quiet for a while, content with her, until the sun peeks over the horizon. I want the peace to last, I want everything else to just go away, but my thoughts eventually stumble into the dark once more.

Astarti, sensitive to my moods, asks, "What is it?

I make myself say it. "I know you said the Leash was cut, but…he's in my head. He's in *here*." I scrape down my sternum, where I feel a constant pressure, a constant wrongness. "I know it."

She sighs.

"Last night I dreamed I was him, standing in the bay at Gruneborg. I—*he*—was excited by what we learned last night. That wasn't *me*."

"Oh, Logan."

It hurts that she doesn't believe me. I understand that it sounds crazy, but it still hurts.

Because I don't know how better to say it, I simply insist, "Astarti, he *is*."

"But, Logan, what you're describing could easily be what you yourself were feeling. This is big, confusing, overwhelming. Your mind is trying to sort through it, and it's all mixed up with the things you went through."

I shake my head, frustrated. I know what I feel.

"Logan."

She tips my face toward hers. I meet her eyes reluctantly.

"I know you think I'm dismissing what you're saying"—She is, isn't she?—"but I just don't like seeing you torment yourself like this. Do you know, I still have moments of panic when I think I'm Leashed? Sometimes I wake up in the middle of the night, unable to breathe, because I think Belos is coming for me."

I pull her close to me again, as though I can shield her from that. She tugs me against her in answer, as though she would do the same for me. For a few more minutes, everything fades away.

When Sunhild comes onto the porch, stretching and cracking her spine, I tense. I don't have any particular reason to distrust Sunhild, but I don't like the way she looks at me, like she knows something. She's doing it now, her eyes sliding to me even as she addresses Astarti.

"Day breaks, sonrsdottur. Come, walk the fences with me."

Astarti's brow furrows. "Walk the fences?"

Sunhild's mouth twitches. "Do you know nothing of keeping land?"

Astarti colors, and I glare at Sunhild for making her feel ignorant. I explain, "She wants you to walk along the fences with her and make sure they're secure." I shoot Sunhild another glare. "Lowly work for a chieftain, isn't it?"

Sunhild shakes her head, laughing. "Foldsmitha."

Astarti shrugs. When we both rise, Sunhild raises a staying hand. All the mirth is gone from her voice when she says, "Only my sonrsdottur."

I bristle, but Astarti squeezes my hand and follows Sunhild down the porch steps.

Chapter 32

My breath plumes in the chilly air. Though the sun shows above the horizon, shadow lingers in this part of the valley. I keep my hands in my pockets to preserve warmth as I walk beside Sunhild along a length of wattle fence. The fence, unsurprisingly, looks fine.

"Do you want to tell me why we couldn't speak in the hall?"

Sunhild darts a look at me, her surprise quickly giving way to approval. "Was I so obvious, or are you so perceptive?"

"A bit of both perhaps. Your Keldan is getting better."

"I have been out of practice with the speaking of it, but it returns."

"Why did you learn it anyway? You seem disdainful of the south, yet you must have traveled there extensively to learn the language."

"My fathir was a great…" She considers possible words and settles on, "traveler—"

"I'm guessing you mean raider." I give her a wry look, and her mouth crooks.

"My fathir was most interested in the suthland, and when he would *travel* to Kelda with his huskarls and my brothir, Wulfstan, I would sometimes join them. In Rune, it is uncommon but not unacceptable for a woman to do this." When Sunhild notices my scowl, she says, "What is it?"

"I do not like your brother."

Sunhild's eyes dance with either mischief or delight. "He speaks his mind."

Several retorts bubble up inside me, but I hate acknowledging how much Wulfstan bothers me, so I clamp my mouth shut.

Sunhild continues, "My sonr grew up hearing tales of the wealth and power in the suthland. I suppose it was inevitable that he would seek those things. Runians can be…covetous."

"His name, Heborian. It doesn't sound Runish to me."

"It is an ancient name, older than the tongue of Rune. I named him for one of the Lost Gods, one who died a glorious death in the battle with his children."

While I find this a rather disturbing approach to naming a child, I have a more pressing concern. "My mother believed that the Lost Gods and Old Ones were one and the same. Do you share that belief?"

Sunhild sniffs. "The Foldsmitha get many things wrong in their tellings, but, yes, I believe this must be true."

"They might say that you get some things wrong."

Sunhild huffs. "And yet here you are, putting your questions to me, not to them."

"They don't seem to remember their history as well."

"And yet, they live long. Why should they not remember?" Sunhild makes a cutting gesture with her hand. "They do not want to."

"Perhaps."

Sunhild scoffs, "It is a certainty. They speak the same tongue as Kelda. Why is that?"

My eyebrows jump. "I don't know."

"I will tell you this. On one traveling to Kelda, I saw a…weaving? Big. Stretched across a wall?"

"A tapestry."

"Ah, yes. I saw a tapestry, faded and frayed, very old, in an old, old house. The landscape in this tapestry was what I could see out the window. It was Kelda. But the figures were using earthmagic to work the land. The Foldsmitha, you see, lived in Kelda in the days before they took themselves away to their moving islands. Why else do Keldans fear Drifters? Because Keldans are descendants of the Foldsmitha, though they have lost their connection to the elements."

"You certainly have a lot of theories."

Sunhild stops and leans against the wattle fence, which creaks with her weight. "I am coming to another theory, but right now it is only a question."

I raise my eyes over her shoulder, looking instead at the shorn ewes and their lambs browsing for new grass on the other side of the fence. "Why do I have the feeling I won't like this?"

"Your Foldsmitha. What is wrong with him?"

My eyes jerk to Sunhild, whose mouth is set in a grim line. "There's nothing wrong with him."

"Have you seen his dath?" She snaps her fingers, looking for that word again. "His energy?"

"Yes," I answer warily.

She crosses her arms, getting to the point at last. "Have you observed it while he sleeps?"

My brow furrows. "No. Have you?"

"Last night I did." When I shoot her a warning look, she says, "I have a right to know who sleeps in my hall."

"It's still rude."

She shrugs. "Do you want to know what I saw or not?"

Unfortunately, I do want to know.

"There's something wrong. Here." She taps her breastbone. "His dath was much too tight. This can happen, yes. But. As he was dreaming, a blackness…uh…*unfurled* inside him, bleeding out from that tight center place. I have never seen such a thing. Now tell me, sonrsdottur: what is wrong with him?"

Her description makes gooseflesh rise all over my body. "Are you sure?"

She ignores the question. "You served the Nottmann. Have you ever seen this?"

Something tugs uncomfortably in my memory, but I can't dredge up any specifics. It is a feeling, no more. I shake my head.

Sunhild warns, "Do not ignore the truth."

"And what *is* the truth?"

Sunhild blows out her cheeks. "I do not know."

"If you don't know, and I don't know, why, then, are you implying that I'm ignoring it?"

Sunhild flicks this away with a finger and moves on to another line of thought. "Even here we heard news of the battle in Kelda, where the Nottmann used a Foldsmitha to crack the wall. The Nottmann had possessed him with his will?"

I cross my arms. I don't like the direction she's taking. "He was Leashed then."

"But he is not now?"

"Of course not. You would have seen it from the Drift. You know that."

"Hmm."

"What?"

Sunhild pushes away from the fence. "It is not the Leash that possesses, but the will." She turns away from me, continuing on down the fence line.

"What is that supposed to mean?" I call after her angrily, but her head is bowed in thought, dismissing me.

CHAPTER 33

LOGAN

When Astarti returns from her walk with Sunhild, her scowl warns me against asking questions. I'm not keen on sitting in tense silence, so I suggest we make use of Sunhild's training yard. She latches onto this suggestion with an enthusiasm that makes me think I'll need a shield more than my sword.

The training yard is little more than a muddy stretch of fenced in ground attached to the back of the hall, but at least it's larger and more stable than a ship deck. Horik, joining us, inspects the weapons rack bolted to the wall. Considering he needs no physical weapon, I suspect his interest in the weapons rack is more about avoiding Astarti's scowl. I keep my own eyes lowered as I set about stretching muscles grown stiff with disuse and injury.

With each of us favoring different weapons, we're forced to be creative in our sparring. Unfortunately for me, wielding a sword against a spear or an axe means I need to be quick, and my left knee is so stiff and weak that I find it buckling again and again. My right shoulder, not yet healed from my night in the taverns of Tornelaine, makes me doubly slow and clumsy.

When Horik knocks my feet out from under me, I hit the ground hard. The air is shocked from my lungs, and in that moment of suffocation, my mind slips.

Is it true, do you think, that they are bound under the sea?

The voice is *his*. I see a wavering image of rocky slopes highlighted by drifts of melting snow, and the far off sheet of the ocean.

Someone calls my name. I roll onto my side, choking for air. When I can breathe again, I stagger to my feet.

Astarti comes to my side, brow furrowed, all her earlier annoyance gone. "Your face is white as death. Maybe you should sit down."

Horik says, "I'm sorry. I should've been more careful."

I look at them stupidly until I realize they're talking about my fall. I step away from them both, embarrassed, frustrated, and confused. Already the vision is fading. "I don't need either of you to coddle me." I correct my grip on my sword. "Again."

Horik and I resume sparring, though he is now overly careful, like I'm some green youth who doesn't know his way around a sword. It annoys me, so I push my body to move faster, strike harder. My left leg is trembling with fatigue, the knee screaming protest, but I ignore it.

I am in the middle of an upward slash when his voice whispers inside me again. *How are they bound? I must know!*

My swing falters. When Horik's axe catches my sword, the blade spins from my hand. Horik, about to throw his shoulder into me to knock me back, checks himself. He stumbles to a halt, red-faced.

"Logan! If you can't stay focused, I won't spar with you! I'll cut you in half!"

Astarti looks concerned. "What's the matter?"

I must know!

I squeeze my eyes shut. I feel like I'm floating, not quite attached to my surroundings. Am I going mad?

When Astarti touches my arm, I jolt.

I don't like how her eyes are searching my face, like she's worried I might be crazy, like she's suspicious of something. I don't like Horik's uncomfortable silence. I turn toward the gate. "I'm going for a walk."

Astarti says, "Do you want me to—"

"*No.*"

As I make a circuit of the fields, my head starts to clear. I can almost convince myself that I imagined his voice. It's so much easier to dismiss nightmares in the daylight.

Farmers stride along their freshly plowed furrows, scattering seed from huge canvas bags. It's almost strange to see such ordinary activity. With all that's been happening, it's easy to forget that people are still living their normal lives, tending to all those tasks that make up a day, a season, a life.

Moisture seeps through my boots from the dewy grass, but I don't mind. Anything is better than the awful dryness of *his* place. I close my mind. I won't think about any of that.

I reach an orchard, where apple blossoms are still folded inside their grayish-green buds, waiting out the lingering cold of a northern spring. My knee is throbbing badly enough that I sit under a tree to rest. Sunlight sparks through the branches into my face, dazzling and blinding. Is it true, I wonder, that the sun is the eye of a god?

Is it true that he is the son of a god? I'm standing on a rocky outcropping, looking down into the valley. I gaze at the distant buildings then across the fields to the apple orchard.

The Earthmaker, says Straton. *He suspects. We must do it soon.*

I look over my shoulder at him and the others, their dark robes still marked with traces of dust from the rubble. I seethe.

Once I've finished with the Earthmaker, I will destroy him for what he did to my fortress. I address all of my Seven, who are my children, my servants, my own self. *We can't risk Astarti's interference. We'll stay close and wait for the right opportunity.*

I crack the back of my head against the tree trunk to clear it. My heart pounds in my throat, choking me. The hair all over my body is standing on end. I stumble out of the orchard to scan the surrounding slopes. I see nothing but rock, snow, and trees. But he's there. I know he's there.

I break into a run. I have to tell them. I am still Leashed. Panic closes my throat. My feet are too slow. I dissolve into the wind.

When I burst through the training yard gate, making it crash against the fence, Astarti and Horik leap apart, their weapons whipping in my direction. I gather myself from the wind and stumble to the muddy earth.

Sunhild, watching from the edge of the field, shouts in surprise at my sudden appearance, but Astarti and Horik run to meet me.

"He's here! I saw him, in the hills, watching us!"

Astarti's grabs my sleeve. "What are you talking about?"

"Astarti, I *saw* him. No, I mean, I saw the valley *through his eyes*." When she freezes with disbelief, I barely keep myself from shouting. "Listen to me! I know it sounds crazy, but I know what I saw; I know what I heard. He wants to know how the Old Ones are bound. He plans to use me somehow. I'm telling you! I'm still Leashed to him!"

She closes her eyes. When I grab her shoulders, she stiffens. I force my grip to ease, but I don't let go. She *has* to believe me. "He's here, Astarti. In Rune. He said they had to stay close and wait for an opportunity. Astarti, he—I think he means to take me again."

Sunhild appears beside us, her gray eyebrows angled sharply. "What's going on?"

"I can hear Belos. In my head." Even as I say it, I feel my face flush. I know it sounds crazy.

Horik says carefully, "I don't see how that's possible. Heborian cut the Leash."

Sunhild wheels on him. "Are you all fools?"

Astarti raises her hands in a let's-be-reasonable gesture. "Sunhild, I know what you're thinking, but it doesn't make sense. Without the Leash, there is no conduit for the will."

Sunhild challenges, "And you understand dath so well that you are certain of this?" She flicks her wrist dismissively. "If the Nottmann is in Rune, we must know."

"Of course," Astarti answers tightly. "But—"

"He *is* here!" I shout. Why won't they just believe me?

Astarti raises her hands in a placating gesture. "I must be certain before I draw any conclusions. There's too much at stake."

Sunhild says sharply, "And how will you be certain?"

"I'll see if I can spot Belos in Rune."

Fear spikes through me. "No! Astarti, no!"

Astarti says calmly, "I can hide myself so he won't see me."

"But—"

"If he's here, he already knows where we are."

"Astarti—"

"I'll be safe. I'll be back." A faint glow surrounds her. I lunge for her, but she vanishes into the Drift.

ꕥ

The rest of the day is a blur. Horik and Sunhild both repeatedly refuse my demands that they find Astarti, insisting that her concealment of her energy will make it impossible to locate her.

At some point, I find myself sitting by the hearth, though I don't have a clear recollection of how I got here. Even though Horik and Sunhild both look comfortable, I find myself pulling at the neck of my tunic, overheated.

She's looking for us.

I bolt up from my stool.

"What is it?"

I look over to see Theron shift in agitation. Soft-hearted fool. I should never have allowed him time with her when she was a child.

"Logan?"

I hear myself say, "We'll wait a while yet."

"Wait for what?" Theron's form wavers, and Horik's overtakes it. Horik's hand curls as though around his axe haft.

I shake my head to clear it.

Sunhild has backed away. Her retainers are on their feet, ringing me.

I scrub at my sweaty face. It's so hot in here, and yet, I'm shivering.

When I drop to my stool, Sunhild motions her retainers away. She touches my forehead with cool, dry fingers. "You're feverish."

I pull away from her hand.

"Maybe you should lie down."

Where is she?

This time, I don't even know who is speaking.

CHAPTER 34

By late afternoon, I've covered the most populated areas along the coast. In Gruneborg, I spotted a handful of Drifters but found no sign of Belos or the Seven. There's a lot of interior space I haven't inspected, but I can't cover the whole country. If Belos is here, he's not near Sunhild's.

For a terrifying moment, in the face of Logan's claims and Sunhild's speculation, I considered the possibility that Logan might, indeed, still be tied to Belos in some way. Though almost everything can be explained as his confusion, I've never quite rid myself of the image of his eyes, threaded with black, when Horik and I woke him from his nightmare on the ship that night.

That image, coupled with Sunhild's insistence that it is the will that possesses, not the Leash, makes something scratch at the edge of my thoughts, a vague, displaced memory of something Heborian said. I will the nagging thought to recede. Right now, I just want to get back to Logan.

I spot him with Sunhild and Horik at the central hearth of Sunhild's hall. She has no barrier, so I slide from the Drift inside the door. Several of Sunhild's men shout and grab for weapons before they see it's me.

Sunhild calls out, "That is considered very rude in Rune."

"Sorry."

Logan is striding toward me, the tension in his body and the worry in his expression telling me what I've put him through. He pulls me roughly into his arms. He's trembling, and I can feel the heat of his body even through his leather jacket.

"I told you I'd be safe."

He eases his grip and leans back a little. "He wasn't there?"

"No."

I watch the color swirl through his eyes before he closes them in shame and defeat. I have just convinced him that he's mad. Like everyone else in his life, I've shown him not to trust himself. My heart sinks. In truth, that nagging thought is nudging me with warning, telling me I'm missing something. Maybe I should admit this to Logan, but I don't want to get him worked up again. Everything can be sorted out soon enough when we have more information. Besides, something more immediate is wrong. He's flushed, his face sheened with sweat. I push damp hair off his forehead.

"You're burning up!"

He pulls my hands away. "I'm fine. I was just worried about you."

"Logan, you're feverish."

Sunhild approaches. "That's what I said."

"How long has he been this way?"

"It's been getting worse all day."

"Is it something you ate?"

Sunhild crushes this hope. "He hasn't eaten. He's refused everything."

I press my hand to his face again, wincing at the heat of his skin. "You're getting in bed, right now."

Sunhild presses a vial into my hand. She leans close to my ear, whispering, "I've been trying to get this into his mead for the past hour. He's putting me on edge." She shrugs at my disapproving look. "Just to make him sleep."

Frowning, I tuck the vial into my pocket and lead Logan to the bedchamber.

"Gods!" I exclaim as I help him out of his jacket and see his sweat-soaked shirt. His fingers tremble on the lacing, so I untie it for him. He leans down so I can grab the hem and pull the shirt over his head. When the cool air hits his skin, his muscles tighten with shivering.

While he kicks off his boots, I go to the side table and prepare a damp cloth. Once he's lying down, I run the cloth down his flushed face and throat, across his sweaty chest and torso. I suppress an edge of panic. Why is he sick? His eyes are half-closed because he's exhausted and ill, but he watches everything I do.

He says, "I guess you were right."

My heart lurches with instinctive denial. "Nothing's been proven. Don't worry about this right now. You need to rest. We'll talk about it in the morning."

He looks like he's about to say something more. I lay my hand on his chest, and he stills. Touch works so well with him.

I hope he'll fall asleep on his own, but he seems to have relaxed as far as he's going to. Even though his eyes are partially closed, I can see he's thinking. When I go to the side table for the water cup, he sits up, restless.

I fill the cup and add the contents of the vial. My fingers tighten around the cup, debating, then I bite my lip, angry with myself. I can't drug him without his knowledge.

"This will help you sleep."

He hesitates, not liking this, but his eyes flick to mine, trusting me. He takes the cup.

He's asleep within a few minutes.

I freshen the cloth and press it to his forehead again. It's probably wrong in some way, but I love watching him sleep. I study the planes of his face, the strong column of his throat, the cut of his muscular shoulders above the line of the sheet.

A slight scuffing sound in the doorway makes me jerk my hand away. Sunhild leans into the room.

"How long have you been standing there?" Embarrassment sharpens my voice.

"You love him. Does he know?"

My throat closes at her words. She can see it and say it so easily. Why do those same words stick in my throat every time I try to speak them? I've never told Logan I love him. *Does* he know?

Perhaps because my uncertainty shows on my face, she adds, with either exasperation or mockery, "Please tell me you realize he loves you."

On some level, I know that he does. But part of me still yearns to hear it. It seems silly that we should need those words when our hearts speak the truth better than our lips. But we do need them—perhaps because we are creatures of doubt and fear.

Suddenly, the need to know that Logan realizes I love him gnaws at me. I want to say it, to see his eyes when he hears the words, to see the knowledge of it settle into him. And to see if he returns it to me.

I huff at myself. Of course I think this now, right after I drugged him. In the morning, I promise myself. I will tell him in the morning.

Sunhild, shaking her head, walks away.

When my back gets sore from hunching on the mattress edge, I move to the chair. The stillness makes my mind skim through everything. I must speak with Heborian. I had planned to wait until morning, when I could talk to Logan about it and hopefully convince him to let me take him through the Drift, but I don't know if I can sit here through the night, waiting. If I leave now, I can be back long before Logan wakes. I will have some answers for him, or at least better guesses. Wouldn't that be best?

I freshen the cloth once more and press it to Logan's face. He's still burning up. No, I decide, I can't leave him.

When Horik comes to the door, I stand from the chair, anxious for change.

"How is he?" Horik inquires.

"Resting but ill. What happened? He wasn't like this when I left."

"He's been agitated all day. He wanted me or Sunhild to go find you, but we told him we wouldn't be able to find you if you had concealed yourself. Later, when we were in the hall, he seemed confused, like he wasn't sure where he was or who I was. Then he looked at me"—Horik cuts off, shifting his feet uncertainly—"and I thought, for just a second, that his eyes were black."

My hands start shaking. No. Oh, no.

I say, not even realizing I've changed my mind about waiting, "Horik, I'm going to Tornelaine to speak with Heborian. I won't be long. You'll watch him?"

Horik's eyebrows draw together. "What's going on?"

I haven't even put my question into words yet, much less my guesses at the answer. "I'll know more when I get back. Please don't leave him."

"You know I won't."

I manage a half-smile. "What did I do to deserve a friend like you?"

He comes to me and leans down, pressing his lips to my forehead.

"I was a young man, but I remember you as a baby. When Sibyl would let me hold you, she would laugh and say I looked like a bear holding a kitten. But I didn't mind." He pauses, gathers his thoughts. "When Belos took you, I knew I'd failed somehow. For not seeing what the king had done, for arriving too late to even fight. It was like losing my young sister all over again. I could not protect her either because I was too slow, too late. I will not be so again."

I am struck dumb by this, wondering: do we all spend our whole lives trying to set right the wrongs we think we've done?

"None of it was your fault, Horik."

"And what did I do to deserve your forgiveness?"

I take one of his big hands in both of mine. "You've never needed it."

His fingers curl briefly around mine then release. "I will keep watch."

Chapter 35

I reach Tornelaine to find Heborian, several of his Drifters, and a crew of what I'm guessing are builders on the city wall.

When I step out of the Drift onto the wall—a prudent ten feet from anyone—Drift-weapons flash into hands, and men stumble back, yelling.

Heborian, unruffled, gives the men a pointed look. "And that, gentlemen, proves my point."

I don't ask what's going on. Heborian's doings are not my concern right now. "I need to speak with you. Privately. Now."

His eyebrows lift at my demanding tone, but he points eastward to the bluffs beyond Tornelaine's harbor. I slide into the Drift and follow his lighted form.

We step from the Drift onto the crest of a high bluff, where the soil has been all but swept away by the wind, scouring the earth down to its rocky bones. A few clusters of spiky grass cling in the divots. The setting sun blazes gold across the sea in the west, catching on a distant mound that might be the Floating Lands.

"Well?" Heborian prompts. "What did you learn of the story?"

I seethe at the way he's turning this into a questioning of me, but I know it's more expedient to answer than argue. "According to Sunhild's telling, it was the Earthmakers who bound the gods. More specifically, the Ancorites did it. Have you heard of them?"

"Sibyl mentioned them. She said they live in a tower on one of the outer islands. She said no one knew much about them, but that a young boy—" His eyes close briefly. "Ah. Logan. So my mother thinks the Ancorites, those very Ancorites living now in the Floating Lands, bound the gods? Surely, if this story is true, they are all dead by now, Ancorites and gods alike."

"No. They are not."

Heborian's eyes narrow at my certainty.

I hesitate, but there's really no point in concealing it. "Logan's father is one of them. At least, it's highly likely. His mother passed into their prison, though she does not know how."

Heborian looks stunned, an expression I have never seen on him before. I'm surprised to find that I don't like it. I prefer him certain of everything.

"But this isn't what I came here to talk to you about." I take a deep breath, bracing myself. "I need you to tell me again about the making of barriers."

He's silent a moment, his eyes showing me he's still thinking about the last topic. When his hearing catches up with his thoughts, he says in surprise, "Why?"

"You Leash someone. And then?"

He tries to stare me into explaining my question, but I only motion for him to speak.

He grunts irritably. "You Take their energy and weave it, just like the lock on the box when we practiced getting to the knife."

"But it's not just the energy of another. You use your own as well."

"It's a dangerous process, but it's necessary if you want to stay in contact with your barrier and know that it's secure."

My heart thumps. "But there's no Leash connecting you to your barrier. I would have seen it."

"You sever the energy from yourself, but it is *your* energy. It gives credence to the idea of the soul, doesn't it? How else could I still be connected with energy I have divided from myself? It should die away, like a severed limb, but it does not. Astarti? What is it?"

The world is spinning. Heborian catches me when I sway. He eases me to the ground and crouches at my side.

He says in a low, demanding voice, "Explain."

I say weakly, "The Leash is a conduit only."

"Yes." He draws out the word, asking me what my point is.

"You have used it to transfer your energy, your will, then you have severed it from yourself, but you are still aware of it." He waits for me to finish. "Could you not do that to a living person?"

Slowly, color drains from his face.

I scrape back my hair. All those times Logan tried to tell me, all those signs I didn't want to see.

Heborian says grimly, "If you're implying what I think you're implying, he needs to be secured. Avydos would be the best place."

I ignore the implications of that. "If you wanted to withdraw your energy from your barrier, could you do it?"

"I don't know. There's no living person, no body with which to make a connection. There's no conduit."

Sudden hope, all out of proportion to reality, flares within me. "But if there *were* a conduit, if there *were* a Shackle connecting you, you could take your energy back. Right?" When he doesn't answer, I say again, "*Right?*"

"In theory. But are you suggesting that Logan be Shackled to Belos?"

"That's exactly what I'm suggesting."

He looks skeptical. "Even if you could somehow pull off this miracle of getting the Shackle on both Logan and Belos, how would you get Belos to draw out his energy?"

"Why should that be necessary? If you can cut out your own energy and cast it off through the Shackle, could you not do the same with foreign energy?"

Heborian frowns thoughtfully. "I suppose. But if Belos is possessing Logan, how will Logan have the presence of mind to do that? How will he even know *what* to do?"

"He can do it," I insist. "Even when Belos was exerting enormous force over him, Logan fought him off several times. He can do it again."

"This is a foolish plan. You'd be endangering Logan and yourself. And putting a Shackle into Belos's hands."

"I don't think Logan can be in much more danger than he's already in."

Heborian falls silent, thinking. Then, "If Belos has been capable to possessing Logan all this time, why hasn't he yet done it? Logan was in my castle, yet he never sought the knife. He was in Avydos, yet never caused harm. What does Belos want him for?"

I mull this over. Several of Logan's comments float up through my memory.

He was excited by what we learned. That wasn't me.

He wants to know how the Old Ones are bound.

My blood chills. "Belos has been using his connection to Logan to spy on us, to learn about Logan's parentage."

"Why? What interest would he have in gods that haven't been seen since the beginning of time?"

He wants to know how they are bound.

I say with numb realization, "He wants to free them."

"But why?"

The question doesn't penetrate. I have other concerns. I have to get back to Logan. When I push suddenly to my feet, Heborian scrambles up, looking twitchy. I've never seen him on edge like this. But, then, I'm shaking too. I think furiously. Should I ask, or should I wait until Heborian thinks I'm gone, then steal it?

"What?" His tone is wary.

"I need your Shackle."

"Astarti—"

"I will get to it, if I have to tear down your whole castle. Can you not have faith in me this once?"

"Do you want it to fall into Belos's hands?"

"As you said once, there are other Shackles. He could already have one in his possession. If he doesn't now, he will someday."

He says tightly, "You take such risks."

"Are you going to give it to me, or am I going to steal it?"

"What if *I* need it?"

"Why on earth would you need it? Unless you want to—" I break off. "That's what you were doing on the wall. You're planning to make a new barrier."

Heborian gazes in the direction of Tornelaine. "We were discussing it. Nothing has been decided."

"Give me the Shackle."

He hesitates. "You must bring it back."

"You know I can't promise that."

"You would rob me of my last resort?"

"Don't be a fool, Heborian. That wouldn't stop Belos anyway."

"No," he admits. "Some days I wonder: what will?"

ꕥ ꕥ

I skim north to Rune with the Shackle blazing white in my hand. I almost gagged when Heborian handed it to me. How can I make Logan wear this thing again?

As I near Sunhild's hall, fear pricks at me. It should be peaceful there, with all Sunhild's men at the hearth, with Horik watching over Logan in the bedchamber. But people are moving about in agitation, Horik is arguing with Sunhild, and I can't spot Logan anywhere.

I slide out of the Drift into the central room of the hall. Several men shout, but I ignore them.

"Horik!"

He spins.

As I run toward him, something overhead catches my eye. The stars. I stumble to a halt and stare at the huge hole in the thatching of Sunhild's roof. Even one of the heavy beams has been torn away.

I wheel on Horik as he reaches my side.

"Where's Logan?"

"I *tried* to stop him."

"*What happened*?"

"He was sleeping. He started having a nightmare, and I couldn't wake him up. All of a sudden, he jumps up, yelling like crazy. He staggers out the door and into the hall. He keeps shaking his head. I didn't know what to do! When the wind started howling, I tried to wrestle him down, but he just vanished! He blew that hole in the roof and was gone."

This is not happening, *not* happening. "You didn't see Belos?"

Horik shakes his head, and yet, I'm not comforted. If Belos has been spying through Logan, he would know every move we're making. He would know just when to hide himself.

"Astarti, I'm sorry. I couldn't stop him. I don't know where's he's gone."

I swallow a horrible taste. "I do."

CHAPTER 36

As I relay what I learned from Heborian, put together with what Logan himself has said, Horik's expression goes from disbelieving to grim to horrified.

He concludes for me, "So you think he's gone to the Ancorites to find out how the gods are bound. Because Belos wants to know."

Chilled by this blunt summation, I cross my arms. The Shackle swings in my grip. It startles me, and I drop it like a snake. I bend down, shamefaced, to pick it up.

Horik eyes it skeptically. "You think that will work?"

"Do you have any better ideas?"

Sunhild, who has been staring despondently at her roof and surreptitiously listening to our conversation, asks, "What will you do now?"

"I have to find Logan."

"We," Horik corrects.

I give him a grateful look. I don't really want to storm the tower of some ancient, creepy Earthmakers all by myself.

Horik says, "But do we know where the Ancorites are? I mean, precisely? And how will we get there anyway? It would take too long to sail, we have no one to take us through the Current, and we cannot drift into Avydos."

"We can't drift *into* it, no."

Horik's eyebrows contract with suspicion. "What are you thinking?"

ꕤ ꕤ

The Drift begins to repel us as we near Avydos. The effect is similar to that of a barrier, but where a barrier is a complex weaving of threads that encircles something, this is more of a steady glow that suffuses the whole archipelago. We get as close as we can, then I look at Horik to see if he's ready. He nods.

I always step from the Drift onto firm ground, so the drop makes my stomach flip. Cold water closes over my head. I kick and wiggle until I break the surface. Horik bursts up beside me, spraying water.

I can't see his expression in the thin moonlight, but I can guess why he's staring. I've barely got my head above water. The truth is, I don't swim well. Growing up in the Dry Land didn't exactly offer a lot of opportunities to learn. But it doesn't matter. I will make it because I have to.

"I'm fine! Just swim!"

Horik kicks ahead, pulling his huge body with strong, sure strokes. I kick along awkwardly behind.

I haven't gotten ten yards before the cold is numbing my limbs. Of course, it doesn't help that I've already expended so much energy traveling the Drift today.

Horik calls my name.

"I'm…fine!"

I kick along, my feet heavy and clumsy in my boots. I wish I could take them off, but I can't stop now.

Panic washes at me as the water laps around my face.

Kick, push, wriggle. Kick, push!

The Shackle in my hand is another impediment, making my strokes halting and uneven.

I lag from exhaustion and cold. I haven't even passed through the arms of the bay. It's too far, much too far.

No! Kick, wriggle, kick, pull, kick.

Cold drags at me.

I suck hard for air, and water shoots up my nose. I cough and hack and kick on a little farther.

Horik is bobbing in the water, looking back. I try to shout at him to go on, but I can't work up any sound.

I cannot make it.

I will drown here, the Shackle in my hand and Logan beyond my reach.

My limbs grow heavy and useless.

I keep kicking—at least I think I do—but I don't seem to be getting anywhere.

Water closes over my head. I flail for the surface, gasping for air before I'm sinking again.

Cold.

Dark.

Nothingness.

I strain for the surface.

I strain for the Drift.

The faintest throb.

The energy, though, is rhythmic, tidal.

Elemental.

Desperate need seizes me. I ease myself into the rhythm as I would the Drift. I meld with it, let it fill me, let it *be* me.

For a moment, the great force of it tempts me to let go of everything, to lose myself completely in something that has no mind, no goal, only the endless need to answer the moon's pull.

But I am not the sea. I am myself, and I have somewhere to be and someone to find.

I surge toward the harbor, rolling and spilling over myself. I toss the boats into one another and crash against the docks, driving them against the stone wall of the harbor road. I rear up and spill across the road.

I stand, shaking, as water crashes away from me, washing against the nearest buildings before rushing back to the bay.

I hear a hacking cough and spin to see Horik flop onto his back on one of the docks. I run toward him on wobbly legs. He turns onto his side and vomits water. I drop beside him.

"Horik?" I touch his back and feel the explosive force of his coughing. It subsides at last, and he pushes to his hands and knees.

He rasps, "You might have warned me! I was coming back for you when"—more hacking—"what *was* that?"

"I panicked. Are you all right?"

He pushes to his feet and braces his hands on his knees. "The two of you! Enough!"

"I don't swim well," I say apologetically.

"A fine time to tell me that!"

I wring out my braid, and water splatters the dock. "I knew you'd say no to the plan."

"You bet your ass I would've said no!"

"This was expedient. Look, we're here, right?"

"Gods!" he swears. "You and Logan both, turning the world on its head. A man can hardly keep his feet!"

I've known for a while that Logan and I make similar use of the elements, but it comes home to me with Horik's words. So does another truth: As my mother believed, the Drift *is* the fifth element. It's all one magic. When I draw on the four earth elements, I must meld with them to use them, and that means I must draw on—reshape—my own energy, as Heborian said. The physical body is made up of the four elements, and that is the source of that connection. As for the fifth element, the energy of the Drift, it's found in that indefinable part of us that makes up our most essential selves. Is it the soul, as some believe?

The sounds of running and shouting jar me back into my cold and dripping wet reality. Horik extends his right hand automatically then grunts when he can't shape his Drift-axe.

Four Wardens thunder down the dock.

I raise my hands to show I won't fight and elbow Horik to do the same. "We need to see the Arcon!"

With four swords leveled at us and four sets of eyes rolling warily in our direction, Horik and I are led through the dark, quiet streets of Avydos. I don't know these men, and I can hardly blame them for their caution. I doubt anyone has ever entered Avydos in the manner Horik and I just did.

Two door guards stiffen at our entrance into the House. I still can't decide whether I'm glad to see the Earthmakers realizing that Avydos might not be as secure as they've let themselves think or sad to see that even here safety is not guaranteed.

Our boots squelch across the gray and white stone floor, leaving a watery trail as our guards escort us to Aron's study. Either they have figured out who I am or else I don't look threatening—I sniff irritably at that idea—because most of their attention has settled on Horik. He, however, seems less concerned with them than with his surroundings.

He mutters, "It's nothing like I imagined."

"How so?"

His eyes rove across a young woman, a servant by her bracelets, who freezes as we pass by. She's wearing the filmy robes so common here. The light from brass braziers and bracketed sconces reveals much of her figure through the robes. Ah, I see. I had forgotten that the only Earthmakers Horik has seen are Wardens.

"Your mouth's open, Horik."

He snaps it shut.

Yes, she was beautiful, like all of them. I cringe at the thought of my own appearance, wet hair plastered to my forehead, clothes hanging with sodden weight.

When we reach Aron's study, one of the guards tries to explain, "Arcon, we found these two, um—"

"Astarti," Aron says in surprise when I peek around the guard.

The guards edge out of my way and bow out when Aron dismisses them.

Polemarc Clitus straightens from whatever he's been reading at Aron's desk, and both Gaiana and Bran rise from their seats.

I push wet hair back from my forehead, trying for a little dignity.

"What happened?" demand four voices at once, then Bran says sharply, "Where's Logan?"

"Horik and I"—all eyes flick briefly to Horik, whom all of them have met but Gaiana, though they are clearly surprised to see him here—"believe Logan has gone to, um, see the Ancorites. We need to know how to get there."

Questions are thrown at me so fast that I can barely distinguish two words in ten.

I raise my voice. "Listen! I know you have questions, but I don't have time to explain everything, and you probably wouldn't believe me anyway."

Horik leans near. "They do need to be warned. If Belos frees the Old Ones—"

"What?" Aron splutters. "What is this? What are you talking about?"

I shoot Horik a dirty look, though he's probably right. I'll try to keep this short. "We've been investigating some rumors about the Old Ones, and we've come to believe that they have been trapped in the ocean"—Gaiana's attention sharpens, but I can't bring myself to meet her eyes—"by the Ancorites." The sound of my own words as much as the incredulous looks on Aron and Clitus's faces tells me how absurd this sounds when laid out so bluntly. I plow on, "We believe that Belos plans to attempt to free them, though we don't yet know for what specific purpose."

Silence fills the room in the wake of this announcement. I glance at Horik for confirmation and find him cringing slightly.

Bran stuns me by saying in a horrified tone, "They would destroy Avydos."

Clitus spins to stare at him. "Branos, you cannot be giving this story credence?"

Bran gives him a shocked look. "Don't tell me none of you have read Gramitus's *Collection of Early Histories*?"

When everyone looks at him blankly, he breathes out irritably. He looks like he's about to launch into what might be a long explanation. All that matters to me, however, is the central question.

"Why do you say they would destroy Avydos?"

Bran's eyes take a moment to focus on me. "According to Gramitus, in the First War, the Earthmakers threw down the Old Ones because the Old Ones were destroying the world. You have to understand that such is their nature: to create and destroy. Constant change, constant motion, chaos." Bran adds, "Did you know that the Dry Land was their first home?"

That tickles my memory, but my look must be mostly blank because Bran explains, "Oh, yes, it was once more beautiful than Avydos, or so says the *Collection*. They built a city that imagination cannot hope to conjure. But the Old Ones could not let it rest, and they destroyed the land in their compulsion for change. That is Gramitus's pressing point: They simply cannot stop. They were on the verge of doing the same to these lands when the Earthmakers stood against them."

My head spins with all this information that in some ways agrees with the Runish tales but in other ways paints a very different picture.

Bran goes on, "Gramitus doesn't speak clearly of the fate of the Old Ones. He implies that they dissolved into the elements, as Earthmakers believe happens upon death. That is why, I suspect, we regard the Old Ones as part of the earth itself, and to speak of them is to speak of the earth."

Aron says, "You're talking about them like they're gods, as the Runians think of gods—beings of power and individual will. But this cannot be. They are only a concept, an expression of the elements. Bran, this account you're giving sounds like nothing more than the theory of an old historian who listened to too many human tales."

I bristle. "My mother believed that the Lost Gods and the Old Ones were one and the same. The Runish tales do, indeed, speak of gods eerily similar to your Old Ones."

Aron insists, "That doesn't prove anything except that the Runians built stories around grains of Earthmaker truth."

Frustrated, I look to Horik. How did we get enmeshed in this debate?

Gaiana clears her throat gently. "I believe Astarti."

"Mother!" Aron exclaims.

She twists her fingers together in her lap. "Everything Sibyl said, everything for which she was Stricken, is true. No one wanted to hear it then any more than you want to hear Astarti now. But I know it from my own experience. I have been to their prison, and they are not bodiless elements. They are individuals. They may not think like us, but they have emotion. The one I met was not happy to be trapped. Who knows what anger they might hold against those who have trapped them?"

I feel the blood drain from my face. Belos, I'm sure, has already realized this.

I say numbly, "That's why Belos wants them released. He wants to destroy you, all of you. That's what he's always wanted. And he will release the Old Ones to do it."

Aron, Clitus, and Bran's heads swing from Gaiana to me and back to Gaiana. No one seems to know which point to question first.

Aron snaps, "Mother, what are you saying?"

I don't want her to reveal the truth of Logan's origins—that is for him to do if he chooses. But Bran is the one who forestalls her answer.

"Belos would be releasing a force he cannot hope to control."

I latch onto this. "Even if Belos can't control them, do you think he cares? If they want what he wants, they will be his allies whether they know it or not."

The room falls silent.

Aron is shaking his head. Clitus looks like he swallowed something terrible. I can hardly blame them. I wouldn't want to believe this either if I were an Earthmaker. I don't want to believe it even as myself. Belos, at least, I understand. Belos, at least, is made of the same matter as they are, even if he has perverted himself with the energy—with the *souls*—of others. But a god? What can we know of such a being?

Bran mutters, "What does any of this have to do with Logan?"

I say, "Listen, you all can believe this or not, you can prepare or not. That is your decision. But I need to get to the Ancorites, and I cannot wait a moment longer. Who will take me?"

Aron and Bran both say, "I will."

I stare at Aron, stunned.

He stares back. "What? Don't you think I care about him, too?"

Clitus says, "Aron, let Bran take them. You and I must focus on Avydos."

Aron's jaw tightens, but he nods.

Gaiana says softly, "Why would he go back there?"

I don't know how to answer this without revealing that Logan is, most likely, still tied to Belos. Should I tell them? I am torn between their need to prepare for the worst and my need to protect Logan.

Horik, apparently, has a healthier conscience than I do—or perhaps he simply has less conflicted interests. "Logan may still be under Belos's sway. You must prepare for the possibility that Belos will use Logan against you." He looks hard at me when he says this last, as though to remind me also.

My mind floods with memories of Logan, possessed by Belos's will, staring cruelly into my eyes with no recognition. I barely hear the questions being shouted around me.

It will not happen again. I will not let it. The Shackle, looped through my belt, hidden under my jacket, is a desperate, frightening promise of hope.

"Stop wasting time, all of you! Bran, let's move!"

Chapter 37

When Bran drags me from the bright, golden flow of the Current into the cool night, I am blind in the darkness. I freeze, waiting for my night vision to correct itself. Horik staggers into me, his thick, muscled torso knocking against my shoulder. He catches himself on a tree.

"That," he mutters, "was unbelievable. The trees are...*alive.* I mean, of course they are, but—"

A flat, grassy plain lies before us, stretching to a finger of land that juts into the sea. At the finger's tip rears a huge tower. I shiver, suddenly chilled, and wish I had taken the time to find dry clothes.

I start across the plain, and the others follow. The only sound is the swish of grass around our feet. The grass thins, exposing sand and rock. As the land channels us into the finger, my scalp prickles. There is something eerily familiar about the shape of this tower. The moonlight catches on uneven planes. Its surface is craggy, raw, elemental. Like the spires of the Broken City.

For the first time, the immensity of all this truly presses down on me. I have been so focused on Logan that I have not allowed myself to fully sense the ancient mystery into which I am stepping. The very air hums with power.

We make our silent way across the rocky terrain, the tower looming ever higher. The moon is behind us, and I can't decide whether I'm glad we're not in the tower's shadow or uncomfortable to feel so exposed. Frankly, I doubt it matters. These Ancorites, apparently, are nearly as ancient as the Old Ones and powerful enough to have bound them. They probably know we're here. If they meant to attack us, they would have already done so. Doubt flickers inside me. *If they are so powerful, what chance do you have?* I close my mind to that. Even if I *knew* I were going to fail, I would still be here, trying.

We stop several paces from the foot of the tower. There are no seams or joints, no windows or doors. I shiver at the strangeness. Horik starts to circle the base, hunting for an entrance. When he returns from his half-hearted search, he announces grimly, "I still cannot reach the Drift."

"No," I agree. "You won't be able to step into it. But can you not sense the power in the air? It's like the Drift itself bleeds through here."

Horik rubs his arms, either for warmth—he's still as wet as I am—or to chase away the strangeness closing in on us. "I feel…something," he admits, "but I don't understand it."

"It's like the air itself is laced with their energy."

"I don't feel anything," says Bran.

"Really? The Drift is…present somehow. It's like, I don't know, I sense…" Premonition, the first hint of understanding, chills my skin, but it takes my brain several seconds to catch up with my instincts. "It's a shield."

Horik's head snaps up. "What?"

I stagger with realization. "That's what's blocking the Drift in the Floating Lands. It's a shield."

"How…"

I say, talking through the idea, "In principle, a shield is much like a barrier, created by one person, an extension of one's energy made to block attacks by the energy, the Drift-work, of others."

I shiver at the thought of Drifters—which, I realize, is precisely what these Ancorites are—so powerful they can cast a shield over an entire archipelago and maintain it without rest for thousands of years. I edge away from the tower.

Horik says, "That's how Heborian shielded Tornelaine during the attack by Belos. He cast a shield before the wall."

I close my eyes as this sinks in. Of course. I did not recognize it as a shield at the time because I did not realize it was possible to make one so big. I recall Heborian's exhortation to understand basic principles. Nothing is really that complicated at its core. The key, he insisted, to learning anything, to doing anything, is to understand the basic, underlying principles.

I say, excitement building, "The shield is not perfect, not absolute, nor is any shield. If you shape one against me but my will, my energy, is stronger than yours, I can pierce your shield, especially as you grow tired. That is how I've managed to shape Drift-light here. It's a small piercing of the shield. That is why the Healers are so rare. They are truly the strongest, the ones able to draw through the shield. That is why, as Gaiana told me, Healing is easier away from the Floating Lands where the Drift is not deadened."

I pace before the tower, following the trail of logic. "But don't you see? They can't cut us off from our energies. No shield can do that. Our energy is *within* us. They can only prevent—or rather, hamper—its external manifestation." My nerves tingle with certainty, with anticipation. "This is why it's possible to blend with the elements here. I'm allowing myself to merge with something the Ancorites cannot block, the four earth elements. The physical body, you see, is made up of the earth elements, and the ability to blend with them comes from the fifth element, our own internal energy."

I look to the top of the tower. I cannot reach Logan through the Drift. But as Logan has shown, as I myself proved in the bay not an hour ago, there are other ways to travel. I have no time to question or fear that power. I need it.

"Astarti? What are you doing?"

Elated, soaring on this understanding, I withdraw into myself, purposefully this time, with clarity, as I never have before. In the past, every time I've accidentally merged with the elements I've done it as I was reaching for the Drift. The first few times, I was here in the Floating Lands, reaching inward, and where I didn't find the Drift, I found something else.

Seeking that inner path, I hover in a strange and nebulous state. I do not even know whether the others can see me, and I can't allow myself to focus on them. I've barely reached an understanding of how to do this; I certainly have no idea how to bring them with me. I am on my own.

I feel for the breath of the wind. It slips around me and through me, and I meld myself with it, weightless and powerful. I ride and direct its currents, balancing its will with mine. I rise higher and higher, swirling around the tower, seeking.

When I reach the top, I find a flat, circular roof ringed with columns, open to the sky, open to the elements. Logan is slumped against one column, his head hanging like he's unconscious.

I spill from the wind so suddenly that I tumble and roll across the roof. Stone abrades my hands as I scrape to a stop. I scramble to Logan, skidding on my knees as I reach him.

Not daring to breathe, I press trembling fingers to his neck. I sag with relief to feel his pulse, but the heat under my fingers worries me. He's still burning with fever.

"Logan." I tilt his head up. "*Logan.*"

His eyelids flicker and part. Moonlight reveals the black threading through his irises.

"*Fight him.*"

His eyes squeeze shut. When they open again, clear this time, he starts to speak but stops, staring at something over my shoulder. My heart lurches and my skin crawls with dark intuition, but when I turn to look, I see nothing.

"I have to get you out of here, before they come back. Are you with me? *Say* something."

Awareness pricks the back of my neck again.

Logan focuses on me briefly. "Star-ti." His eyes drift over my shoulder again.

Dark, brooding energy hums behind me. I know, deep down, that they are there, waiting, watching, unseen.

"Get up," I command, tugging at him. At first I think he's resisting me, then I recognize the buzz of energy surrounding him. He is bound with Drift-work. And air?

A quiet laugh, elusive as the wind, slips behind me. I scramble to my feet. A shape hovers, like a mirage in the Dry Land. The hair rises on the back of my neck.

"Show yourself!"

That laugh again. I close my eyes, then open them slowly. Five forms begin to take shape before me. Even though I've been expecting this, my heart leaps into my throat. I stagger back, my heel knocking into Logan's toe as he strains against his bindings.

The five shapes take on greater substantiality. They are skeletal, their faces and bodies worn away until they look like little more than skin stretched over bone and hung with tattered robes. How can beings so frail be so powerful?

One of them, with one claw-like hand curled over the other, drifts toward me. Behind me, Logan grows frantic. The Ancorite flicks his wrist. Something—insubstantial but laced with deep power—brushes past me. Behind me, Logan goes rigid, then stills.

The Ancorite's voice floats on the air, not quite real. "Our children have grown careless in their breeding. Perhaps we should bind this one also."

For all the horror that is Belos, never has he frozen me with the primitive, elemental fear that seizes my body at the sight of these ancient beings.

When I get my voice to obey, it comes out as only a whisper. "Let him go. He's done nothing."

"It matters not." The Ancorite's accent is strange, with harsh sounds that remind me of the language I've heard Logan mutter on occasion. "Our only concern is that he be contained, like his father. We must keep the balance."

"He's not a danger to you."

Ancient, drooping eyes regard me steadily, without emotion. "Intention is nothing; his power itself is unacceptable. If only we had bound him the moment he set foot in our tower, all would be well. But time has made us soft, and we were not certain, and he escaped. We will now correct that mistake."

I eye the harsh lines of the Ancorite's body, the coldness of his expression. I picture the scars on Logan's back and the horror in his face at any mention of these creatures. Soft?

I grope behind me for Logan. When my fingers find his face, his flesh is hot and too still.

I whisper, playing for time, "I don't understand."

"We have a sacred charge, and for all the ages of this world we have kept it. We will bind him with chains of water and stone, air and fire, with his own deepest energies. He will be woven into the fabric of his own prison, like the others."

I shiver at his certainty, his coldness. "Are they so terrible?"

"You're a Drifter. You have seen a sliver of their power and fury in the great wind within the Drift. Since the beginning, they have strained for freedom there."

I reel. He's talking about the Hounding.

He nods to the four flanking him. "It's time. He must be bound."

All five of the Ancorites reach past—reach *through*—me. I strike out at them, but my fists sail through air. And yet, the Ancorites latch onto Logan with very real hands, dragging him away from the column. They are as fluid as water, as strong as the earth. They mutter in that ancient, eerie language.

I hear my own inhuman sounds as I grab at Logan, tearing at his clothes. Suddenly my fingers scrape through to stone. Like the Ancorites, he is fading from sight.

For the first time in my life, I pray for Belos to come. For the first time in my life I understand the desperation that drives some to strike deals with him: right now, I would sell my soul to stop this.

CHAPTER 38

LOGAN

Fingers like claws, hard as iron bars, latch onto me.

I am a child again, screaming, begging.

But everyone has abandoned me. This must be what they want, what I deserve.

Is he one of them? We must know!

Through every lash of the whip, I clench more tightly around that storm building within me. I must not let it out. I must not let them see.

Force him!

I try to let my mind float away.

They cannot hurt me if I am not there.

A different voice slithers into the void. *They are old and weak! Rip them apart!*

I shrink from the familiar presence as it violates the innermost part of me.

They will bind you! Get up!

Fear spikes.

Their dry, rasping voices chant the ancient language. I feel myself dissolve. They are changing me, making me into nothing. Again.

"Stop it! Let him go!"

Her voice. I catch a glimpse of moonlight-painted cheek, of dark, flying braid. Astarti.

The past washes away. The present reasserts itself. No. I am no longer a weak and frightened child.

The ancient chanting intensifies, dry voices rasping louder.

One of them mutters, "Bind her also."

The storm builds inside me, raging for freedom.

I feel the stone under me, the air around me as I force my body to reclaim itself.

Yes! Kill them! Rip them!

"He's reforming!"

Wind howls within me. Part of my mind grasps desperately for control, for awareness and logic. Another part screams a wild, desperate, *Yes!*

I am wind, water, air, fire. I am everything.

I throw back my head and yell.

I will tear this world apart.

The storm breaks. Wind screams, rain pours, the earth trembles from its fiery core to its cold, hard stones.

My vision returns. I am on the tower roof. Ancient, watery eyes stare at me in horror and mad fear. Rage floods me.

Kill them! Rip them!

I don't even know whether that is my will or *his*, but I answer it. I dive for Dioklesus.

Invisible bonds loop around and through me, trying to reshape me, but I howl. The binding bursts. Dioklesus staggers back.

My hand clenches on his thin neck. He starts to fade, but I am the master now. His body is nothing but earth and fire, air and water, and I force him to obey, as he once forced me. His skeletal hands claw at me, but I am rage.

Break him!

The voice is past and present, spoken to me, through me, by me.

His neck snaps. His body crumples.

The energy humming around me falters.

Somewhere, deep under the sea, stone cracks and booms. Water roars.

CHAPTER 39

When the Ancorite's lifeless body crumples around Logan's fist, the boom from out at sea ripples through the earth, shaking the tower. I feel the first tingle of the Drift as the Ancorites' shield wavers.

I sprint toward Logan, who is staring down at the body of the man he's killed. He wheels on me, eyes burning for destruction. Wild, uncontrolled energy rolls from him.

Then his expression clears, and he's just Logan again. He reaches for me.

Suddenly, his body seizes, and his eyes pool with blackness.

I draw back instinctively. Though I need Belos to arrive, though I've all but begged for it, my blood runs cold.

The air shivers beside Logan.

Belos steps from the Drift.

His face is gaunter than I've ever seen it. His eyes are hungry, elated. Mad. He smiles. "It is good, isn't it, Astarti, to feel the Drift here at last?"

My mooring tingles with promise as the shield continues to fade. Waves crash against the base of the tower. Worry pricks at me as I think of Horik and Bran down there.

"Old men!" Belos calls grandly. "Do you laugh at me now? Would you now let me wander around your tower for three days, a beggar? You did not even think me worth binding or driving off!" He shouts, "Do you still think me so unworthy of your notice?"

One ancient, skeletal Ancorite, his form as insubstantial as wind, rasps, "You fool! Do you know what you've done?"

Belos's jaw tightens at the insult. "I know exactly what I've done."

Logan steps forward with a stride not his own, a cruelty and purpose not his own. He has gone from one binding to another.

Logan latches onto the neck of the Ancorite who taunted Belos. The ancient thing tries to fade, but Logan seems to be forcing him to hold shape.

Belos laughs, delighted, as the Ancorite writhes.

Another boom vibrates from the sea through the land.

I slide the Shackle from my belt. This is my chance.

As I slip behind Belos, I draw energy from the Drift. It responds sluggishly at first, then comes rushing along my mooring.

I whip a lash of energy around Belos, binding him tight. He cries out in surprise. I have only seconds before he breaks the binding. I shove the Shackle onto his wrist and yank him toward Logan, who has dropped the frail, lifeless body of the Ancorite. I slap the other Shackle onto him.

With my hand on the bone chain, I wrench them both into the Drift.

Chapter 40

LOGAN

The awful compression of entry releases me suddenly, and my nerves dance with sudden weightlessness as the vast expanse of the Drift floods out in all directions. My wrist tingles with raw energy, and I recoil at the sight of the Shackle, white and gleaming, clamped on my wrist. Wind howls around me, further fraying my already confused thoughts. Time bends and folds. I don't know where I am or what is happening, but I want this thing *off*. I claw at it, but my fingers pass right through it.

Yet, despite its insubstantiality, it has real power. Like the Ancorites. My energy roils with fury. *Kill!* Snarling, I spin to seek them, but what I see is *him*.

At the other end of the Shackle.

His energies rip and tear at each other, a hundred trapped souls clawing for release. All those he's Taken, as he will Take me.

No. He will do worse than that, for he has done more than simply Leash me. My mind splinters, shards of it slicing into the past.

I peel open my good eye. Dusky light, tinged with the red of sunset, glints along the shoulder studs of Belos's vest as he studies me where I'm lying on the stone table in his study, my leg throbbing under the hot compress. Belos's jaw is set with determination, and there's something in his eyes I don't like. Uncertainty, maybe, or excitement.

He turns and paces away from me. I follow his progress to the far wall, where a map hangs. Belos halts before the map, blocking my view. His shoulders hunch and his head lowers in thought.

Straton's voice calls, "My lord, are you sure—"

Belos raises a hand for silence.

He turns away from the map, but his finger lingers on a point in the Southern Ocean. When his finger drops, I shiver to see what it covered. Not the Floating Lands, as I expected, but a burn hole where they should have been.

Shoulders hunched, head lowered, Belos paces the study. When he walks past a pedestal table, I shrink into myself, start shaking. The Shackle, which began all this, lies coiled on the table, sunset gleaming over its smooth, white links of bone.

Belos clamps a hand on my arm.

Knowing instinctively that this is the end, the final measure, I throw myself open to the elements in a last, foolish attempt to escape whatever is coming. Wind screams through the deep-cut window, whipping dust over all of us. The earth rumbles, shaking the floor and walls until a crack splits from the window up to the ceiling and lets in a blade of light. I reach for the wind, willing my sluggish, unresponsive body to dissolve into it. Belos smiles, letting me believe for a second that I might succeed, then he wrenches me through the horrible compression and into the Drift.

I try to wrench my arm free of his grip, but his other hand closes on the dark Leash that pulses between us. Nausea rolls through me. I might collapse if not for his grip on my arm.

My Leash is not the only one snaking out of his body. Dozens travel into the distance, some fading from sight as they reach the Green Lands, others ending somewhere within the fortress. Mine, though, is thickest and the only one blackened by his will. I am frozen with it, my own will suffocated by his.

Belos reaches a hand deep into his energies, somewhere around his heart. His face contorts with pain. A silent scream splits his lips. When the Leash sends a booming pulse deep into my being, pain slices through my heart. He is killing me, splitting me in half. I try to scramble away, but I am dragged back by my Leash. When his hand plunges into my heart, I scream, but the sound is swallowed by the nothingness of the Drift.

Past and present fold over one another until I can't distinguish the layers. Is this happening now? Or is it memory? I claw at my chest. That *wrongness* pulses inside me. I shudder.

Logan!

The voice is distant and strained, but it's her.

I'm in the Dry Land. She's come for me!

No. That already happened, that—

Wind whips around me, howling through the Drift.

Her lighted form catches my eye. A sword flashes at her. She spins away, her spear catching and deflecting the blow. Belos lunges again. Belos! Attacking her!

I yank on the Shackle's chain. Belos soars back, his sword sweeping harmlessly away from Astarti. Midflight, he twists to face me. His eyes latch onto mine as he barrels into me. Nausea rolls through me even before impact. He drives me onto my back, pinning me. My hands latch on his throat. Everything feels wrong. My hands are there, but not. His throat is there, but not. I do not like the Drift.

I freeze when oily blackness floods the chain. It snakes through me, straining toward that dark, aching point in my chest. No.

No, no, no.

I am a child, cringing as the bloody lash rises again.

I am a man, screaming inside myself as I split a city wall.

I am a child, clawing for escape from invisible bonds.

I am a man, clawing for escape.

Always, trying to escape.

Enough!

I am sick of my fear, sick of waiting for them to break me, sick of believing they have power over me. I am myself!

And I am strong.

Belos's black will oozes through me, seeking that piece of himself lodged in my core. I do not accept that. I am myself!

My own will surges against his. I am!

Something opens in my chest.

Power and need surge through me.

I am stronger.

My energy expands, bursting from within, and the wrongness that is him breaks from me like a sword pulled free.

The oily blackness washes clean, driven out by my own blazing silver and gold. Both our wills surge along the chain. I drive the blackness back into him.

I am bursting with power, elated, soaring on it.

I drive him to his back, riding high on the sudden fear in his eyes. I will do to him what he has done to me. *I* will Take *him*. He will know what it means to submit.

But when my very essence reaches into Belos, brushing the dark and torturous heart of him, I recoil. Would I taint myself with him of my own free will? I draw back. I don't want that. I don't want any part of that.

In that moment when my will falters, he wrenches me through the tight passage and out of the Drift.

Bluish light glows around me as I pin Belos to the ground. Snow floats through the diffused light. The earth rumbles. Waves crash.

I tighten my hands on his throat, and the glow brightens.

I am surging, pulsing with power like I've never felt before. I want only to expand, to reach the highest point, to kill him with it. Belos twists in my grip, but I force his body, his elemental matter, to hold still under me. I let my rage and need expand, filling me, flooding out of me. The release is so, so good.

Blue flashes all around me, highlighting the snow. The earth rumbles warningly. People shout; weapons clash. I ignore all of it until a boom shudders through the earth, and the stone under my knees shakes with terrible violence, sending me and Belos tumbling. I scramble to hold onto him, but stone crumbles beneath me. My stomach lurches. I am falling.

Instinctively, I blend with stone and wind, tumbling through it all in a confusion of substance. Wild energies course through the elements. Something in me yearns to answer their call, but other energies tug at my awareness. Belos. Astarti.

Astarti!

I streak toward her.

When I reshape myself beside her, the rumbling earth makes me stagger and fall among tumbled rocks. I have no idea where I am, but I reach for Astarti, to make sure she's there, to make sure she's safe. Her hands answer mine, tugging at me in turn. We shout each other's names. The sound of exploding stone drowns us out. At the end of a narrow spit of land, the tower crumbles into the raging, frothing sea.

The tower?

The Ancorites!

I lurch to my feet, hunting for them, staggering as the earth trembles. With a faint blue glow, Horik appears, startling me.

Astarti shouts at him, "Where is Bran?"

"Safe! I sent him back to Avydos!"

Bran? Here? Confusion dizzies me as the events of the day crash through my mind piecemeal. Rune. Sunhild's hall. A dream of power and vengeance. An uncontrollable need to confront the old men. *His* will and greed surging through me, driving me on. Astarti, coming for me. Again. Of all that's happened, *that* is all that really matters. I turn to her, but she's pointing toward the end of the spit of rocky land.

"Belos! He has the Shackle!"

My blood roars at his name. He's standing near the rubble, at the edge of the ocean spray, looking out to the turbulent, moonlit sea. With a faint blue glow, the Seven appear around him.

Belos. He started this, all of it. But I will end it. I will kill him.

I take off at a run. The rocky ground trembles, making me clumsy, making my weak knee almost buckle, but I will not stop. I've almost reached Belos and the Seven when water explodes in a giant fan, crashing over the rocky land and all of us.

In the shallows, a figure breaks the water's surface. The moon paints highlights on a head and shoulders like the very bones of the earth. The ocean crashes madly around him. My blood hums with recognition. I know him. In my very blood, I know him.

Somewhere in the distance behind me, fiery light flares, rendering everything in brief clarity. Snow dusts through the air. The figure tumbles from the water toward the rocky land. Belos, with the Shackle dangling from his hand, vanishes only to reappear beside the figure—the Old One. The Old One roars, wrenching away, but Belos latches onto him, and they vanish in a flash of blue.

The sound that follows is a boom, a scream, a breaking of the very earth. It comes from everywhere and nowhere. Water crashes onto the rocky spit. Wind rages, nearly blowing me off my feet. Astarti and Horik stumble into me from behind. The

Seven are nearly swept away by the raging waters. A blue glow surrounds them.

They vanish.

I hear nothing but wind and water and the horrible scream lacing through them.

I shout, "Astarti! Take me into the Drift! He's Leashing the Old One!"

My voice is drowned out by the scream, but Astarti latches onto me and wrenches me into the Drift.

Wind howls through the Drift. Blazing shapes tear at each other from the heart of the wind. One is huge and blinding, like the sun. I have to look away. Lights flare and explode in the vastness. Wind pummels me and Astarti, tearing at us, tearing *through* us. My energies start to unravel. My mind splinters. My last, horrifying thought is that I will dissolve into this madness.

Astarti wrenches me from the Drift.

We fall to the rocky ground. I huddle, twitching, as too much energy courses through my body. Astarti moans beside me.

Eventually, the tremors pass, and I notice that the wind has subsided and the ocean is settling.

I stare at the spot where Belos and the Old One vanished. "He's going to Leash him."

Astarti says, "If the Old One cannot stop him, we certainly cannot."

I push shakily to my feet. Horik helps Astarti to hers.

The earth rumbles its warning again. In the distance, light flares, illuminating the snow falling around us. Astarti rubs a sleeve across her face. Something smears.

Not snow.

Ash.

I spin to watch in horror as Mount Hypatia belches flame from the heart of Avydos.

Horik shouts, "They have to get out of there!"

I look from the distant, fiery mountain to the dark, empty sea and back again. Astarti is right. There's nothing we can do for the Old One.

Chapter 41

Logan takes me and Horik to the heart of the city. We tumble from the wind to the smooth stones of the Arcon's courtyard. The air is heavy with swirling ash and smoke. People rush past us. Everyone is shouting.

A voice booms from the porch, "Move, move, move! Take only what you need!" The Warden is ushering people out the door, and they are hurrying down the steps with their arms full of blankets, wooden boxes, and children. In the city beyond, the streets are flooded with people. With every rumble of the earth, people scream. Water sloshes in the bay, crashing into the harbor. Wind whips and spills through the city and the courtyard.

Someone rushes past, knocking me into Logan. He pulls me behind him and starts toward the Warden, pushing through the stream of people.

When we reach the porch, Logan shouts to be heard. "Where is the Arcon?"

"The Arcon, Branos, and the Polemarc are helping evacuate the other islands! Everyone will gather outside Tornelaine! The Prima is already there!"

The earth jerks and shudders underfoot. The central mountain of Avydos belches flame, illuminating the sky. For one brief moment, I see a woman's huge and fiery form within the bursting flame. Liquid fire trickles down the mountainside.

When the last Earthmaker has fled across the courtyard, the Warden shouts, "Come on! There's nothing to be done!"

Horik shouts, "But there are still people in the city!"

The Warden nudges us down the steps. The wind all but steals his words, but I think he shouts, "They know what to do!"

We follow the stream of people toward the grove of trees beyond the courtyard. The trees creak and moan as earth and air tear at them.

Light floods the sky once more. Liquid flame bursts from the mountain and streams down its rocky face. The burning river surges toward the Wood that lies between the mountain and the city.

Everywhere, people rush to the trees, many of them dropping their burdens.

Logan grabs the Warden's shoulder as we reach the trees. "Take these two to Tornelaine! I have to find my brothers!" The Warden nods, grabbing for my hand.

I snatch at Logan, desperate not to be separated, but he is already gone.

The air has grown heavy with smoke. I cough, choking on it. The trees shake and creak. One by one, they begin to twist and fall as though torn by huge, unseen hands. The Warden lunges for Horik and drags us both into the Current.

The golden stream churns and rages. Branches lash and writhe. The Wood is like an animal in its death throes. A face appears and disappears among the thrashing branches. I watch, horrified as hands, impossibly huge, rip and tear, moving in and out of sight. When the hands reach toward me, my energies spike with instinctive fear, and I flee with the Warden, Horik, and everyone else.

When the Warden drags me and Horik from the turbulent golden Current and into the cool night, I suck in the cool, clean air in desperate breaths. Horik and I follow the panicked Earthmakers from the trees and onto the plains outside the walls of Tornelaine.

Heborian's soldiers ride among the mass of people, shouting for order. Figures dot the top of the city wall. When I point, Horik nods. Not trusting the Drift to be safe, we push our way through the crowd.

We reach the city gate to find it shut. I shout to the top of the wall, but caught in the crowd, I begin to fear I won't be heard. I would try to manipulate the wind once more, but I don't want to leave Horik.

"Astarti!" Heborian shouts from above.

The gate inches open and Horik and I squeeze through. It booms shut behind us, and the soldiers lower the bar into place.

Horik and I race up the steps to the top of the wall. Heborian latches onto me. "Thank the gods!"

"I wouldn't exactly say that!"

"Astarti!" Prima Gaiana pushes past Heborian. "Where is Logan?"

My heart leaps with the question, but before I can answer, wind batters me, nearly knocking me down the steps. Logan, Aron, Clitus, and Bran tumble from the wind. They roll and skid across the stone battlements, knocking several men off their feet.

I rush to Logan, who turns onto his side, coughing smoke from his lungs. His face and torso are smeared with ash.

He gasps, "We couldn't get into the Current," before another fit of coughing seizes him.

I hear Aron shout, "Why aren't you letting them in?"

Heborian answers with a sharp, "They must calm down first. I cannot let this panic spill into Tornelaine."

"We had a deal!"

"And I will keep it! But they *must* first be contained."

The ground shakes. People scream.

Logan pushes to his feet, and we pace along the wall until we can see the ocean beyond Tornelaine. Fiery light pulses in the sky above Avydos.

"Did everyone escape?"

Logan's voice rasps from the smoke he inhaled, but the desolation of his answer is clear enough. "No."

ꕤ

The rest of the night is both exhausting and tedious. When the crowd settles, Heborian's soldiers and Aron's Wardens begin the long process of bringing the Earthmakers into the city and constructing temporary sleeping shelters in the open marketplaces. The people of Tornelaine, frightened by the sudden influx of Earthmakers, make the process even more difficult. Through it all, everyone is on high alert, both jittery and sharp-tongued, expecting an attack from Belos or from the earth itself.

As Logan and I help set up tents, I worry about him constantly. His shoulders droop with fatigue. His hands shake so badly that he drops his mallet several times. When I try to get him to leave the work to others, he says, "I'm staying with you."

It's nearly dawn before we withdraw to Heborian's castle, leaving the soldiers and Wardens to maintain the tenuous peace of the Earthmaker encampment.

When I get Logan into bed, he's asleep so fast that he'd never know if I left. There's so much to do, so many problems to address. But as I watch his face relax in slumber, I know I cannot leave. This is the only place I want to be. The rest of the world can wait.

Chapter 42

LOGAN

I wake beside Astarti. Sunlight slips through the curtains to lie in a bright band across her throat. I brush dark hair away from her face. Her eyelids flicker and part.

There is so much to talk about but only one thing I really want to say. I've let it burn inside me, unspoken, for too long. I cannot hold it back anymore, no matter the consequences, no matter her reaction. "I love you, Astarti."

Tears spring into her eyes, but she smiles. "I love you, too."

My chest seems to open, and for once, it feels whole and clean and right. I slip my arm under her and draw her against me. I'm holding her so tightly I fear I might hurt her. But no. She hugs back just as hard.

I must fall asleep again because the light has shifted by the time I wake. Astarti is still in my arms, and I'm stirred by the press of her body against mine. I bury my face in her neck. She strokes my hair.

I smooth a hand down her side to her hip, but I stop myself there, not sure what she wants. But her hands mimic mine, tracing a path down my chest and belly. I groan as her hand brushes low, instinctively seeking that most intimate part of me. Her fingers are shy, uncertain, and I let her learn me in her own way.

I'm trembling, yearning to learn her body as she is learning mine, yearning to know her body as I know her soul. Both are so beautiful.

When she is ready, I lay her down. I kiss her lips, her throat. I take my time because this is best and purest moment of my life, and I don't want it to ever end.

ꟾ ꟾ

We wake later, lazy and contented, our arms and legs entwined. I want this to be my full reality, but soon enough my mind shuffles through what has happened. Astarti stirs in my hold.

"What is it?" Her voice is husky with sleep.

"Why did they stop? The Old Ones?"

Her brow furrows. "I don't know. What could we possibly know of such beings?" She must feel me stiffen because she grips me more tightly. "I didn't mean—"

"It's all right. I know what you meant."

"What do you think happened in the Drift? Do you think the Old One could have won? Do you think Belos is dead?"

"Do you?"

"I once stabbed him in the chest and he didn't die. I won't believe it until I see his lifeless body." She pauses, looking worried. "You understand, don't you, why I Shackled you to him?"

I comb my fingers through her tangled hair. "Yes. Thank you, Astarti. For your faith in me."

She clutches me to her. "I thought I had lost you."

"I'm not going anywhere," I whisper into her hair, and I do my best to prove it.

EPILOGUE

BELOS

I claw my way onto the rocky spit of land. This island is largely untouched, but the blackened hulk of Avydos smokes in the distance. I throw back my head and laugh. The sky spins, and I fall to the rocky ground.

The Seven are dragging themselves from the water. They are white-faced and shaking, drained almost to emptiness. It was necessary.

Straton casts me a malevolent look. He has always been resentful of his position, but I don't care right now. I don't even care that I've lost the Shackle. I don't need it anymore.

"My lord?" inquires Rhode. "Where is he? The Old One?"

I recline on the rocks, shrugging. "Here. Nowhere."

"But he's—"

"Oh, yes. He's mine."

ABOUT THE AUTHOR

Katherine Buel grew up in Kansas with two passions: stories and horses. She's taken both of those with her through much of the upper Midwest, then out to Maine and back again.

She also loves mountain biking and kayaking—and too many other things that there's never enough time for.

Printed in Great Britain
by Amazon

67432299R00201